A
SUITCASE
IN BERLIN

Also by Don Flynn

Murder in A-Flat
Ordinary Murder
Murder On the Hudson
Murder Isn't Enough

A
SUITCASE
IN BERLIN

Don Flynn

WALKER AND COMPANY
New York

*For C. B., who nudged me up
the first gangplank.*

The author wishes to thank Sam Graff, fellow newspaper scrivener and world traveler, for shooing the pigeons
out of his German, and contemporary American painter
David MacKay for his art expertise.

Copyright © 1989 by Donald R. Flynn and
Charlotte J. Flynn

First published in the United States of America in 1989
by Walker Publishing Company, Inc.

Published simultaneously in Canada by
Thomas Allen & Son
Canada, Limited, Markham, Ontario

Library of Congress Cataloging-in-Publication Data

Flynn, Don.
A suitcase in Berlin / Don Flynn.
p. cm.
ISBN 0-8027-5742-1
I. Title.
PS3556.L84S85 1989
813'.54—dc20 89-34322
CIP

Printed in the United States of America

10 8 6 4 2 1 3 5 7 9

$$\triangledown$$

Chapter One

We came up the steps of the Kochstrasse U-Bahn station in Berlin and walked along, checking the street map once, and then went around a corner onto Friedrichstrasse and there it was.

"Checkpoint Charlie," Claudette said under her breath.

I could see it about a block and a half ahead of us, where Friedrichstrasse dead-ended into the Allied checkpoint. Beyond it were East Berlin and Communist East Germany.

"Come on," Claudette said softly.

We walked up to the squat, prefab, very temporary-looking hut set in the middle of the street, with painted American, British, and French flags on the front. Just ahead, where Friedrichstrasse zigged through the control point into East Berlin, stood two East German border guards with slung AK-47 automatic rifles.

To each side of us, stretching away as far as the eye could see, was The Wall, a bland, concrete monstrosity fourteen feet high, spattered with indignant graffiti.

Where The Wall Begins, Freedom Ends!

A red, round peace symbol with an upside-down Y in the middle.

An American comment: Communism Sucks!

A man in an overcoat paced to and fro in the December chill, wearing a sandwich board of protest scrawled in German, and a woman paced to and fro with him. They crisscrossed ceaselessly in front of the two border guards, only a few feet away beyond the invisible line that marked the border.

Just behind The Wall rose a square guard tower, with shadowy figures moving around inside behind the glass. Dead ahead of us was the sign:

SIE VERLASSEN DEN AMERIKANISCHEN SEKTOR. VOUS SORTEZ DU SECTEUR AMER-ICAIN. BЬ1BЬ1E3HAETE N3 AMEPNKAHCK-ORO CEKTOPA. YOU ARE LEAVING THE AMERICAN SECTOR.

We stood there surveying The Wall as it snaked through Berlin. We noted the wide, cleared expanse on the East Berlin side—an open field for firearms—and saw the wooden cross driven into the ground on the West Berlin side marking the spot where a young East German died trying to get out.

"My God," Claudette breathed. Amen, I thought.

"Now what?" I asked her.

Claudette breathed in deeply. "I have to see if the painting is there, first," she said.

"First . . . ?"

"Well, yes. And then . . ."

I turned away in exasperation and drew her back toward The Wall Museum, which graphically depicted escapes into West Berlin. There were photos of hollowed-out cars,

tunnels, cables rigged onto the roofs of East Berlin down
which fleeing East Berliners had slid to freedom in the
West. There were also photos of the bodies lying on both
sides of The Wall of those who didn't make it.

"You're really going over there?"

"Fitz, I have to!"

I lighted a Tiparillo and pondered the necessity. Let's
face it, I was also pondering the necessity of my going
through The Wall with her. I had been sent there to cover
preparations for the 750th Anniversary of the founding of
Berlin for the travel section of the New York *Daily Press.*
All I needed was to get involved in some hopeless, bun-
gled, international mess, get locked in a Communist cell,
like Nicholas Daniloff, and have my city editor, Ironhead
Matthews, come totally unglued.

Ironhead hadn't wanted me to come to Berlin in the
first place, you understand, but he'd been unable to prevent my being loaned to the toy department for this
assignment. He had made it clear that I was to write a
kitschy beer and oompah travel piece and then get the hell
back to New York to cover *real* news. Naturally, he acted
as though I had arranged the whole thing—but how the
hell could I have imagined that a blue line up Fifth Avenue
in Manhattan would lead all the way to Berlin?

The way it had happened was that the committee of the
Von Steuben German Day Parade in Manhattan wanted a
blue line up Fifth Avenue because, after all, the Irish had a
green one for St. Patrick's Day. So I had been sent to cover
the "blue line" squabble, and that led to covering the
parade, too, and the high jinks up in Yorkville.

I think it really resulted from my brilliant idea of putting
that cutesy touch in my byline on the Von Steuben Day
story: By EDWARD "VON" FITZGERALD.

Mrs. McFadden, the publisher's wife, had spotted that
"Von," decided I was the perfect one to cover the 750th
birthday party in Berlin, and I had been consigned to
Barrel Rawlins, the travel editor. Ironhead flew into a
titanic sauerkraut rage and accused me of a Teutonic plot
to get myself sent to Berlin for a "goddamn wurst and
oompah festival," as if I'd told Mrs. McFadden what to
do. I admit I wasn't unhappy to get such a lark of a travel
junket, even though it meant working for the toy department for a week or so, but I couldn't help it. Neither could
Ironhead, and that's what got him worked up, because he
doesn't like any of his reporters sent on any story that he
doesn't think up first.

That had been bad enough, but while Ironhead was
standing at the city desk screaming at me that I'd better
get back to New York in time to cover the Prissy Ryan
trial, Claudette Barry had shown up. After somehow
talking her way past Denny at the reception desk, she
came sailing right up to the city desk and stuck the
Associated Press clipping from Berlin about *La Chambre
Verte* into Ironhead's face.

"This story about my painting was in your paper Sunday," she announced. "It would be a great story for you if
you could help me get it back."

"What?" Ironhead had foamed. "How did you get in
here? What painting?"

"*The Green Room,*" she had explained. "See, it was
hanging in the Louvre in Paris when the Germans marched
in, and Hermann Goering stole it."

"Hermann Goering?"

". . . and he took it back to Berlin, but it got lost when
the Russians took the city, and now it's in the National
Gallery in East Berlin. But it belongs to my family . . ."

"Madam, what the hell are you talking about?" Iron-head had demanded. "This is an AP story from Berlin. We don't know anything about it! Bobby!"

Bobby, the head copyboy, had shown Claudette Barry precipitously out of the city room that day, but Claudette had overheard that I was going to Berlin, and I guess that's why I later found her sitting across the aisle on a Lufthansa jet to Frankfurt.

I was sipping a St. Pauli Girl beer when I heard the voice order a white wine.

"Well, hello."

"Fitz, isn't it?" She smiled prettily. "I'm Claudette Barry."

"Oh." I considered that a moment. "Where are you headed?"

"Berlin."

"Oh, yeah," I said. "I heard you talking to Ironhead."

"Who?"

"My city editor at the *Daily Press.*"

"Oh . . . *him*," she snorted. "Appropriate name."

"What was it about . . . a painting you want returned?"

"Yes. *The Green Room.* The Nazis stole it from Paris in 1940 and took it to Berlin. Then, when Berlin fell, the Russians took it somewhere and it disappeared. Your paper had a story that it's on display in the National Gallery in East Berlin."

"I see. For the Anniversary. So you're going to ask them to give it back?" I glanced at her, wondering a little at her naïveté.

"Oh, I'm through asking," she said. "I've been through all that. My grandfather left that painting to my family, and now it belongs to me and I'm going to get it."

My St. Pauli Girl beer tasted suddenly flat. "What? How?"

"Never mind," she said.

I got up and moved over to sit beside her. I was annoyed and determined not to get involved.

"What the hell are you talking about?" I hissed. "You think you're going to walk into a communist museum and walk out with that painting under your arm?"

"It belongs to me."

"Listen, are you totally crazy? You want to end up in some Siberian gulag?"

"Don't worry about it. I don't expect you to help me."

Even then I had realized that she meant just the opposite, and that helping somebody whom Ironhead had thrown out of the city room was a prescription for disaster.

So why was I standing at The Wall with Claudette Barry? I don't know. Maybe because a story in the *Daily Press* had launched her on this bizarre mission and then Ironhead had dismissed her. Maybe because I felt responsible. Maybe because Claudette Barry was earnest and winsome and, let's face it, a lovely French-American girl with a Catherine Deneuve face and coal black hair that disintegrated my reason.

Now Claudette was edging forward toward the prefab hut.

"Now, listen," I said, "what the hell do you think you're going to do? Do you see those guards? Do you see that goddamn wall? Do you see that sign?"

"Americans have a right to go into East Berlin."

"Yes . . . to look around."

"Well, that's what I'm going to do."

"Just look around?"

She pulled her arm free and gave me the kind of look

that Napoleon must have worn when he asked a captured Russian general in Vilna, "Which is the shortest way to Moscow?"

She walked along to the Allied Checkpoint Charlie hut in the middle of the street. I followed. A window in the hut slid open, and there stood a middle-aged American GI who sounded like a Cajun from Louisiana.

"Yes, ma'am," he said in a practiced singsong, "you just walk through the checkpoint holding your passport up for them to see. You go into that building over there on the other side, and they'll check your passport. If you're polite to them, they'll be polite to you. Don't jaywalk or they'll arrest you, be out by midnight, and don't drink the Coke or you'll have the trots for two weeks."

"Thanks," said Claudette, and with a glance at me started walking toward the two Grenzenpolizei stationed just beyond the border. Then she paused and looked back.

"Coming?" she asked.

An insidious viper sidled up and whispered to me, "Hasten then to the goal which you have before you. Throw away vain hopes and come to your own aid, while yet you may, if you care at all for yourself."

Marcus Aurelius, the Roman emperor-philosopher who had adopted me, was at my elbow as usual, prodding me when he considered it necessary. Sometime I'd like to get my hands on him and shake his teeth loose.

There she went, mad as a hatter, strolling into East Berlin past Grenzenpolizei and guard towers manned by shadowy gunmen, right past the You Are Leaving the American Sector sign. Well, let her go. It was none of my business. No doubt the KGB was preparing a goddamn dungeon for her in some Arctic Circle gulag. I was not going to get myself even higher on Ironhead Matthews's shit list by going into East Berlin on an idiotic wild-goose chase, and that was final!

"Wait up!"

$\triangledown$

CHAPTER TWO

I WALKED with her through the checkpoint, directed by signs for pedestrians: *Fussgänger*. Through an unmarked door into a low, institutional-looking building and to a door marked *Eingang*. The guards were in brown uniforms with green epaulets decorated with gold dingbats.

I watched a man coming back out of East Berlin. A guard was holding his pack of cigarettes, taking each slim tube out to peer at it. Then he put the pack into an X-ray machine.

"Passport," a Grenpo said and took my passport. He looked like any clerk in the basement at Manhattan State Supreme Court, except for the uniform. There is something crazily European and even Third Reichish about passports. There they have you in their hands in paper form, and it's as though you aren't quite official unless they approve your paper persona. Maybe they'll put you into some drawer someplace, and then you won't have an official existence.

The Grenpo fixed a baleful glare on the photo in my passport, which resembled that of a sofa salesman in John's

Bargain Basement in Brooklyn, and then squinted directly at me.

"Wie heissen Sie?" he said.

"Edward Fitzgerald," I said, and was relieved that the passport did not identify me as a New York newspaper reporter.

He nodded gravely, stamped a piece of paper, and handed it and my passport back to me. "So!" Then he did the same thing to Claudette Barry. "So!"

We were each asked for five deutsche marks for one-day visas, and then we moved on through another door to a subway-token-looking booth, where we had to buy twenty-five East German marks, for twenty-five West German marks, even though a West German mark is worth about four or five times as much as an East German mark.

Then we went along a corridor, watched by a hooded cobra of a television monitor, around a corner, through an electric gate, and we were in East Berlin, on Friedrichstrasse.

The first time you walk along Friedrichstrasse in East Berlin, you walk hand-in-hand with Franz Kafka. You are on your way to The Castle where they're going to put you on Trial. Kafka looked a great deal like the lovely and vulnerable Claudette Barry, however, and the prying eyes watching our every move were apparently ghosts from World War II that existed mostly inside my own head.

I had first sensed the ghosts that morning when we landed at Tegel Flughafen and rode a taxi into downtown Berlin.

The first thing you notice are the street signs, which in their dignified, black-letter Deutsch characters seem like directions for Von Rundstedt's army. *Bismarckstrasse.* Then you cross over the *Hohenzollernkanal,* which is only a little stream for such a majestic name. A *Spielpalast* turned out to be a gambling joint with the name emblazoned on the front: Dallas. So Berliners are watching our TV as much as we are remembering their city as the crucible of the last big war.

Then we had come out onto the Kurfürstendamm, and it looked like Fifth Avenue in New York, both sides packed with an unbroken line of smart shops and stores in new glass buildings, and with double-decker, psychedelic-colored buses going back and forth. We could have been in New York or Chicago, except for the thing in the middle of the street. A blackened, bombed-out, preserved ruin sat on a traffic island, a thing I had seen on postcards from Berlin: the Kaiser Wilhelm Memorial Church, a forget-me-not to World War II.

We had checked into the Hotel Bristol Kempinski off the Kurfürstendamm, where the people who had arranged the travel junket had gotten me a room.

I had hardly unpacked when Claudette was on my phone asking me if I knew how to go to East Berlin.

"What are you talking about?"

"That's where the painting is."

Somehow since the story about *The Green Room* had appeared in the *Daily Press* and I was in Berlin, she seemed to have decided that we were in this together. She didn't say anything directly, but why else would she be asking me how to get to East Berlin?

My hesitation must have betrayed my thoughts, because then she said, "I don't expect you to take me there. I just thought you might know the way."

"How would I know? I just got here, too."

"Well, okay. I'm just going to go have a look around."

"Wait a minute . . ."

Claudette wasn't in the mood to wait, however, and the next thing I knew we were at the Zoo Station of the U-Bahn, then transferring at the Hallsches Tor Station, and then at Kochstrasse and Checkpoint Charlie.

In East Berlin, we walked a few blocks along Friedrich-strasse and we were at Unter den Linden, the main intersection of prewar Berlin.

"Look," said Claudette, pointing west.

There was the Brandenburg Gate topped by the Quadriga, and beyond it I could make out Die Mauer and West Berlin. Not all the ghosts were inside my head.

So, jumpily, Kafkaesquely, looking over our shoulders for Communist storm troopers who weren't there, we walked along Unter den Linden toward Alexanderplatz, past East German soldiers wearing salad-bowl steel helmets, goose-stepping up to change the guard in front of a museum in honor of the "victims of fascism and militarism." We went by Frederick the Great on a horse, and across a bridge over the River Spree, and came to Marx-Engels-Platz.

Across from Marx-Engels-Platz is an immense, open, cobblestoned area, big as a parade ground; and set back from Unter den Linden is the majestic, blackened Altes Museum, fronted by eighteen fluted columns, its roof studded with stone eagles. We walked across the parade ground, past the graceful Berliner Dom to the museum, its steps flanked on both sides by naked Greek heroes slaying lions. Inside, we were in a circular lobby surrounded by sixteen Greek gods and goddesses; I could pick out Diana, Venus, Paris, Bacchus, Hera, and Zeus.

"*Ja?*" A *gnädige Frau* smiled at us.

"Haben Sie hier Gemälde von neunzehnhunderts?" I blurted out.

"Ahhh!" She smiled and pointed back out the door. *"Gehen Sie links um der Ecke. Der Deutschen Kunst."*

"What?" asked Claudette.

"This isn't it," I told her. "Come on."

"Fitz," she beamed, "you speak German! That's wonderful."

"I speak German like a three-year-old," I told her. "I took it at college, but *Ich habe alles vergessen.*"

Outside, I led Claudette around to another museum, behind the Altes Museum. There on the Bodestrasse was Der Deutsch Kuntsmuseen, the National Gallery, surrounded by a Greek portico, with another horseback statue over the entrance of *Dem Gedächtnis Koenigs Friedrich Wilhelm IV.*

"Frederick the Great?" she asked.

"I don't know. I get my Fredericks mixed up."

We had to pay three marks, and then we wandered through several exhibition rooms of paintings and sculpture: Cezanne's *Stilleben mit Fruchten und Geschirr,* which was a still life with fruit; also Rodin's *Der Denker,* and a Raul Dufy, and a Degas. I was looking at another Rodin sculpture, of Joseph Falguiere, when my arm was squeezed and held.

"Fitz!"

"What?"

"Look!"

I looked. A brilliant green painting of a French room in heavy, flowing contours, with luminous patches and dark corners. I immediately looked at the brass plate on the bottom of the frame: *La Chambre Verte.* Claude Gramont. It was her painting.

"For crissake," I muttered.

"That's it." She stood there, stunned, as though amazed
to find it, even though she had traveled all the way from
New York believing it was there.

She sank down slowly on a little wooden bench, and sat
there devouring it. There it was, *The Green Room, her*
painting, left to her family by the Postimpressionist painter
Claude Gramont, and now, she insisted, legally her property, even though it was currently in the custody of the
National Gallery in East Berlin.

I wish I could tell you that I was overwhelmed by the
painting, but the truth is it didn't seem much different
than other paintings I had seen from time to time, even
though I don't pretend to be the sort who goes to art
museums every Saturday. But if the arcane wonders of the
bilious French room were not obvious to me, Claudette
was transfixed. After almost fifty years, *The Green Room*
had surfaced again, and she was seeing it for the first time.

I sank down beside her, and realized that I had hoped
she wouldn't find it. It had all been so simple, though.
And yet, having found it, what could she do? There it
was, two feet away, but as good as on another planet.

"I didn't think you'd find it," I told her.

"Neither did I."

"Really?"

"Well, no, not really. I mean, it had to be here. But it's
like a dream. It's as though it never really existed before
this minute. My God, Fitz, what are we going to do?"

"Listen," I finally said, "what do you mean, 'we'?"

"I can't believe it," she murmured. "I've really got it."

"You haven't got it."

"Well . . . I mean . . . I've *found* it."

We sat there, like tourists in the Tower of London

looking at the crown jewels only inches away, or like window-shoppers on Fifth Avenue looking into Tiffany's at a necklace worth some immeasurable amount of money. Such voyeurs, of course, know they can only look and admire and fantasize, but Claudette Barry felt that she was looking at her own property.

"How are we going to get it out of here?" she asked, and never in my life had I heard a question that alarmed me more.

$\triangledown$

CHAPTER THREE

OUTSIDE, we retraced our steps across the football-field-size yard in front of the Altes Museum to Unter den Linden and back along it again. Claudette marched determinedly along, her head on fire, wheels spinning. All I wanted was to get her out of East Berlin.

"What the hell's the matter with you?" I'm afraid I snapped. "Are you totally out of your skull?"

"It's mine," she hissed stubbornly. "They always said they didn't know where it was, so they couldn't help me."

"Who?"

"The State Department."

I had hoped that seeing the painting impossibly beyond reach in an East Berlin museum would have allowed her to put it out of her mind. But, no, now that she had seen it, she must have it.

"I told them it was here, but they said they didn't have anything official." She smoldered. "All I ever got was a runaround!"

She halted and glared at me, as though I were somehow part of the State Department. "Well, now I've seen it! With witnesses."

I was about to ask what she meant by "witnesses," when she set sail again along Unter den Linden and led me back to Friedrichstrasse. "Where is it? Right here somewhere?"

"What?"

Then I realized she was looking for the Brandenburg Gate, because off she went toward it. I was about to ask why she was going toward the Brandenburg Gate, with The Wall beyond it, when she veered off to the right, down a side street.

"Hey!"

Around a corner onto Neustadische Kirchstrasse and up to a building guarded by several uniformed officers. I looked up and saw the American flag. The United States Embassy of East Germany.

"What are you doing?"

"I'm going to tell them where my painting is," she said pointedly.

We went into a small, carpeted lobby, where there were steps going up on the right and a little table with a man behind it.

"Yes?" he said, with what sounded like a British accent.

"I want to see the ambassador."

"How's that?" He was a Brit, all right.

The short-haired Brit stood up and looked at us. Behind him, inside a little glass office, stood a U.S. Marine in full dress uniform, peering out at us.

"Yes, yes. What about?" he asked officiously.

Claudette stepped closer to him, and I guess all the frustrations of a year or so of official obfuscation and bureaucracy exploded in her, triggered by actually seeing her painting in East Berlin.

"Listen, I am an American citizen and I want to speak to the American ambassador! *That's* what it's about!"

The Brit frowned and told us to come in, go up the
stairs and into the embassy, past the U.S. Marine in his
glass booth. We were shown into a carpeted room with a
table and a smiling, official photograph of President Reagan on the wall. In a moment, some kind of an attaché
came in and sat across the table from us. He looked at me.

"Shelbourne McNamara. How may I help you?"

"Not him. Me!" Flap! Her passport slapped the table in
front of the attaché. She had built up a head of steam by
now.

"Oh." He got his head turned around to size up Claudette Barry. "How can I help you?"

"The Russians have my painting in the National Gallery," she started, "and I want it back."

The youthful attaché, who looked like somebody who
went to Duke University or maybe Vanderbilt, shot a
glance at me, as though to confirm that this woman was
on the level, or maybe in an unconscious solicitation of
sympathy from a fellow male.

"Your painting?" he finally asked.

Claudette sighed deeply. I had the feeling she had had
conversations like this with a long string of American
officials, which accounted for her exasperation. I knew
how it was, to explain a complicated foul-up to some
secretary guarding the gates of a politician's office and
then get passed on to a third subassistant, and then another
and another, and finally to reach a first subassistant and be
asked, "What's this all about?" You find yourself talking
like a flamethrower. That was Claudette as she sat across
from McNamara.

"Did you ever hear of Claude Gramont?"

The attaché searched the air a moment, but came up
with only a shrug.

"He was my grandfather, a French painter. Postimpressionist."

"Postimpressionist?" It didn't seem to help McNamara. "You're talking about one of his paintings?"

"La Chambre Verte," she said proudly. "It's a masterpiece."

She explained that Claude Gramont's greatest achievement, *La Chambre Verte,* was hanging in the Louvre in Paris in 1940 when the Germans marched in, and that dirty Reichsmarshall Hermann Goering swiped it, along with every other art treasure he could lay his fat, greedy paws on. That was the last her family had heard about it for years. After the war, they had been able to confirm that yes, indeed, *La Chambre Verte* had been carted off to Berlin, but the trail was lost in the rubble after the Soviets took the city.

Claude Gramont had sent his wife to relatives in New Jersey on one of the last ships to come across before the war, and with her she carried the documentation for the painting. Then he had joined the French Resistance. Claude Gramont and the painting had both vanished during the war, but ownership was handed down, until it was now Claudette's. Now *La Chambre Verte* had resurfaced in East Berlin.

Out came the clipping from the New York *Daily Press* that had brought her into my life.

"Here, read it. It was in this man's Sunday paper two weeks ago."

Shelbourne McNamara took the clipping, shot an uncertain glance at me, and read it over quickly: an Associated Press story with a Berlin dateline, announcing that *The Green Room* would be on display in East Berlin for the 750th Anniversary.

McNamara slid the clipping back to her across the polished table top, and was immediately presented with a document, which Claudette pulled from a well-worn envelope. "The catalogue for the 1940 *Peintres Français Contemporains* Exhibition in the Louvre listing *The Green Room* and there's a photograph of it."

McNamara examined the catalogue with considerable reluctance, frowning perplexedly.

"See there," Claudette pressed him, "he wrote under the photograph, 'Sophie: This one's for you.' That's what it says in French. And there's his signature."

"Yes," dragged out of McNamara.

"And under it, see there, Sophie signed it over to my mother."

A nod.

"And under that, see this? It's signed over to me." Then she pulled out a letter on Louvre stationery and shoved it at him. "Here's a letter dated 1939 from the Exhibition Committee requesting *The Green Room* for the exhibit."

"I see," said McNamara, nodding over the catalogue and the letter. "Well, yes, of course, Miss Barry. We'll file a claim at once."

Claudette's gray eyes filled with interest. "You will?"

"Yes, certainly." Shelbourne sat up straight, and wrote on a form. "It will be handled with the others."

"Others?"

Well, yes, he said. Surely Claudette Barry didn't imagine that she was the only person seeking the return of property from the German Democratic Republic?

"How long will it take?"

Shelbourne McNamara bounced his ballpoint pen off the wooden tabletop and sort of glanced around at Ronald Reagan, as though checking with the chief.

"Well . . ." That was the extent of his commitment.

"Well, what?"

Then Shelbourne began talking, and I was back in New York again listening to a court clerk explaining the criminal justice system. Claudette's claim would be duly filed, Shelbourne explained, and would be given every possible consideration, as soon as arrangements for the settlement of claims against East Germany were completed.

"What?" asked Claudette, which is what people also ask court clerks in New York.

Claims against the Federal Republic of Germany had pretty much been taken care of, or were being dealt with, said McNamara, but for those with the Deutsche Demokratische Republik, or Communist East Germany, procedures were still being negotiated through Washington. As soon as these negotiations were completed and a procedure established for the return of property, Claudette's claim would be handled with timely dispatch along with others.

"As soon as *what?* You mean to tell me there isn't even a . . . *procedure* . . . with East Germany?"

"There have been discussions."

"What kind of discussions?"

"Lengthy ones." He smiled rather hopefully.

"You mean nothing has been agreed on?"

"Not yet."

"Not *yet?* Are we talking about since the end of World War II?"

Shelbourne McNamara smiled wistfully. Apparently he could think of no words.

"Let me ask you this," said Claudette, putting both elbows on the table and giving the attaché the full muzzle velocity of her penetrating gray eyes. "How many claims have been settled with East Germany?"

"None."

"So, the truth is, you can't do a damned thing."

Shelbourne's ballpoint pen bounced on the table. "All claims are being processed through channels on the Allied side," he declared rather unhappily.

Claudette Barry gave the attaché the kind of look a shopper gives a clerk at Macy's who says all the sensibly priced coffeepots are gone, and then she glared at me. "See?" her glare shrieked.

"So I have to get it back myself, then?" she flung at the official American representative in East Berlin.

"Uh, pardon me?"

"I said, so I have to get the damned painting back myself!"

McNamara didn't bounce his pen. He dropped it. "But, you can't do that," he concluded.

"If the American government won't help me, what else am I supposed to do?"

"That's quite impossible," he said, on firmer ground now. "Any claim filed with the D.D.R. by an American citizen has to come through official channels."

"Claim?" Claudette distinctly snorted. "Hmmph! Obviously, possession is everything here. I've already got the documentation. Now I'll have to get the painting."

"I'm not sure I understand." He floated to Claudette.

"You will!"

Alarm crept into the attaché's organization face. "You wouldn't . . . uh, attempt anything . . . uh, you're not thinking of . . ."

"That painting's mine, and you sit there telling me you haven't been able to get anything back from the East Germans in forty years!"

"There are signs of progress."

"Forget it," said Claudette. She was on her feet.

"But . . ." Shelbourne was also on his feet. "I'm afraid I can't, Miss Barry."

"What?"

"I can't let you . . . endanger yourself. You have no idea of the seriousness of such a step."

I had the idea that he meant he didn't want this kind of headache. Well, I didn't blame him. I found myself admiring Claudette's determination in the face of all this maddening official gobbledygook, but I didn't want this kind of headache, either, and was glad to remain silent and thus in no way part of the proceeding.

"*You* can't let me?" Contempt radiated from the lovely Claudette. "Obviously, you can't do anything!"

But she was wrong there. The attaché suddenly had that rather calm look of a Marine under fire. Imperturbable, I guess you'd call it.

"I'm afraid I'm going to have to deny you further entry into East Berlin," he said flatly.

"What?"

"I'm sorry. I'm going to have to give your name to the East German Grenzenpolizei and suggest they deny you reentry. The last thing we need is some sort of . . . incident."

Claudette Barry stood there glaring at this imperturbable FBI agent-attaché-college-punk-Yuppie-robot clerk and saw her dream of getting her painting back collapse.

"Is that so?" she flung out, in what I was sure was a mere empty show of bravado. "And how would you like a story about that in every newspaper in America?"

An electric cattle prod thunked me in the neck.

"Excuse me?" Shelbourne looked a little whey-faced.

"This is Ed Fitzgerald," said Claudette, indicating me,

"who has been assigned to this story by the New York *Daily Press*."

Shelbourne blinked. He looked at me. Then at Claudette.

"But . . ."

"You want Fitz to write that the American Embassy in East Berlin has joined forces with the Communists to stop me from getting back my property?"

Shelbourne looked at me and a frown of considerable annoyance grew across his forehead. I had the feeling it was as nothing compared to how Ironhead Matthews would react when he learned I had dragged the *Daily Press* into this dreadful muddle.

▽

CHAPTER FOUR

W E walked back out to Unter den Linden and up toward
Friedrichstrasse. Claudette's face was still flushed. She kept
looking away from me, and when she finally did turn her
head, her face was troubled.

"God, I'm sorry, Fitz," she mumbled. "I didn't mean
to bring you into it like that, but . . . it just makes me so
mad! I won't hold you to it, of course. I mean, I can't,
anyway. But you see what I'm up against?"

Before I could figure out how to answer that, the
reddish mustache appeared. Standing there on Unter den
Linden, barring our way, muttering something.

"What? *Was sagen Sie?*"

"Passports!"

I got focused and there stood a Volkspolizei, an East
German cop.

Claudette seemed frozen. She managed to fish her passport out of her purse and handed it over. Like the border
guards, the Vopo examined the papers as though looking
for coded secrets. A train for Siberia was leaving in ten
minutes.

"So," he said, and handed her back her passport.

He turned to me. I gave him my passport, but felt my neck reddening. What was this? The Vopo looked like some Transit Authority cop on the Broadway-Seventh Avenue IRT line in Manhattan. What the hell right did he have to stop people on the street? "Because this is East Berlin, Fitz," said a voice inside my red ear.

"So!"

We walked away along Unter den Linden, both of our heads racing around in their own little courses.

"My god, Fitz! They know!" The bravado had vanished from Claudette Barry.

"What? Don't be silly."

"They *must!* They've been following us."

I plunged on, annoyed in my own way. "You're imagining things."

"Let's get out of here," she breathed.

But the intrusion of the green Vopo had had a different effect on me. We came up to the intersection of Friedrichstrasse and Unter den Linden and on the corner I spotted a modern-looking hotel. Hotel Unter den Linden, it said, not surprisingly. We still had almost fifty East German marks between us, and we couldn't take them back into West Berlin.

"Come on," I said, and led her into the hotel.

Inside, there was a nice, carpeted lobby like in any pretty good hotel in New York, and off the lobby a bar, flanked by a floor-to-ceiling mural of Berlin at about the turn of the century.

"Fitz," she was murmuring as I led her through to the bar. "Let's get out of here."

But I was suddenly determined not to be shoved out. They had made us buy fifty East German marks to get in, hadn't they? And we couldn't take them back, right? Okay, we'd spend them.

"Sit," I commanded.

She sat. I climbed onto a bar stool beside her and plopped down the East German money on the bar.

"*Bier!*" I commanded the pleasant-looking bartender.

He nodded and smiled at Claudette.

"*Noch ein,*" I told him, which means "another."

I sat there, rather like a stubborn, territorial bullfrog on a lily pad, croaking away to tell anybody within earshot that I had a right to be in this pond, goddamnit, and just try to kick me out.

I lighted a Tiparillo and glared at Claudette.

"Fitz," she murmured, "I feel strange here."

"Listen, goddamnit, it's just a bar."

The slightly beefy, easygoing bartender brought two large bottles of Radeberger Pilsener. I sipped some, puffed on my Tiparillo, and tried to make sense of it.

"It had to be a routine check," I suggested.

Claudette cocked her head at me doubtfully. "They were watching us! Nothing is routine here. Oh, God, Fitz, you're right that I should forget the whole crazy thing."

That only annoyed me more. I hadn't told her to forget it. I had suggested she was out of her mind, that's true, and had told myself I would have nothing to do with it, and, yes, I had been annoyed when she threatened the American Embassy with the *Daily Press,* but goddamnit! The thing was, it was none of my business, even if she did show a lot of spunk and certainly needed help, and even if she was in the right. Let the American officials help her, even though I could see they weren't going to. All I had done was walk with her on the street and there's a goddamn mustachioed Vopo stopping us, trying to intimidate us! Well, I wasn't going to get involved, but I also wasn't going to be intimidated by things I couldn't even understand.

That's the way it is with a New York newspaperman, or maybe any reporter, for all that. You more or less mind your own business until somebody tries to order you around. Then you get your back up and want to know why. Of course, I had to admit that I wasn't in Brooklyn, either.

After the first Radeberger Pilsener, Claudette and I both calmed down a little, although we still couldn't figure out what had happened. If anything.

"Maybe that attaché McNamara told them about us," she suggested uncertainly.

"How? We were barely out the door."

She gazed at the big wall mural. *Deutsche Frauen* in long yellow dresses were about to board fat, ungainly-looking double-decker buses in 1912 Berlin.

The bar began to fill up. A stout young man sat beside me, and I noticed he was listening to our English. He turned to smile. I smiled back.

"*Amerikaner,*" I said. "*Ich spreche nicht zu viele Deutsch.*"

"*Ahh, sehr gut,*" he said amiably. "Very good."

The Communist East Berlin monster, intent upon destroying freedom, sat there looking and talking like any bricklayer in a bar on Metropolitan Avenue in Middle Village, Queens, New York City.

"*Woraus kommen Sie?*" I asked him in faltering German.

"Dresden," he said in English.

"He's from Dresden," I told Claudette. "And look—no horns."

Dresden grinned unknowingly.

Well, since we had those almost-fifty Ostdeutsche marks, I insisted on buying Dresden a drink. "I can't take *das Geld zürück,*" I told him.

"*Ja, ja.*"

Through the medium of Dresden's uncertain English
and my wobbly German, we exchanged the information
that we were visiting East Berlin and that he had come up
from Dresden to have his manager's car checked out.

Dresden bought back some beer—even though I insisted
we use my East German money until it was gone—and as
I studied him I reached the conclusion that this was no
undercover spy.

"Tauschen Sie Geld aus?" he finally said to me, looking
at my money on the bar.

"What did he say?" Claudette had caught the conspira-
torial tone in his voice.

"He wants to exchange money," I told her. "I guess he
wants West German marks. They're worth about four or
five to one against East German marks."

Dresden was smiling at us.

"Oh, my God!" hissed Claudette. She saw a Soviet
colonel at the very least. I toyed with the idea that this was
a Nicholas Daniloff case building again, with me as the
bait.

Maybe it was the Radeberger Pilsener, or just a gradual
return of common sense, but I knew that this was an
absolutely chance meeting. This affable Dresdener was no
spy, just a driver looking to pick up a little extra *Geld* by
trading with a rich *Amerikaner*. There was some simple
explanation for the Vopo stopping us, although I didn't
know what it was. Nevertheless, I was not about to engage
in an illegal currency exchange with an East German
stranger in the public bar of the Hotel Unter den Linden.
A bullfrog I might be, but not a goddamn idiot.

"Maybe he can help us," came the hopeful voice of
Mademoiselle Barry at my elbow.

"What?"

"If he wants to exchange money, maybe we can get him to help us." Claudette's courage had returned, it seemed.

"What are you, crazy?" I mumbled.

I decided maybe we ought to get going. We had to walk back down Friedrichstrasse to Checkpoint Charlie to get out. It was only about four o'clock, but it was already pretty dark. I looked at the Dresdener and shoved the rest of the East German money along the bar to him. He looked at it, then at me.

"Wir müssen gehen," I told him. "It's yours."

We went out and crossed Unter den Linden and were about half-a-block along when Dresden came huffing up beside us.

"Bitte. Warten Sie," he puffed, and walked along with us.

Claudette's hand tightened on my arm.

"I valk wiz you," he smiled.

"Wenn Sie willen." I watched him out of the corner of my eye. *"Wie heissen Sie?"*

"Gerhardt," he said, and bowed as best he could while continuing to walk.

"What does he want?" came the hiss.

As though understanding, Gerhardt from Dresden again said softly, *"Tauschen Geld aus? Ich möchte einen Computer kaufen."*

"He wants to exchange money. He wants to buy a computer," I told Claudette, who was peeking across me suspiciously at the East German.

"We're going to West Berlin. Can't spend East German money there," I told him.

Gerhardt eagerly pointed to a store window. *"Hier!* Buy you some *Schmuckstücke* for your wife! *Etwas kaufen für ihre Frau!"* There was jewelry—*Schmuck*—in the store window. He gestured at Claudette.

"Nein," I told him. We walked on toward the check-point.

"He wants to exchange money," I told her. "He says I should buy something in a store for you."

"If we were only sure he isn't a Commie fink," she muttered.

I looked at Gerhardt. *"Sind Sie KGB?"* I asked.

"Vas?" he said, frowning.

"Are you a cop . . . *Polizei?"*

Gerhardt stopped and waved his arm. *"Nein, nein!"* He dug into his jacket pocket and pulled out a wallet. He insisted upon showing it to me. Pictures of himself, a woman, and a little boy. *"Meine Familie! Kein Polizei."*

We walked along and I noticed the street was quite dark. There were no advertising signs in the state-owned store windows, only the street lamps overhead.

"I don't think he's a cop," I told Claudette. "He's just trying to make some money by doing a little exchanging."

"Maybe he could help us," she breathed.

"What? How?"

"To get the painting. Ask him when he'll be in the hotel again."

"Wait a minute," I protested.

"You be in hotel again?" she asked Gerhardt. He cocked his head and tried to get it.

"Hotel? *Ja, ja."*

By then we had Checkpoint Charlie in sight, and there were four other people—two couples—walking along behind us. Gerhardt the Dresdener slowed and stopped and stood watching us. When I looked again, he was gone.

$\bigtriangledown$

CHAPTER FIVE

THE next morning in the Kempinski Ecke, the hotel dining room on the corner of the Kurfürstendamm, I had breakfast with Hans Dieter, the man assigned to show the New York *Daily Press* reporter and others around Berlin to hear about plans for the 750th Birthday celebration to be held the following summer. With him was a reporter for *B.Z.,* West Berlin's version of the old *Berliner Zeitung*. The *B.Z.* man was Franz Hoppenrath, a gregarious, ruddy character who spoke about as much English as I spoke German.

"Zo, vas zinken you about Berlin?" asked Franz, and lighted a pipe.

"Well, I haven't seen much yet," I told him, and lighted a Tiparillo. "I was in East Berlin yesterday. Unter den Linden."

Franz Hoppenrath and Hans Dieter gave each other a look and smiled indulgently.

"Yesss! Under the lime trees. But there are no more lime trees, isn't?" The *B.Z.* reporter smiled congenially. It occurred to me that my German must sound about the same as his English; that is, faintly comical.

But if Franz and I were fellow reporters, and thus only half plugged-in, Hans Dieter was something else. His English was better than mine; or at any rate, more elegant.

"There is a news briefing, yes? With the Bürgermeister"—he smiled at me—"the mayor of Berlin. We shall go, shall we?"

Well! The Bürgermeister. I was beginning to feel rather important for a visiting newspaperman, when I happened to notice a familiar form across the Ecke. The hair was dark and short and beautifully coiffed, and the profile was pure Joan of Arc.

Claudette Barry sat at a table with a rather slick-looking number in a brown suit who was all attention to her. I found myself wistfully fantasizing that Claudette was simply a lovely American on the loose in Berlin, a romantic little fling over Wiener schnitzel, but, alas, she was a woman with a quest, interested in me not as an eligible male but as a champion from the Fourth Estate whose help she needed.

Among ink-stained wretches there's a sort of rule that you can't make a pass at a woman who needs your help, because that makes it some kind of extortion or something. Of course, this conflict-of-interest cloud hanging over me helped clarify things, because it meant the only way I could get involved with her was by helping her in an insane quest that could only cause me to be drawn and quartered by Ironhead Matthews—if it ended in disaster, which seemed an absolute certainty.

No, there could be nothing between the tantalizing Claudette and me. Yet there I sat in the Ecke, staring at her and the brown-suited stranger, worrying and wondering what she was telling him.

"Pardon me," I told Hans and the *B.Z.* man, and walked over to say hello.

"Fitz!" she smiled, reaching out as though delighted to see me.

"Morning," I said, and my eyes were fixed upon the gentleman across from her, who wore gold-rimmed glasses, his hair parted in the middle, and the look of a clock salesman.

"This is Ed Fitzgerald," Claudette said. "Ed, meet Erik Grosse-Mund."

Erik Grosse-Mund the clock seller immediately swept the napkin off his lap, stood up, clicked his heels, and thrust out his paw.

"Herr Fitzgerald!"

"Hello."

"Sit for a minute." Claudette said with understated urgency.

"I'm with people," I muttered with as much offhanded importance as I could manage. "We have to see the mayor."

"He's an art dealer," she whispered to me.

I glanced at Erik Grosse-Mund of the brown tailored suit and the clicked heels and sank into a chair between them.

"An art dealer?"

"I went into Leo Spik's on the Ku-Damm," she bubbled on.

"Where?"

"That's what they call the Kurfürstendamm," she explained. "The concierge told me Leo Spik is the biggest art dealer in Berlin, so I went around to find out if he knew about *The Green Room,* and that's where I met Herr Grosse-Mund." She smiled and hissed, "Isn't that a dynamite name?"

Erik grinned rather sappily over all this clucking by the

glorious American Fräulein, and produced a finely engraved business card, which he extended toward me between two fingers with a practiced twist of his wrist. *Komissionär für Auktionen,* it read, and listed his address as Hamburg.

I can't say I was too pleased that Claudette was fooling around with an art dealer, because that could only mean she was still trying to figure out how to get herself tossed into some damned communist gulag.

"You are . . . a *Freund?*" Erik studied me. "American, yes?"

"That's right. From New York." I don't know why I was so antagonistic toward him, except that I didn't like his unctuous manner or his arty hair-parted-in-the-middle looks.

"Fitz," said Claudette, "he says *The Green Room* is probably worth several million dollars!" She smiled eagerly at me. "Maybe more."

Erik beamed, as though he himself was conferring all this wealth upon Claudette.

"You told him about the painting," I muttered, not making it a question. "Beautiful."

"He's all right," she said. "He's a West German. Besides, he's an art dealer."

I really might have been annoyed at her dropping confidences like that, except that it was none of my business and I was not going to get involved in any over-The-Wall craziness.

"What else did you tell him?" I asked her quietly.

"Oh, everything. He wants to help."

Erik beamed at us. *"Ja, ja,"* he chirped. Yes, said Erik Grosse-Mund, *Das Grüne Zimmer* was a famous, lost Post-impressionist painting, and everybody in the world of art was very excited to learn that it was once again being exhibited in East Berlin. And now, to meet the actual owner! Well, he was absolutely at Fräulein Barry's service! And mine, too, of course.

Wonderful.

"I will be *sehr* happy to handle zee whole zing," he declared. "Venn do you take possession?"

"Well, you see, Herr Mund," gushed Claudette, "it's still in East Berlin. And the Communists don't recognize my claim. They think it belongs to them as a spoil of war or something."

Herr Mund sipped his coffee. He studied people outside strolling on the Ku-Damm. "So . . . zen you do not have possession, yet?"

"Well, no. It's in the National Gallery in East Berlin."

"*Ach.*"

"But it's mine," she dashed on. "I have the documentation for it."

Grosse-Mund emitted a Teutonic grunt. "You have the documentation, but the Communists have the painting?"

"Can you help me?" Claudette wheedled, and I could see by Erik's glance that he would be very happy to help her in the same way I wanted to, which annoyed me even more.

"*Ja,*" he said. "When you have the painting out of East Berlin. When you have it in West Berlin or Hamburg, then I can handle the sale for you."

"The sale?" said Claudette, frowning. "I hadn't even thought about that."

"What do you plan to do? Take it back to America?" Erik wanted to know.

"I don't know," she admitted. "I guess I hadn't thought that far ahead."

The brown clock seller wagged his head gravely. "You vill never get it out of Europe. Oh, no! I zink you must sell it here."

"You can do that for me?"

Erik nodded professionally. "Yes, yes, of course. Quite. Here or in Hamburg." He fiddled with his teaspoon in his coffee cup. "But, you say, you must get it out of East Berlin? Get it out—*wie?*"

"He wants to know *how* you're going to get it out of East Berlin," I told her. I also considered that an interesting question.

She leaned across the table. "I think we're going to have to steal it."

I tried to kick her under the table, but apparently I missed.

"*Ach! Was haben Sie getan!*" grawked Herr Mund.

"*Bitte . . .* sorry."

Erik squared himself around, moving his legs away from me. "What do you say? Steal *Das Grüne Zimmer* from the East Berlin museum?"

"Yes," said Claudette. "It's mine, so it's not really stealing it."

Erik sat back in his chair and wagged his chin. "*Unmöglich.*"

"What did he say?" she asked me.

"He said, 'impossible.' "

"But it's not impossible," said Claudette, her gray eyes narrowing. "Not if you and Fitz help me."

I was considerably outraged by this remark, and as for Erik Grosse-Mund, he seemed quite dumbfounded.

"*Ich?*" he pointed to himself in alarm. Then he shook his head energetically. There was clearly some gigantic misunderstanding. "*Unmöglich!*"

"Impossible," I translated, but Claudette had already figured that out.

"Look, I have to go," I told them.

"Ja, Ich auch," said Erik, standing.

"You can't help me?" Claudette asked plaintively.

"Ich gehe nicht nach Ostberlin," he said.

"He doesn't go into East Berlin," I told her.

"Do you know anybody who does?" she went on, and Erik paused to look at her again, new hope glimmering in his speculative eyes.

"Hmmm! *Ich weiss nicht. Aber, veilleicht.* Maybe."

I almost had her in tow when Erik piped up again. *"Bitte,* Fräulein Barry. I am at *das Schloss."* He got out another of his cards and scribbled the hotel name and address on it. "Or you can find me at the Exil."

"The Exil?" she said, looking at his card.

"It is, how you say, an artist's bar. In Kreuzberg. If you get the painting out, you contact me at the hotel or the Exil. I do not have an office here, you know, but, of course, like all Germans I have a suitcase in Berlin." He smiled fondly.

"A what?"

"It is a saying, you know. Everyone who comes to Berlin wants to stay. But if you can't, you say, *'Ich habe noch einen Koffer* in Berlin.' It means you will come back again one day."

"Like a coin in a fountain in Rome?" I asked uncertainly.

"Vas?" he said, confused.

Claudette listened to this idle chitchat impatiently, and then broke in. "If I get the painting out," she told Erik, "I won't need you anymore."

"*Ach,* but you vill! Vat vill you do wiz zee painting, eh? It must be kept somewhere safe. It must be sold. *Nein,* you vill need an art dealer more zan ever."

"The Exil?" she asked.

"*Ja.*"

"Listen, thanks a lot," I told him, "but it's all right." I dragged her across to my table, where Hans Dieter and Hoppenrath were casting glances toward us. "What's the matter with you," I snapped. "How do you know who that guy is?"

Claudette glared at me. "Well, at least *he's* willing to help. And he's right. I will need him."

I hadn't planned on taking an international adventuress with me to meet the mayor of Berlin, but I didn't dare leave her alone with the wily art dealer, so we all got into Hans Dieter's car and drove out to the Berliner Rathaus, or city hall, in the Schoneberger district.

Berlin City Hall turned out to be a fine old imperial structure that was once the Schoneberger Rathaus. There was a plaque on one side of the front door honoring President Kennedy, who gave his *"Ich bin ein Berliner"* speech there, and a plaque on the other side quoting the Gettysburg Address: *"Moge diese Welt mit Gottes Hilfe eine Wiedergebort der Freiheit Erleben."* Terrific. JFK and Abraham Lincoln propping up the Berlin Rathaus.

Inside the lobby were more bronze plaques honoring the *"Heldentod für Vaterland,"* the honored dead from World War I, and then we walked along carpeted corridors lined with paintings of past Bundespräsidents. It was like City Hall in Manhattan, and maybe like any city hall anywhere.

We were led upstairs and into a large room where lunch was being served to about forty journalists from around the world who had been invited to Berlin to trumpet the great birthday celebration.

They were from everywhere—South America, Singapore, China, Canada. There were women reporters from India wearing saffron robes with red dots on their foreheads. A big guy with dark, wavy hair and a sort of Joe College manner, complete with striped tie and tweed jacket, slid into a chair beside me at the expansive luncheon table. I glanced around for Claudette and saw her on the other side of the table chatting with Franz Hoppenrath, the ruddy *B.Z.* reporter, who seemed quite transfixed with whatever she was telling him.

"So, how do you like Berlin so far?

"Oh, great," I said. "Ed Fitzgerald, New York *Daily Press.*"

He stuck out a big paw. "Stew Faulkner, Milwaukee. I'll tell you something, Fitzgerald, they got terrific beer here. Almost as good as in Wisconsin. Been to East Berlin yet?"

"Yeah."

"You have?" He was all ears. "Spooky or what?"

"Naw. Nothing to it."

Big Stew Faulkner looked me over and seemed impressed. Then he sort of slanted his head. "Well, you'd better watch your step over there, from what I hear."

"What?" I looked at him.

Faulkner looked grim. "I heard a reporter went over there and lifted something, just for fun, you know—a souvenir—a little statue of a bear or something, and . . . boy!"

"Boy, what?" I inquired.

He hesitated, as though unwilling to say more. Then, with a sigh, "Well, he *disappeared!*" He nodded his head soberly. "I think we'd all better stay the hell out of there, except for the organized tour we're taking."

I didn't much appreciate Stew Faulkner's confidence, under the circumstances, and turned away to watch the Bürgermeister come into the room and proceed to the head of the table. He was an attractive young politician dressed all in blue, like all politicians anywhere, and he launched into a discussion of how Berlin was the only natural capital of Germany.

". . . zee heart of a divided city, a divided nation, a divided world, a symbol of freedom . . ."

I took some notes and noticed that, across the table, Franz Hoppenrath was nodding and nodding as Claudette spun her tale into his willing ear.

"Zis Wall will not exist in history, zis is an inhuman zing. In my lifetime and in history, zee German nation vill be reunited . . . Berlin is zee capital of zee German nation. One nation, one language, one people, one German literature . . ."

When it was over, we all strolled out, and Stew Faulkner asked me if I was going back to East Berlin again.

"I don't know," I dodged. I could tell that, like any reporter, his curiosity was growing and that he'd be over there, too. How could any newspaperman go to Berlin and not go through The Wall for a look?

When I caught up with Claudette in front of the Rathaus, she informed me that she had invited Franz the *B.Z.* reporter back to the Kempi for a drink, because there was something vital to discuss. We caught a cab outside and rode back together, and she led us into the bar off the lobby.

"Fitz," she said when we were seated at the bar. "Franz knows how to get the painting out."

My heart sank. I looked at Franz Hoppenrath, who seemed quite self-satisfied that he was helping us.

"Oh?" I managed.

"If this is really important to you," said Hoppenrath, rather portentously.

"Oh, yes," gushed Claudette. "It is everything to me."

Franz seemed to weigh that. "It is . . . valuable, yes?"

"Very."

"I only ask because it must be, as you say, worth the candle," he said gravely.

"Herr Hoppenrath," she confided, "it's worth several million . . . maybe more."

"Hmmmm," he grunted. "Well . . . there is really only one way." He took his pipe from his mouth. "The painting must come out in the trunk of a diplomat's car."

"A diplomat!" Claudette glowed agreeably.

"Yes, you must find a willing diplomat. Preferably impoverished," said Franz.

"And can you come over and help us bring it out?" she wanted to know.

Franz Hoppenrath lighted his pipe. "*Ach!* No, no. I have been on zee East Berlin blacklist for some years now. If I go zere, zey vould shoot me."

$\triangledown$

CHAPTER SIX

As we sat in the Kempi bar with Franz Hoppenrath, some of the other reporters began wandering in. Apparently, the fact that I was a New York reporter caused quite a stir, because several of them immediately congregated around us at the corner of the bar.

"Fitzgerald, New York *Daily Press*," I said nonchalantly.

"Bibi Nelson, Rio de Janeiro."

"You're really from Rio?" enthused Claudette, and Bibi Nelson smiled and explained that he was the " 'Phil Donahue of Rio.' I have a show in the morning and in the afternoon. Have you ever been to Rio?"

I began to realize that it was not entirely my exciting New York presence that attracted Bibi Nelson. He seemed to think Claudette Barry was the reporter. Or else he didn't care.

"Do you know any diplomats?" Claudette immediately asked Bibi Nelson, and I wanted to give her a kick.

"Why don't you broadcast this over Voice of America?" I hissed into her ear.

Of course Bibi Nelson knew diplomats. He was the Phil Donahue of Rio, for God's sake.

"Oh, yes, my dearest friend in Europe is in the office of the Brazilian Ambassador to East Berlin," he said brightly, and I thought Claudette was going to eat him alive.

"Wait a minute," somebody said, but nobody listened to me.

Bibi had that smooth, unwrinkled television look, like somebody out of a movie who could talk nonstop without coming up for air. I imagined him as somebody who walked around in lounging pajamas swirling an oversized brandy snifter.

Reporters, and even television personalities—who are not considered actual reporters by ink-stained wretches like me—have to seem to know everything. Bibi quickly promised Claudette that he would introduce her to his man in the ambassador's office.

I lighted a Tiparillo and asked the bartender for a German beer. It occurred to me that now Claudette—and maybe I—had "cased" East Berlin, that we had an "inside man" in Gerhardt the Dresdener, and now maybe a goddamned diplomat, not to mention the Phil Donahue of Rio, who was undressing Claudette with his eyes and holding onto her arm, apparently unbothered by any silly ethical twitches.

"I'm from New York," I told the dark-haired bartender, who wore a tux. "What's a good German beer?"

"Ach." The bartender smiled. "Budweiser."

"We have that in New York," I told him. "I want something Deutsch."

"No, no. What you have in America is not *real* Budweiser. *This* is," and he put a mellow goblet of amber beer on the bar.

"*Sehr gut,*" I told him, and he brightened.

"Ah! So you speak German!"

"Well . . . *ein wenig. Waren Sie in Berlin geboren?*"

"No, no. Milano."

Well, it was quite pleasant sitting there chatting with an Italian-born bartender in Berlin. "Ed Fitzgerald *aus* New York," I told him.

"Angelo!" he smiled.

I realized, of course, that I was trying to ignore the possible catastrophe building at my elbow. Finally, I turned back to Claudette and Bibi.

"Fitz," she said, beaming, "Mr. Nelson is going to arrange a meeting with a diplomat for us."

Us, she said. Just like that. I felt I might need several more German Budweisers before long.

Claudette Barry may have had a French grandfather, but the fact is she was very American. She blithely assumed that anybody in West Berlin was quite willing to help her get back her property from the unscrupulous Communists because it was the right thing to do, and because she was, after all, the deserving American owner. I wasn't so sure. In fact, it seemed to me that everyone she told about *The Green Room* was actually interested in getting their hands on either the painting or her, and even though I wanted to ditch her, I was perverse enough not to want to ditch her into the arms of the Phil Donahue of Rio or that goddamn clock seller. Don't even ask me. Besides, I guess I felt sort of responsible for her.

I glanced at Franz Hoppenrath, who was studying Bibi Nelson with a fine newspaperman's skepticism from behind his pipe, and realized he saw through the varnished performance just as I did. He saw my look and removed his pipe.

"This is a friend of yours?" he said, rather too politely.

I shook my head. "One of the reporters."

Franz sort of chuckled. "Yes, we have them here, too."

"What's it like, covering Berlin?"

"Oh, well, you know, very interesting." He smiled. I could see he was an understated person, either through natural characteristic or because his English was limited.

"You're from Berlin?"

"Yes," he said easily, and suddenly I realized that he must be somewhere over fifty, old enough to have been in Berlin during the war.

I sipped my beer, wanting to ask him about it, but not wanting to pry. My long newspaperman's nose won out. "You were here during the war?"

He didn't react much. "Yes," he replied calmly, and then sort of laughed a hopeless little snort.

"Must have been something," I said, rather vaguely.

Another brief shrug. "I was seventeen years old in 1942," he said flatly. He seemed to remember that occasion quite distinctly, and I could only imagine what it must have meant. He would have become a soldier in time for the Eastern front. I didn't press it any further.

I was happy to find that bigmouthed Bibi Nelson turned out to have clay feet in about ten minutes. That's how long it took for him to telephone his VIP ambassador connection and come back to tell us there was a slight hitch.

"Uh, the man I know there is too busy," he said brightly, not exactly eating crow, which is something television journalists are incapable of doing. "I gave him your name. He'll see if he can get somebody else," he finished rather lamely.

Franz and I exchanged rather smug, knowing glances, I'm sorry to admit.

That might have been the end of the whole bollixed-up mess, except that later in the afternoon, while I was taking a nap in my room, the phone rang.

"Fitz!"

"What's the matter?"

"Can you come to my room?"

I sat up and considered the invitation. Go to her room? Certainly I would. After all, we were fellow Yanks and she had probably dropped the whole mad scheme of stealing that painting, and we could slide into a less complicated relationship. I hopped up and walked down the hall to her room. The door was open.

I walked in, but instead of finding Claudette in a filmy negligee, I found she was with somebody. The man rose from a chair, smiling, a little black mustache above his mouth.

"Good day, sir."

He wore a gray suit and a sweater, with a white shirt and a tie, and looked like some sort of government clerk.

"Hello."

"Fitz, he wants to help us," Claudette jumped in.

"Michel Granger, at your service," he smiled blandly.

"Granger?"

"*Oui.* Yes." He flipped open his wallet to flash some sort of ID. "*Direction de la Surveillance du Territoire.*"

"What?"

"Sureté Nationale," he explained.

Sureté? I searched my mind for some context. That would be the French police, as far as I could figure it. I looked him over. Yeah, he looked like a detective, all right. But what in the world was a French detective doing in Berlin calling on Claudette?

"Ed Fitzgerald, New York *Daily Press*," I told him, and took out my press card to show him. He took it into his hand, studied it a moment, and then gave me a look that was not so bland any more.

"*Journaliste?*"

"*Oui.* Yes."

"Hmmmm."

"Fitz." Claudette darted in. "He says he wants to help me get the painting back."

I studied Monsieur Granger. "Is that so?"

"But, of course! Zis painting is of great interest to us," he smiled.

"You mean, because it was hanging in the Louvre?"

"Exactly. Mademoiselle Barry, you say you have documentation for *La Chambre Verte?* May I see it, please?"

"Oh, yes!" Claudette took a step as though to find the papers, but I put my hand on her arm and nudged her into a chair.

"Wait a minute," I said. "What do you want with the documentation?"

Monsieur Granger's eyes flicked. "To see that all is in order, of course. Once the painting is in West Berlin, we would be pleased to assist the mademoiselle in getting it back to France."

"I see."

"He says I might have trouble getting it out of West Berlin," said Claudette. "He'll help us."

This called for some thought. I sank down onto Claudette's bed and lighted a Tiparillo.

"What happens when you get it back to France?" I asked him.

Monsieur Granger now studied me. "What is your interest in this?" he wanted to know.

"I'm a friend."

The black mustache quivered. I didn't like this Michel Granger of the Sureté Nationale. He didn't like me much, either. He turned to Claudette.

"We would simply like to make sure that all is in order," he said smoothly. "We will be pleased to take possession of the documentation, to assure the safety of them, and when you have the painting we would be pleased to guarantee safe transport. It is all quite according to regulations." He smiled Frenchily.

"Who told you about the painting?" I asked him.

"Pardon?"

"How did you happen to call on Claudette?"

La Chambre Verte came from the Louvre," he declared. "Naturally, we are interested." I noticed he had not answered my question.

"Listen, who sent you?" I demanded, realizing I was dealing with a regular *flic* here. I was back in Manhattan talking to some 17th Precinct detective.

"Monsieur . . ."

"Fitz!" questioned Claudette, "What's the matter with you?"

"Never mind. Thanks a lot, Granger."

He looked me up and down—rather menacingly, it seemed to me—and again turned his attention to Claudette. "I would appreciate it if you would apprise me of your movements, Mademoiselle Barry. If I can be of assistance, please do not hesitate. You have my card."

"Yes . . . thanks." Claudette was uncertain now, glancing at me.

I watched Monsieur Michel Granger of the French Sureté as he walked out.

"Where the hell did he come from?"

"He just knocked on my door. Why? He wants to help."

"Sure."

"What? I don't understand."

I puffed on my Tiparillo. I didn't understand, either, to

tell the truth, but it was obvious that we weren't in New York anymore. I couldn't call up somebody, as I could in Manhattan, and ask who this Michel Granger was.

"Did it ever occur to you that the French government might consider the painting their property?" I asked her.

"What? But . . . it's mine."

"You heard him. It came from the Louvre."

"But I have the documentation."

"Yes, which you were about to hand over to him."

Claudette sank back into her chair. "Oh!"

How did the French Sureté, if Granger was in fact from the Sureté, find out about Claudette and the painting to begin with? Of course, she hadn't exactly kept it a secret. In fact, she had dropped the story of her mission into so many ears in Berlin that it was common gossip along the Ku-Damm. Or else . . .

"That damned American attaché!"

"Who?"

"Listen, somebody sent that French cop after you, don't you know that? Who could have done it? That attaché in the American Embassy in East Berlin?"

"But why?"

I chewed on the plastic tip. I didn't know that, exactly.

Before I could ponder over the question, the phone rang. Claudette answered.

"Hello?"

She made a face of helpless bewilderment and gestured to me.

"Fitz . . . somebody's talking German." She shoved the phone at me.

"Hello? *Ja?*"

"Ich bin Diplomat," a voice said.

"What?"

"Treffen Sie mich gegenüber dem Zahn."
"Was Sagen Sie?"
"Cafe Möhring. *Ja, ja? Ich gehe.*"
The phone went dead. I hung it up and looked at Claudette.

"What the hell was that?" I asked her. "He said something about being a diplomat."

"Fitz, it's our man! He wants to help. What did he say?"

"He said meet him across from the Tooth."

∇

CHAPTER SEVEN

"THE Tooth?" Claudette asked blankly.

"That's what he said. Cafe Möhring."

"Come on!"

"Wait a minute," I protested. "What are you going to do?"

"Why, we have to meet the diplomat, of course." She seemed surprised I had asked.

"Listen," I told her, "you've got to stop saying 'we.' I can't get the *Daily Press* involved in this thing."

"But, Fitz, I'm not talking about the *Daily Press*. I was thinking that you could go with me, just as a friend." She frowned and looked away. "I guess you're right, though. I do seem to be leaning on you. I'm sorry . . . I'll go by myself."

"You're not going alone," I decided. "I guess it won't hurt to at least meet the guy."

That's how we ended up going down to the lobby and into the bar to Angelo. "Angelo, what's the Tooth?" I asked.

"The Tooth?"

"Yeah. We're supposed to meet somebody at Cafe Möhring across from the Tooth."

"Ahhh!" Angelo smiled. "The Kaiser Wilhelm Church! Some Berliners call it the Tooth."

We walked up to the Ku-Damm and down the wide avenue until we saw the Cafe Möhring across the street, a nice looking tearoom with orange awnings in front and a big M over the door. I glanced across the Ku-Damm at the Kaiser Wilhelm Church and the bombed-out, blackened church tower. It did sort of look like a rotten tooth.

Cafe Möhring could have fit nicely into the lobby of the Grand Hotel in prewar Berlin, with little marble-topped tables and marbled columns. It was all pale green and tan-colored, with padded upholstered benches along the walls. Chandeliers hung on brass chains, with clusters of little light bulbs in yellow lamp shades.

We walked to a table against the side wall. We could see the Tooth out the window, across the Ku-Damm. After a blond waitress wearing a black uniform and a pink apron served us tea, we looked around.

"How are we supposed to know him?" she whispered.

"You got me."

We needn't have worried. A man sitting at a table in the corner walked over to us and smiled.

"Fräulein Barry?"

"Yes!"

He was a nondescript character with a thin mustache, wearing a felt hat and a black sort of raincoat, about forty by the looks of him. He sat in a chair across from us, lighted a cigarette, and gazed at a spot between us.

"Don't tell me anything."

"What?" I said. I didn't like the sound of that, or the looks of him, either.

"Don't tell me anything," he repeated in clear, precise German that I could understand. He was a diplomat, all right. I wondered if he was a West German, or even an East German.

"How are we going to talk?" I asked softly in exasperation. "Did Bibi send you?"

"What?" he said, frowning.

"Are you from the Brazilian Embassy?"

He leaned back in his chair a moment, seemingly aghast. Didn't these bungling Americans understand the delicacy of such transactions?

"*Bitte!* I cannot go into such things," he pleaded in good English. "You must talk, but do not tell me things." He flicked his eyes evasively over us.

I lighted a Tiparillo, which didn't seem to go too well with this genteel tearoom, and pondered the ridiculous situation. I believed he was a diplomat of some sort, because of his correct German, which even I could make out easily. He didn't sound Brazilian, though even I realized that I wouldn't recognize a Portuguese accent in German if it would save me from the Gestapo. My instinct told me he was a German, and for the moment that's all I had to go on.

"Now, listen," I told him, "whether you're a German or a Brazilian or whatever, we have to communicate somehow."

He waved a hand across the conversation, blotting it out, put his cigarette into his mouth, and explained everything.

"I drive over, I drive back, I don't know anything," he explained. "The rest is up to you. *Verstehen Sie?*"

"I guess so."

"What time of the day or night?"

I made rapid calculations.

"As soon as it's dark. Somewhere between four and six."

"Good! The best time." He puffed studiously. "I will park the car wherever you say in East Berlin at four o'clock. I will give you the key to the trunk. I don't want to know anything. At six, I will come back to the car, drive it to West Berlin, and park it wherever you say. I will leave the car parked for two hours, and then come back for it. You will leave the key under the rear tire. Do not get caught putting anything into the trunk or taking anything out. I don't know a thing."

He puffed on his cigarette and examined the wall behind my right ear.

"How do we know who you are?" I asked him.

"You don't. I don't know you. You don't know me. I don't even know what you're doing. It is better if we are total strangers."

"How do we know you can do what you say?"

"Nobody will stop me. I have diplomatic status," he said. "There's nothing to it. But don't tell me a thing."

"Okay," said Claudette. "You'll bring it to the Hotel Kempinski, then?"

Herr Don't-Tell-Me-Anything gave her a straight-on look for a change. "Kempi?" His head wagged vigorously. *"Nein . . . unmöglich."*

"Where, then?" she asked.

Black Raincoat thought it over. "I don't wish to park in front of major hotels, or on main streets. It's better for you, too, without many people or lights. You have to open the trunk, remember. And I will know nothing."

"He's right," hissed Claudette.

Yes, some nice dark, deserted street someplace would

be marvelous, I thought. Deliver a multi-million dollar painting to a deserted street in the middle of nowhere. Beautiful. I would have to think of a place not too deserted and not too dark.

"You will give me fifty thousand dollars American in advance," he added.

Claudette tensed and gulped. I looked at him and tried to figure out if this was a joke. He obviously caught our reactions and launched into a soothing salesman's pitch.

"You realize what a dangerous undertaking this is for me," he said earnestly. "You are not doing this for some unimportant little trinket. This . . . whatever it is . . . must be worth a lot to you." He smiled smugly.

"Fifty thousand dollars? What are you, crazy?" I asked him.

"How much were you planning to offer?"

I glanced at Claudette. She rolled her eyes. I don't think the question had been seriously considered until that moment.

"I don't know," she murmured. "But not . . ."

The little diplomat's words had considerably sobered me. If he wanted that kind of money, this was a far more dangerous caper than I had thought. Or he was used to dealing with American millionaires.

"Herr Diplomat," I said, "we're not even on the same planet here."

"Well . . . twenty-five then."

I tried not to react. He was coming down from the stratosphere rather swiftly. But, still.

"Fräulein Barry is not a Rockefeller."

Black Raincoat frowned in disappointment. "I could not possibly do this for less than . . . ten thousand dollars American." He nodded in finality.

"The whole thing will take about two hours," I protested.

"Ahh . . . but the peril!" He looked at me sternly. "My entire career."

"Five?" floated hopefully from Claudette.

I studied the diplomat as he considered this presumably insulting pittance, for which he was to risk life, career, and reputation. An indignant refusal hovered in his eyes, and then he said, "Well . . . all right."

It occurred to me that we were not dealing with a full-fledged ambassador.

"Listen, Herr Diplomat," I told him. "We'll have to figure this out and get back to you. Where can we call you?"

The head shook. "*Unmöglich.*" Impossible. He knocked the ash off his cigarette. *He* was impossible, as far as I was concerned.

"And we have to know who you are, too."

The head shook. Ashes flicked.

I started to get up. "Well, then, this whole thing is *unmöglich*. We'll find another diplomat."

Looks of consternation from Herr Diplomat and Claudette. Two against one, here. Both idiots. But there was a trade-off, of sorts. Claudette wanted her painting, but our diplomat certainly wanted money. The way he clung to this deal made me think he was desperate for money and terrified of being caught.

He finally had an idea. "I will be here every morning for the next three days, at ten."

"Okay!" Claudette piped up. "We'll be back."

That was as good as we could do, for the moment. I led Claudette outside onto the Ku-Damm, and she was bubbling with ideas as we walked along.

"Fitz, we need a place to deliver the painting if he won't come to the hotel."

"Yeah, and we have to know who the hell this guy is, too," I said, and then caught myself. What the hell was I doing, I wondered. "Please remember, I only came along to help you talk to this guy."

"Sure, Fitz, I know," she said, and held my arm as we walked. "It's really very sweet of you, and I promise not to get you in too deep."

It gets dark early in Berlin in December and a gloom had settled over the Ku-Damm. Off to the right there was an archway that led from the Ku-Damm through a covered pedestrian walkway into a courtyard, on the far side of which was a "Bilka" German department store where the concierge had told me I could find Tiparillos.

"Come on, I want to get some Tiparillos," I told Claudette, and led her into the covered alleyway. I didn't notice at first that we were suddenly all alone in that dim tunnel until something—I don't know what—raised the hair on the back of my head, and I stopped abruptly and looked back. Probably it was reflexive experience from New York, where you always have to watch your rear.

The figure was bathed in gloom, but the stance left no doubt. I shoved Claudette down and against the wall as the *BLAM!* crashed through the tunnel, echoing off the walls, ceiling, and concrete walk in a reverberating crescendo.

Something between a gasp and a shriek popped out of Claudette. I shoved and dragged her along the walk toward the courtyard.

BLAM! Another explosion, and dust came down on us as we crawled like a couple of demented crabs. Then we were out of the tunnel and around a protecting wall, listening in terror for the sound of footsteps.

∇

CHAPTER EIGHT

I DON'T know how long we huddled there, straining to hear the sounds of an approaching gunman, when we should have been scurrying away across the courtyard to the Bilka store. Finally, we heard voices and footsteps—people coming through the tunnel and across the courtyard, attracted by the sounds and our crazed actions.

I peeked back around into the covered tunnel, but the gunman wasn't there anymore. Instead, there were curious passersby—one in a uniform—advancing cautiously along, looking at the tunnel wall.

"Come on," I commanded Claudette, and walked her as quickly as I could through the tunnel, noticing the two white gouges in the wall where the slugs had left gashes.

It was only a couple of blocks back to the Kempinski, but it took a hundred years to walk there on rubber legs. We didn't stop until we were back inside her room, where she sank in a trembling ball onto the bed and stared at me with wide, questioning eyes.

"My God, Fitz," she blurted.

"Yeah."

"Who could it have been? What did it mean? Maybe they thought we were somebody else?"

I dug into the minibar and fetched out a can of Heineken, trying to think. I didn't believe it had been a mistake, not when we had just come from meeting a shadowy diplomat in a public café on the busiest avenue in West Berlin. I couldn't make any specific sense out of those shots, but it didn't take a genius to figure out that somebody had observed our rendezvous and didn't want there to be another.

"It was no accident, Claudette, don't kid yourself."

"But," she gasped wildly, "we haven't done anything. All we did was . . ."

No, I thought, all we had done was go into East Berlin and case an art theft, alert U.S. Embassy officials that we were thinking of stealing it, babble everything to an art dealer, ask a flighty Brazilian TV character to find us a crooked diplomat, attract a Sureté *flic,* meet the goddamn flaky diplomat in public, and get outselves shot at. Hardly anything.

Then the telephone rang, and Claudette levitated about a foot off the bed. I picked up the phone cautiously. "Yes?"

Only breathing. I could sense somebody on the line, however.

"Hello?"

"You were lucky."

"What?"

More silence. Then, "Berlin is not a place for fools. Stay out of East Berlin."

I was trying frantically to get my head working. "Who is this?"

"No mistake next time. Stay out of East Berlin."

I was holding the phone in a death grip by then, straining to hear, to pick up on the voice, to detect some kind of inflection. But it was flat, cautious, uninflected, with no tinge of an accent that I could get a fix on.

"Listen," I said, "who are you calling? What's this about?" By then, I was talking to myself.

"What . . . ?" came from Claudette's white face.

I hung up the phone and took a swig of Heineken. "I don't know. Somebody with a message—stay out of East Berlin."

"But . . ." She couldn't figure out how to finish.

I was spinning by that time, my own head full of "buts" and some "whys," too, and even more with some "whos." Was the voice faintly French? Was it our inquisitive Michel Granger from the Sureté? There was no way to know.

"Fitz, I don't see how anybody . . . maybe it's because you're a reporter!"

She was grasping at straws, all right. Well, so was I. I shook my head at her in exasperation. Then another thought penetrated my disorganized head.

"How could he have missed?" I wondered out loud. We had been sitting ducks, alone in that tunnel, and he had been no more than twenty yards away.

"There wasn't much light," Claudette offered hopefully.

"We saw him, didn't we? He not only missed—he missed twice."

"But who? Why?"

I tried to figure that one out. "What about your arty patron, Herr Grosse-Mund?" I suggested. "You blabbed everything to him, and he was all ears."

"But that doesn't make sense!" she protested.

No, I had to agree, it didn't, but then nothing did at the moment.

"I think it's because you're a reporter," she said then, apparently liking that solution better. "Erik wouldn't want to stop us from getting *The Green Room!*" She settled herself on the bed. "In fact, I think he's the only one who can really help us. He's an art dealer, he knows about these things."

"What are you talking about?" I complained.

"He is! We need him, Fitz! When we get the painting, that diplomat said he won't bring it to the hotel. Even if he did, we need somebody to hold it for us. Erik!"

I don't think it was until that moment that I finally realized how deeply I was immersed in this crazy escapade of trying to pull off a multimillion dollar art theft from Communist East Germany, when I was supposed to be in Berlin doing a simple, kitschy travel story. What the hell was I doing? What the hell was I thinking of? Obviously, I wasn't thinking at all, but blithely following in the wake of the attractive and persuasive Claudette Barry of Tenafly, New Jersey. Well, those shots in the tunnel off the Ku-Damm had reminded me that we were not in Queens staging a Halloween prank.

"Listen," I told her, "didn't you notice those goddamn bullets? Don't you understand what that crazy maniac said on the phone? Goddamnit, drop it!"

"Drop it?" Her face registered astonishment and runaway disappointment. "But, Fitz . . ."

"Don't 'but Fitz' me," I yelled. "I'm not going back over there! Are you completely out of your mind?"

"You don't understand!"

Oh, I understood, all right. So the painting was hers, and she wanted it. So it was worth several millions. What good would it be to a DOA? More to the point, what difference did it make to me?

"I'm sorry," I said, with as much finality as I could.

She bowed her head a little then, and when she looked up again there was a different expression on her face. I was looking into a set, determined glare.

"Fitz, I'm not asking you to do anything," she said angrily. "I'm not asking you to endanger your precious newspaper."

"Good," I said.

"Do you think I want *The Green Room* for the money?" she said fiercely. "Is that what you think? The hell with the money! Oh, I want it, all right—but not for me."

"Claudette, whatever the reason, you're not in a damned movie here! Somebody's playing for high stakes."

She was on her feet, walking back and forth, fired up as I had never seen her.

"It was a crucifixion, Fitz! What they did to my grandfather was a crucifixion! He was killed in the resistance, you know. We found out after the war. He put Sophie on one of the last boats to come over, with documentation to his paintings—including *The Green Room*. Then he went to fight the Nazis."

"Sophie . . . his wife?"

"Yes. She'd been his model and mistress, I guess, but they got married at the last minute. She was pregnant. There was nothing else to do. Anyway, Sophie gave the painting to my mom—it was all she had to give—and it passed down to me, though we never expected to see it again."

La Chambre Verte had been the most celebrated painting Claude had accomplished, she said, during twenty years of struggle. He had gradually become an important Post-

impressionist and *The Green Room* was hung in the Louvre
in the 1940 Exhibition of Peintres Français Contemporains, contemporary French painters. At the age of forty-
eight, Claude Gramont had finally made it. And then had
come World War II.

"They didn't just kill him," she went on bitterly, "they
stole his work! Except for the few Sophie brought over,
most of the important works were lost or destroyed in the
war. Well, they're not going to keep *The Green Room*! I'm
going to find his old studio—we have the address in St.
Germain des Prés in Paris—and I'm going to restore it.
And I'm going to have a scholarship . . . the Claude
Gramont Scholarship . . . for painters. And *The Green
Room* is what's going to make it all possible."

Claudette Barry, the beautiful, seemingly lightweight
adventuress, was weeping on the bed.

Well, *Gott in Himmel.*

$\bigtriangledown$

CHAPTER NINE

Dʀɪᴠɪɴɢ along in the cab, I wondered if Claudette had ever studied the island-hopping warfare of General Douglas MacArthur, because when she got to minor problems like people shooting at us, five thousand dollars in bribe money, or a diplomat who wouldn't identify himself, she just outflanked them and headed for the next major objective, leaving the dogface soldiers to mop up behind her. This is fine if you're General MacArthur, but I seemed to have been cast as the dogface.

Nothing would do except to go to the Exil and find Erik Grosse-Mund, because we "needed" him, and if somebody was onto us, it was even more important to act quickly and get *The Green Room* out before anything else happened. I didn't tell her that my reason for wanting to see Erik was a little different.

"If the diplomat won't bring the painting to the hotel, we can have him deliver it to the Exil," she explained. "Erik will help us set that up."

I didn't even want to think about what would happen at the Exil, because I was still trying to figure out how to deal with the diplomat.

"What make you think he'll deliver the painting to the Exil?"

"What?"

"He could take it and go to Heidelberg."

Claudette spoke as though she were explaining the obvious to a child. "But we're paying him."

"Yeah. That'll pay his way to Heidelberg."

"We have to trust him, Fitz. He's taking a big risk, too."

Some risk, I thought. There had to be a way to guarantee he would show up with the painting. If there was, though, it eluded me.

"Now I understand why people say newspapermen are cynical," she declared.

I lighted a Tiparillo and wanted to twist her nose off. How many people already knew about this hopeless caper? The American attaché in East Berlin, who wanted it stopped. The art dealer, who could be an Erik the Swindler. The *B.Z.* reporter, with his amiable willingness to send us where he knew a bullet awaited him. Bibi Nelson, the Technicolor television voice, who couldn't keep anything to himself between thirty-second commercial breaks. The French Sureté, who just might want the painting for themselves. Some unknown maniac with a gun. And now a Black Raincoat who wouldn't tell us his name, rank, or serial number. Wonderful! Here we were, dealing with a painting worth millions which, once stolen, would really belong to nobody, except the person who could keep his hands on it.

"The whole thing's impossible," I told her irritably.

"But why?"

"In the first place, we have no idea who that guy is, or who sent him," I said. "We don't even know if he's a diplomat."

"But, he said . . ."

"I don't care what he *said*. People have been known to lie, you know. There are people who make their living by lying and that includes diplomats."

Claudette sat back in the seat and sulked. "Fitz, it's our only chance."

"You can't just give him the money and the painting and let him drive away."

"We could rent a car and follow him," she suggested.

I had considered that, too, but while going through The Wall I had noticed cars being stopped and searched. Everybody had to get out, trunks and hoods were opened, the inside searched, and a mirror on a long pole held underneath to see if any spies were hanging onto the exhaust pipe. A diplomat's car whipped right through without being examined.

"We'd lose him at the checkpoint."

"I'll get in the trunk with the painting," she said brightly.

"No, you will not."

She made another face. "Well, then, what?"

"I don't know," I admitted.

The Exil was like any artist's bar you ever visited in lower Manhattan, which is to say it was all atmosphere and very little substance, with a round, iron stovepipe going up and across the ceiling. It sort of reminded me of McSorley's Ale House on the edge of Greenwich Village, with a lot of artistic types sitting around smoking over their beers.

We went in past a steam counter and into the back room, where there was a real billiard table, tables around it, and wallpaper depicting glasses of beer growing out of flowerpots. I could tell we were in the artist's quarter, all right.

"Why do they call it the Exil?" Claudette wondered, taking it all in with delight.

"Zwei bieren," I told the *Ober* when he came over, and then asked about the name.

Oh, he explained in German, the place had been started by an artist from Vienna, who felt like an exile in Berlin. I told Claudette, who was quite thrilled. Personally, I also felt like an exile in Berlin.

"Do you see Erik?" she asked me, craning her neck around, but I wasn't looking because I didn't want to find the damned clock seller, or anybody else.

"Listen," I reasoned, "don't you think this is getting a trifle cuckoo? Why don't you hire an international lawyer or somebody?"

"Lawyer," she said distastefully, jerking her head around irritably. "How? With what? It would take forever and bleed me white, and besides I've tried all the legal, official channels, and it's all bullshit!" She blushed and added, "Excuse my French." She picked up a coaster and turned it over and over restlessly. "There's no other way, Fitz." She sighed, tossed the coaster aside, and sat back in her chair to look away, inner wheels turning.

"What's the matter?"

She gazed at me again, leaned. "I don't know, Fitz, it's just . . . I don't know. I wish you *were* an international lawyer, a hired hand, somebody impersonal, so that . . ."

"So that what?"

She shook her head quickly. "Never mind." There was a bit of a tremor in her lovely voice.

I don't know if I've gotten across just how fetching Claudette Barry was, with her glowing skin and provocative figure and Catherine Deneuve face framed by short, coal black hair. The more I was around her the more maddening it became to maintain any kind of independence or indifference. God knows I wanted to take her in my arms, too, but one couldn't be at the price of the other.

She turned her head toward me then and gave me such a wistful smile that I experienced the sensation that things were getting much better and much worse. I put my hand over hers.

"I don't want to ask for your help, Fitz, but I have to. There's nobody else. And yet . . ."

"And yet what?"

"I don't want to use you, Fitz. I don't."

I held her hand and thought of no better way in the world of being used than by Claudette Barry of the luminous gray eyes.

We were on the brink of a sea change in things. I don't know where the conversation might have gone, if she hadn't looked across the bar and announced, "There's Erik!"

I glanced up, and there came Erik Grosse-Mund the art dealer, sauntering toward us through the tables like some kind of a boulevardier, a brown coat draped over his shoulders.

"So! How do you like it?" He surveyed the beer-glass plants.

"*Wunderbar,*" said Claudette, and Erik sat at the table.

"So, you think maybe you would like me to handle the sale, after all?" He smiled genially.

Claudette leaned across the table. "Well, maybe," she said. "Why did you say it would be difficult to get it out of Europe?"

"Vell . . ." He gestured.

"The French Sureté called on us today," I told him.

Erik sat up and paid attention. "*Ach!* I thought so."

"But why?" asked Claudette.

Erik's brown head went back and forth. "Vell, they vish to get it back to Paris. *Ja?*"

"Yes. Then what?"

He shrugged. "You vill never get it out of France. They vill claim it as a national treasure. It vas stolen from the Louvre, you said."

"But what if I don't go to France," said Claudette. "What if I take it straight to New York."

He nodded. "*Ja.* But, you must go zru customs, *ja?* And if the French have a claim on it viz the *Vereinigen Staaten* . . . with your government . . . ?"

I sipped my beer. That sounded like McNamara, all right.

Erik smiled warmly, however. "But, you see, I can sell it for you, and zat vill be zat. The buyer will worry about such zings. All you have to do is get it out of East Berlin."

"That's all set," Claudette blurted out before I could get my leg against hers.

"That's right," I put in.

Erik glanced at me and at Claudette and then back at me. He would certainly have preferred dealing only with the naive American Fräulein.

"How will you do it?" He smiled easily and took out a long, thin brown cigarette.

"Never mind," I told him. "What we want to know is, what happens when we deliver it to you?"

"You'll give us a receipt?" Claudette got in.

"A receipt?" Erik smiled broadly. "Oh, *ja, ja.* You bring it to me, and then we can handle it any way you wish," he said earnestly. "You deliver it to me, and we will take it to a dealer and put it into his vault until the sale, *ja? Und* you keep the receipt. And you have the papers, too." He smiled.

Claudette cast a questioning glance at me. It was all quite in order, wasn't it? she seemed to be saying.

"When will you deliver it?" Erik wanted to know.

I put my elbows on the table and leaned toward him. "Before we talk about that, have you blabbed to anybody about this?"

Erik caught my tone and leaned toward me. "*Was ist das* . . . blabted . . . ?"

"Did you tell anybody about this?"

"*Ach, nein!* Well, only Siggy, you know."

"Siggy?"

"*Ja,* Dahlem, the art dealer. He must hold it in his vault."

"Where were you this afternoon?"

Erik's eyes widened. "Did zumzing happen then?"

"Where were you?"

"*Mit* Dahlem . . . his *Büro* . . . *Sie kann ihm telefonen . . .*"

I examined Erik Grosse-Mund and decided he couldn't have been the gunman. He was too short, for one thing. And his hand shook even while holding a brown cigarette.

"We'll bring the painting in the evening," I said. "About seven or eight, maybe."

"So late?" Erik Grosse-Mund's eyebrows were up.

"Yes," I said, not bothering to explain something that might require even more explanation if I started.

"Well," he said, "we can meet at the dealer, then. On the Ku-Damm."

"No," I said. "We'll deliver it here."

"Here?" He looked around, apparently wondering if we planned to walk into the Exil with it under our arm.

"Outside," said Claudette. "We'll drive to the dealer from here."

Erik shrugged, looking from Claudette to me and back again, and nodded. "Well, okay, fine. When will this be?"

"We'll call you at the hotel," I told him.

"I have talked viz Siggy Dahlem, Fräulein Barry, *und zee* Gween Woom is maybe the only important Gramont left."

"You mean it isn't worth as much as you thought."

"*Nein, nein.*" He gave her a meaningful stare. "The market today . . . comparable works . . . It is worth *vielleicht* twelve . . . sixteen million deutsche marks."

"How much in U.S. dollars?"

"Six . . . eight million." Grosse-Mund sat back and beamed happily.

"My God!" Claudette gasped.

"So, you see, there is plenty for all."

Erik sat forward in his chair, pulled his coat closer around him, and then looked from Claudette to me and back again. He took a puff on his brown cigarette. "So, you are really going to do it?"

"Yes," Claudette said at once.

The cigarette shook a little, he slanted his head thoughtfully, stared intently into Claudette's eyes, and said, "It will not be . . . um . . . *gewöhnlich* . . . ordinary sale. *Ich muss Funf-und-Dreizig Prozent* . . . ah, zirty-five prozent commission haben." He stared at her with his alert eyes.

"Thirty-five percent!" Claudette was stunned. She had realized, too late, why I didn't want her dropping those big figures around into peoples' ears.

"It could be *gefährlich* . . . dangerous," he explained unctuously.

Claudette said the figure again under her breath and sat

there dazed, possibly adding up the additional bribe that had to go to the diplomat.

"Vell, you zink it over," said Erik. "I vill be *zu* Schloss through tomorrow, and zen come *wiederzurück* in two weeks."

"What?" she said, alarmed. "After tomorrow you're going back to Hamburg?"

"*Ja.* I come again in two weeks *nach* Berlin."

Claudette looked at me. "Fitz, you'll be gone by then." She fixed Erik Grosse-Mund with an angry glare that gradually slid into resignation.

Erik hunched forward again, and so did Claudette and I, so that we all had our heads together over the little table, talking in low voices.

"What is it you say?" Erik asked.

Claudette looked at me. "Fitz, we can't wait. All right, it's a deal, Erik," she told him.

Erik smiled and looked at her, then at me.

"We do it tomorrow," I said.

∇

CHAPTER TEN

RIDING back to the Kempi in a taxi, I kept wondering at myself. All I had planned to do was go with Claudette to meet that diplomat, and now I had told Erik Grosse-Mund that we were going through The Wall into East Berlin tomorrow to steal *The Green Room!* Somehow, these things kept sneaking up on me and decisions kept getting made for which I was not prepared. It was like agreeing to take a kid to Great Adventure to let him ride the carousel and then finding yourself on the goddamn Runaway Train. And this train kept gathering speed.

We rode back along the Ku-Damm through the center of Berlin, past the Tooth. Claudette snuggled beside me silently, lost in her own deep thoughts. At the Kempinski, we went into the bar and sat in a sort of banquette in the corner, where Angelo the amiable bartender from Milan served me Bud and Claudette a white wine.

"Fitz," she said glumly, "there's something we've forgotten."

"What?" I said, not overly surprised. I felt I had forgotten about ten things, among them how to keep my mouth shut and also why I was in Berlin.

"The money," she said miserably. "That diplomat has to have five thousand dollars before we can do anything."

I lighted a Tiparillo. I had forgotten that, too, or had at least shoved it out of my consciousness.

"I don't have five thousand dollars," she murmured sadly. "What am I thinking of?"

"Erik says the painting is worth six million dollars at least," I suggested.

"Well, yes, maybe, but where do I get the five thousand now? I've got about seven hundred," she said. "I could get another thousand from my credit cards."

"I've got about five hundred in expense money," came out of me idiotically. "So, that's five hundred, and seven, and a thousand . . . twenty-two hundred."

Claudette sighed glumly. "Not nearly enough."

You know how it is when you want to buy something that's totally out of your financial reach and you get lost in the calculations? You want to buy a car for $4,000, but you find out that you're dreaming and that what you want really costs $21,000. So you look over these $20,000 cars when you can barely afford $4,000, and the next thing you know you're tickled at finding a "bargain" at only $18,000. You wind up trying to buy a car for $18,000 when you can only afford $4,000. That's what was happening to me as we pyramided money we didn't have.

I wish I could tell you that it didn't occur to me that I could draw money against my *Daily Press* credit card, but the Runaway Train was still carrying me faster than I could think.

"If I drew a thousand against my credit card," I found myself saying, "that would be thirty-two."

"Still not enough," she lamented.

I puffed on my Tiparillo and conjured up the face of our

diplomat. If he was willing to take five thousand when he had asked for fifty, maybe he would take less.

"Let's offer him thirty-five hundred," I concluded from the depths of my economic wisdom.

"You think he'll take it?"

"If it's cash in hand, I think so."

"But we're three hundred short of even that," she pointed out.

"I'll draw thirteen hundred," I announced grandly.

"Oh, Fitz!" she breathed, and kissed me, and I almost asked if I should draw out another thousand.

Somehow, the idea of drawing out only another three hundred from the *Daily Press* credit card didn't seem so monumental, because I had conveniently rationalized away the previous thousand dollars that would also have to be accounted for, not to mention every last bit of my existing expense money. I don't want to hear a lot of screaming about how I should have realized that all this would eventually put me across a desk from Ironhead Matthews, trying to explain that I had laid out eighteen hundred in *Daily Press* money to help a busybody whom Ironhead had thrown out of his city room as a crackpot. Claudette sat next to me on the banquette in the Kempi bar, her hand on mine, and the overwhelming female nearness of her disintegrated my brains.

As always seems to happen when things are starting to work out, our intimate tête-à-tête was interrupted as Stew Faulkner, the big, friendly reporter from Milwaukee whom I had met at the Bürgermeister's lunch, sauntered into the bar and joined us.

I introduced Claudette and Faulkner gave her a good looking over, as any man would.

"Stew tells me that people who go to East Berlin disappear," I tossed out.

Claudette's head popped toward Faulkner. "Who told you that?"

Faulkner sort of turned his head, as though sloughing it off. "I just heard it's better to stay out of there," he mumbled, apparently a little annoyed at my jab.

"A reporter comes to Berlin and doesn't see East Berlin?" I scoffed.

"We're taking that tour," he said defensively. "You smart-ass New Yorkers—can't tell you anything."

I don't know why I was puncturing Stew when I wasn't all that enthusiastic about going back over there myself. Maybe I was scoffing at myself a little, too.

Then a pretty, chic Fräulein in a blue patterned dress slid over next to Faulkner and made it a foursome.

"Melanie," she said when Stew introduced himself.

You know how it is when you're in a situation and you get vibes that you at first don't quite interpret correctly? It was easy to see that Stew Faulkner was perfectly willing to flirt with Claudette, and of course she was so unknowing—or maybe knowing—that she went along with it and let him drool over her, even though he had to lean over me to do it.

But Melanie, a blond with shoulder-length hair and a look about her that said she knew her way around a bar, seemed to be more or less hanging on my every word. It was as though fate were trying to rearrange things to put Stew with Claudette and me with Melanie.

Somehow or other, after I made a quick trip to the john, I came back to find myself standing beside Melanie and Stew sitting on the banquette beside Claudette.

I was annoyed at first, until I realized that (A) Melanie was thoroughly stunning and leaning against me every chance she got, and (B) Claudette was getting considerably annoyed. I lighted a Tiparillo and foolishly allowed myself to bask in this unexpected and maybe even unprecedented outburst of attention. What was I supposed to do? While Claudette and I had developed this sort of lawyer-client relationship or whatever it was, there was no problem concerning Melanie of the shoulder-length blond hair and willowy frame who apparently found me irresistible. There was no reason why I couldn't flirt with Melanie, and I'm sorry to admit that I found it wonderful that Claudette didn't like it.

It wasn't so wonderful when she excused herself to go to the ladies' room and didn't come back. I didn't notice it for a while, bewitched as I was by the smoky eyes and welcoming body language of Melanie, who seemed quite fascinated by the reporter from New York.

"You live in Berlin?"

"Oh, yes."

"What do you do?"

"Do?"

"Arbeiten Sie hier?"

"Oh, yes. I am working woman." She turned up her mouth. "Why do you smile, *Herr Schreiber?*"

"Oh, nothing." I was thinking of what she had said unawares. In New York, hookers call themselves working girls.

It was about then I realized Claudette Barry had apparently fallen in. I looked at Melanie.

"Melanie, will you do me a favor?"

Melanie edged closer and tried to perform a skin graft.

"Ja?"

"Would you check on Fräulein Barry?"

"Wer?"

"Claudette. *Sie war hier. Sie ging an die Toilette.*"

"Ah!" Melanie took her bag and walked out of the bar. "Hotsy totsy!" Stew Faulkner was still standing there smiling. "Is she in business?"

"What?" I was annoyed. Did every attractive woman who seemed interested in me have to be a hooker?

"Don't you think she's for sale?" Stew went on gregariously. "Not cheap either, Bucky." He motioned for Angelo the bartender. "Excuse me, do you know the Fräulein who was here?"

Angelo glanced at me and smiled noncommittally. "Oh, no." Angelo was quite the diplomat. There would be no opinion from him.

Stew from Wisconsin turned back to me, winked, and sipped his beer. "Bet on it, Bucky."

The topic of our conversation walked back in, smiling prettily, to report that *die Toilette* was quite *leer*. "Nobody zere, *Herr Schreiber*."

Wonderful.

I quickly signed my bar tab, slid it to Angelo, and hurried out through the lobby to the elevators. In a few minutes, I was knocking gently on Claudette's door.

"Yes?"

"Hey? What happened?"

Silence.

"Open the door."

I knocked again. The door gave. I pushed it open and Claudette was back inside the room, sitting on a chair in a green robe. The look on her lovely Gallic face was part apologetic, part annoyance.

"Why'd you disappear?" I asked, moving toward her but stopping when I recognized the look.

"I was getting tired, Fitz, and I thought maybe I ought to get out of your hair for a while."

"I like you in my hair," I said rather absurdly.

Claudette blushed at that, and smiled in amusement. "Yes, but here I am dragging you all over Berlin, asking you for money."

"You didn't ask."

She sat there watching me, something silky-white under her green robe, and my pilot light flared up uncontrollably.

"But if you're tired . . ."

"Wouldn't it be terrific if we were just a couple of people who happened to meet in Berlin?" she said wistfully. "Just hanging out, a girl from New Jersey and the ditzy reporter from New York?"

"Ditzy?" I said, and moved closer.

She laughed warmly. "A little . . . but very nice in spite of himself."

She stood up and paced away, agitated. "Oh, Fitz, I'm just so crazy over the whole thing!" She came back again, walking in her green robe and white teddy or whatever under it. Claudette Barry knew how to walk.

"It'll be okay," I said idiotically.

"Okay! What do you mean? Going back over there . . . what if they know? Fitz, I'm so afraid."

Then she was in my arms, trembling. I was trembling, too, but not from tomorrow's fears. My arms were around her, my hands on her back, and she turned her mouth up to be kissed. I pulled her tightly against me and dispatched *The Green Room* and East Berlin and The Wall into the future to wait for us. I needed the present, that moment, and Claudette straining against me. Whatever cloud there had been around us swallowed us up.

"Don't leave me alone tonight," she murmured.

$\triangledown$

CHAPTER ELEVEN

Dᴇᴀʀ world, is there anything more fulfilling than to wake up in the morning in Berlin under a *Plummel* and see tousled black hair framing the dewy-eyed face of Claudette Barry on the pillow next to you?

"Hello."

She snuggled against me, her lithe body a silken thing, and I was instantly back to life. We became one again, and how wondrously her body fitted mine. I could have stayed there skin-to-skin forever.

Gazing into her beguiling gray eyes so close to me now, I realized that whatever reservations I had had about us and the whole sappy adventure were gone for good. Probably my chances of remaining indifferent to her and her quest never really existed in the first place. From the first moment when she shoved that news clipping into my face I had been in for a penny; now I was in for a pound.

We got up and had coffee together in her room. With the first sip it all came back to me. This was the day we were to go over The Wall for *La Chambre Verte*. I went back down the hall to my room to shower, shave, and dress, and as water poured down over me it seemed to wash away all the pretty illusions I had been building. Had I in the spell of Claudette's disarming loveliness actually promised to draw thirteen hundred dollars on my *Daily Press* credit card?

I had. As I got dressed, calculations swirled around inside my head, all of them dire. I would have to call the *Daily Press* to Jack Milligan to get approval, of course, because this was more than a thousand dollars extra over and above my expense money. What time was it? Nine in the morning. That meant it was about three in the morning in New York, and how could I make a call now?

I knotted a tie around my neck, and it felt just like the claw hands of Ironhead Matthews. From the mirror his storm cloud of a face glared back out at me, a glowing dirigible in his downturned mouth.

"You want thirteen hundred dollars for *what?*"

"Well, you see . . ."

"Maybe you think this is the Morgan Guaranty Bank?" he suggested in the levity before the volcano.

"It would be a helluva story, Ironhead. *Daily Press* aids lady in distress."

"By lady in distress, you mean that dippy quiff who snuck in here and jabbered bullshit at me?"

The image faded, along with my hopes of pulling this off in some quiet, underhanded way.

Marcus Aurelius wrote admiringly of his adoptive father, the Emperor Antoninus Pius, that he never "carried anything to the sweating point." But then, Antoninus Pius never had to deal with a New York city editor. I was in Berlin, a more or less foreign correspondent on a hot adventure with a delectable creature at my side, I had just showered, and yet I felt sweat pouring out all over me.

Of course, rationalizations slowly crept into my enamored skull, since I could not possibly disappoint the silken Claudette Barry, and crises can always be dealt with better if they are put off until tomorrow or next week.

I would draw the money now, and call Jack Milligan later when he was in his office at the *Daily Press*—in about seven hours—and tell him an emergency had arisen. In seven hours, surely I could dream up something suitable. Besides, what business was it of a mere office manager to question a reporter in the field?

I lighted a Tiparillo and held onto that good thought. Of course! Who was Jack Milligan? Nothing but a grubby bookkeeper who served the reporters out there fighting for the New York *Daily Press*. It was none of his business what I needed the money for. He was acting as though it were his own dough, for crissake. I resolved to *tell* him I had drawn the money, that seemed at least reasonable, but there would be none of his boring questions about it.

Thus having resolved this formerly sticky problem, which now was recast into its proper form as an unimportant administrative trifle, I went down the hall to collect Claudette.

The room service man was just coming out as I approached her door, and then I realized he wasn't wearing any sort of uniform. At the Hotel Bristol Kempinski, where bellboys wore green livery out of the Grand Hotel, everybody wore some kind of uniform.

"Hey," I called out, but whoever he was, he was around a corner and gone.

I hurried down the hall and looked around the corner. Elevators, and another hall going further. No room service man or anybody else.

Back at Claudette's door, I found it standing ajar. I slid inside and heard the shower running. The room was in spectacular disarray.

"Claudette!"

The shower stopped, and she peeked out at me, wrapped in a towel and such a vision that I almost forgot The Wall, the painting, and the fact that her room had just been ransacked.

"What?"

"How long have you been in there?"

"I don't know. Why?"

"Jesus!"

She glanced around and saw the mess. "Fitz!" She stepped out, in her towel, and her eyes were saucers. "Was somebody in here?"

"Get dressed."

She jumped back into the bathroom and I looked her room over. Drawers were pulled out, their contents spilled on the floor. Her luggage had been tossed like a salad. Claudette dressed in no time, it seemed, and came out to help me examine things.

"Somebody ran away from your door as I came up."

"Oh, my God! What does it mean? Somebody was in here searching the room while I was in the shower!"

"Looks like it. Is anything missing?"

She quickly went through her things, but couldn't tell.

"I had my purse in the bathroom with me," she said. "Thank God! What did he want?"

"Have you got the papers for the painting?"

She dug quickly into her purse and brought out the documentation. She breathed a sigh of relief.

I tried to think. "Maybe somebody knew we were supposed to have five thousand bucks," I suggested.

"But . . . who? Only that man, that diplomat."

"Yeah."

So we weren't slipping around unnoticed in Berlin, after

all. I cursed Claudette's free-and-easy discussions with strangers about what she was doing here, and realized any number of people must know. Whoever it was, he had to have been after the money or the documentation for that painting. I glanced at her and wondered if that intruder would have gone into the shower after her if I hadn't arrived when I did. I said nothing, though.

Claudette was sitting on the bed, staring eagerly at me, waiting for an explanation, or some words to make it all right.

"Well, maybe it was the room service man." I dodged.

"Room service?" She surveyed the cyclone of her room. "Fitz, that was no room service man, and you know it."

"All right. He didn't get anything. Let's get going."

"But I can't leave anything here now!"

"Yeah. You're right. You've got the papers, that's all that really matters. Let's go draw some money. We have to meet that diplomat."

Claudette restored some order to her things, clucking away under her breath all the time. We were almost out of her room before I remembered.

"Bring your camera," I told her.

"My camera?"

"Yes. Do you have film?"

She grabbed her Polaroid camera and we left. In the lobby, we walked off the elevator into a crush of people all standing around, and there was Hans Dieter coming toward me, smiling, his hand out. "Well, there you are. Ready?"

"Ready . . .?"

"Today, we go to Martin-Gropius-Bau. This will be certainly quite fascinating."

The journalists swarmed around chatting, the Indian

women with their red dots and the South Americans in their formal suits with vests. I remembered I was supposedly in Berlin to learn about the city to write a travel piece.

"The bus is ready," one of Hans Dieter's people was blustering, shooing the reporters out.

Stew Faulkner was next to me. "This should be good," he confided. "The Gestapo headquarters is right next door to the Martin-Gropius building."

"Gestapo?"

Something bumped me. Claudette Barry was beside me.

I drew Faulkner aside. "Listen, Stew, would you cover for me? There's something I have to do."

Large Faulkner smiled knowingly, glancing at Claudette and then back at me. "Where're you going?"

"It doesn't matter. Pick up some press handouts for me, will you?"

The Joe College face lighted up and his eyes opened knowingly. "Sly dog," seemed to be the message.

I slid off through the lobby and ducked into the bar, followed by Claudette, and we waited while the big red-and-cream bus loaded and pulled away from the front of the hotel.

"I'm supposed to be covering a story," I groaned.

"Stew will cover for you," Claudette assured me.

When the bus was gone, we came out of the bar and back through the lobby and walked up to the Kurfürstendamm to find a bank, where I nervously took a thirteen-hundred-dollar cash advance on my *Daily Press* credit card. Then we walked along the Ku-Damm to the Cafe Möhring.

"Now, listen," I told her as we went, "don't try to talk business with this character. Leave that to me."

"Yes, Fitz."

She had her arm hooked in mine and stayed very close to me. We went into the tearoom with its rather formal air of *preussische Gemütlichkeit*. In the corner at the same table sat the Black Raincoat. He glanced up, then away, and I took that to mean we should not join him, but that we should take the upholstered bench along the side wall as before. We sat and were served tea by the waitress with the pink apron. He came strolling over to us.

"Wie geht es Ihnen?" he smiled politely, and sat across from us. "Do you have the money?"

I sipped my tea, lighted a Tiparillo, and studied him a little. "Do you have any identification?"

"Ganz unmöglich."

"What does he say?" Claudette nudged me.

"He won't show any I.D. The whole thing's idiotic."

The Black Raincoat sat there and smoked a cigarette. "You must trust me," he finally said.

It was wonderful. We had to trust him, give him money, give him Claudette's painting, ask nothing, and tell him nothing. It was like dealing with a New York divorce lawyer.

"Forget it." I stood up.

His hand came across the table, waving me back down. "Wait . . . wait . . . wait. *Sitzen Sie. Bitte.*"

I sank back into the chair. Claudette had not stirred.

"What do you want?" he asked softly.

"For crissake, something. We may be Americans, but we *are* from New York."

"Command me. I will do it. Tell me where to park the car, and for how long."

"Bodestrasse," Claudette slipped in. "For two hours."

"Bodestrasse?" He puffed and nodded. *"Ja, ja. Bei der Kuntsmuseen."*

"Yes!" She gripped my hand enthusiastically. "See, he understands."

"Yes." I puffed my Tiparillo. "We'll pay you at the Exil."

"Nein." He didn't even bother to shake his head. *"Jetzt."*

I told Claudette he insisted upon payment now.

"We have to trust him, Fitz," she pleaded.

"Half now. Half at the Exil."

"Nein."

"He seems all right to me," from Miss Trustful.

I didn't like it, but then I couldn't imagine any situation that I would like. "Your car will be parked on the Bodestrasse from four to six," I told him. "Backed into the curb in front of the National Gallery."

He nodded.

"At six, you will drive to the Exil and wait for us."

Another nod. "You have the money?"

"Yes." I took the money out and held it in my hand so he could see it. "Outside."

"Nein."

"Ja." I swallowed the money into my hand and got up. "Come on," I told Claudette, and walked her away without looking back. Outside on the sidewalk, I drew Claudette away toward the street and waited until he came out. He looked at us, and then came over.

I let him see the roll of money again, then closed my hand. "We could only get thirty-five hundred," I told him.

He halted, backed up a step, and turned away. Then, he came back again, sighed, and said, "All right."

"Not here," I told him. "Where's your car? We have to be able to recognize it."

Black Raincoat seemed distressed and moved his head around uncertainly, but I wouldn't show the money again.

Finally, he walked along the Ku-Damm and down into a
side street, Rankestrasse, and stopped by a parked Opel
with red license plates. We followed slowly.

"Now, listen," I told Claudette, "when you pay
him . . ."

"You want me to pay him?"

"Yes. But when you do, I want you to stand in front of
his car and hand him the money."

"What?"

"Right in front, and make sure the money's in plain
sight when you give it to him. Give me your camera. Walk
right up to the front of the car and make him come to
you. Go."

She went. I stopped and turned around to face the other
way for a moment, and then looked again.

For once, she did what I told her to, and when Black
Raincoat came in front of his car with the red diplomatic
license plates, the Polaroid camera was out and focused on
both of them. I popped off a picture as they stood there.
Raincoat looked at me full-faced, startled, and it was
perfect. He grabbed the money and ducked around into
the car, but by then I was standing beside the driver's side
window. He rolled it down slightly.

"Now, listen," I told him, "I've got a picture of you
and your license plate and Claudette giving you money.
Verstehen Sie?"

I pulled the backing off the Polaroid photo and looked
at it. It was perfect. I held it up so he could see it through
the car window.

He sat behind the wheel, frozen, blinking at the photo,
and looking at me. What he was thinking, I don't know.

"You won't tell us who you are," I said. "Well, this will
tell somebody who you are, and whose car you're driving.
And that somebody gave you money."

He looked down and lighted a cigarette, his hands shaking, and grumbled something. If a gun was going to appear through the car window, this could be the time. But Herr Diplomat sat huddled there, seemingly immobile.

"You can have the photo when you deliver, *ja?*"

He nodded.

"See you at the Exil."

$\triangledown$

CHAPTER TWELVE

AFTER leaving the diplomat, we went back along the Ku-Damm and walked anxiously through the pedestrian tunnel where we had been shot at to the Bilka department store. We bought our supplies: razor blades, plumber's putty, safety pins. What a cop back in Queens would call burglar's tools.

Then we stopped at a photo shop and Claudette gave them her Louvre catalogue to get a photographic blow-up copy of *The Green Room* in the same size as the painting, two feet high and three feet wide, which she rolled up into a cardboard tube. We hurried back to the hotel and went up to her room to go over the plan we had hatched the night before under the *Plummel,* but in the most exquisitely distracting of conditions. She ordered coffee from room service, and we went over it all again.

I realized I was doing most of the talking. The whole crazed expedition was now in the hands of somebody who had sworn blue that he wouldn't have the slightest thing to do with it.

"Let me see it," I told her, and she unrolled the photo blow-up of *The Green Room* and spread it on the bed.

"All we have to do is get the real one and leave this in its place," she informed me brightly.

She made it sound easy, all right, but there were the minor problems of how to carry the copy into the museum and how to bring the original one out, not to mention a few additional terrors that I ignored for the moment.

"How are you going to carry it?"

She rolled up the photo copy again, slid it into the tube, and slipped it up the sleeve of her raincoat. Then she looked at me expectantly.

The next question was how to bring out the original *Green Room,* which couldn't be rolled up as the photo copy had been.

"Put the safety pins in," I told her. She spread my London Fog raincoat on the bed, reached up between the coat and the lining, and put the safety pins in. Then she took out the copy and pinned it into the lining.

"Try it."

I put the coat on and walked around the room. It seemed to be all right, but of course it wasn't the real thing, which would be stiffer.

"You can't even notice it," she exulted. "I guess we're ready!"

"Yes," I managed.

Oh, we were ready, all right, as ready as the Polish Uhlani Lancers were when they charged Nazi Panzers on horseback.

I put in a phone call to Erik Grosse-Mund at the Schloss Hotel, but of course he wasn't in, so I left a message for him with the striped pants at the front desk to meet us at the Exil that night at six-thirty.

We left the Kempi again and walked up to the Zoo Station on the Ku–Damm and caught the U–Bahn to

Hallesches Tor and then to Kochstrasse and Checkpoint Charlie. We walked through as before, doing the rigmarole of buying the one-day visas and exchanging twenty-five deutsche marks for twenty-five East German marks. We weren't searched.

It was after two by the time we got through the checkpoint and headed along Friedrichstrasse. I didn't feel this time that ghosts were watching us. Nobody seemed to be paying any attention to us, I thought.

At Unter den Linden, we went into the Unter den Linden Hotel and into the bar, where we sat in the corner and watched. It wasn't too long before Claudette spotted Gerhardt from Dresden walking in.

I sauntered to the bar, sat beside him, and ordered us both Radeberger Pilseners.

"Ah, der Amerikaner," he beamed.

"Wie gehts?" I said pleasantly.

"Gehts gut."

I invited him to come sit in the corner with Claudette and me, and then asked if he still wanted to exchange some money.

Gerhardt the Dresdener perked up. *"Ja!"*

Would he do something for us?

"What?" He searched our faces intently.

"Kommen Sie." I told him.

We walked outside and along Unter den Linden toward Marx-Engels-Platz, and I told him in my stumbling German what we needed him to do.

The stout engineer listened and wagged his head around and listened some more and kept walking with us. We crossed the River Spree and came to the big parade ground area in front of the Altes Museum across from Marx-Engels-Platz, and there he stopped.

"So," he pondered. *"Und das ist alles?"*

"That's all," I assured him.

"Und wie viele tauschen wir aus?" he wanted to know.

I then dropped the convincer. There would be no exchange at all, but we would give him two hundred deutsche marks outright. He blinked, sounded the *"zwei hundert"* silently with his lips, and then nodded.

We let him walk ahead of us across the cobblestoned court next to the Berliner Dom and then sauntered along after him. He went straight as an arrow to the museum, up the stone steps between the Greek statues slaying dragons, and inside. We went in after him, bought our tickets, and strolled along like a couple of tourists, keeping him in sight. As in the National Gallery, there were no soldiers or guards around, and we walked through the exhibition rooms without being watched.

In the third room, Gerhardt paused and glanced around. Then he moved in closer on a large, gilt-framed painting of some long-ago battlefield, and bumped the painting frame with his shoulder. We halted and watched.

Nothing.

He glanced at us, and I indicated he should do it again.

This time, Gerhardt gave the frame a good whump with his shoulder, and that did it.

The frumpy, middle-aged housewife caretakers whom we had noticed as the only guardians of the art treasures suddenly appeared and descended upon Gerhardt like furious harpies. Two came around one corner and two more around another.

"Was haben Sie getan?" I heard one of them snap at Gerhardt, and then others were talking loudly and Gerhardt was gesturing with his arms wide, complaining that he had only accidentally bumped a painting.

They were all still gabbling and waving their arms when Claudette and I walked away and back outside. Claudette looked at me. I looked at her.

After a few minutes, Gerhardt came huffing outside and back down the wide stone steps. We walked across the large yard and back across the Spree and waited.

When he caught up with us, I led us all into the Opfern Cafe in the Arsenal Museum beside the Spree and we sat at a table.

The waitress served us tea in short glasses with glass handles. I lighted a Tiparillo and puffed thoughtfully, exchanging glances with Claudette. There was nothing more for us to do at that point except to wait until it got dark. It was after three, and Black Raincoat was to park his Opel on the Bodestrasse in front of the National Gallery by four.

Gerhardt watched us both frowning and finally asked why we wanted him to bump a painting.

"Macht's nichts," I told him.

"Gehe ich nicht ins Kuntsmuseen?"

I assured him that, no, he did not have to go into the National Gallery. He seemed relieved.

Just after four o'clock, we left the Opfern Cafe and walked outside. Happily, it was quite dark already.

"Come on," I told Claudette, who had once again slipped into silence.

We walked back over the river and across the cobblestones that led to the National Gallery. On the Bodestrasse in front I spotted the cream-colored Opel parked with the trunk backed up to the sidewalk, and relief mixed with alarm slid through me. It was all working, and that was both good and terrifying. What the hell were we doing?

"Hier," I told Gerhardt, and positioned him at the Opel

looking up the street toward Unter den Linden. The street dead-ended into Unter den Linden, into a large, official-looking building on Marx-Engels-Platz.

"What building is that?" I asked him.

Gerhardt looked somber. *"Der Deutsch Demokratik Republik Völkskammer."*

Great. We were pulling this caper in the shadow of the East German Communist Government's parliament building. There was no turning back now, however. The Opel was parked and waiting, it was good and dark, it was after four, and the museum closed at six.

The National Gallery is fronted by a little yard and surrounded by a sort of Greek portico, which was being worked on. Flimsy wooden construction walls had been erected along the portico, obscuring the street from the museum for much of the way.

Claudette and I walked under the portico and along the sidewalk through the little yard, going under whichever Frederick-on-horseback it was who surmounted the entrance, and went into the lobby.

Buy the museum tickets, and then up the carpet-covered marble steps. One, two, three . . . there were fourteen steps. Then into the exhibition rooms to the right, and in a few minutes we once again stood in front of *La Chambre Verte.*

It was a question now of being alone in the room, without the middle-aged Frau harpy guards, long enough to do it. I sank down onto a viewing bench to collect my thoughts and calm my nerves and then glanced up and saw something that almost gave me a heart attack.

"Well, well. Bucky."

Stew Faulkner the reporter.

$\triangledown$

CHAPTER THIRTEEN

"I THOUGHT you went to the Martin-Gropius building," I told Stew Faulkner haltingly.

"Oh, yeah, I did," the big Milwaukeean said, moving over to have a closer look at *The Green Room*. It was nothing. Just a building not far from The Wall."

"What about Gestapo headquarters?"

He shook his head. "Hole in the ground. Just an excavation. So, I decided I really should come over here and have a look. And here you are." He smiled oafishly, glancing at Claudette. She gave him a look that could have melted Frederick the Great's statue. Stew squared around to get a head-on view of the painting.

"Let's see, now," he said, sizing it up. "What's this? *La Chambre Verte*.

"*The Green Room*," Claudette managed. "It's Postimpressionist."

"Ahhhh," said Stew, and it sounded hollow to me. He didn't know any more about Postimpressionism than I did.

"Have you seen the Pergamon Altar?" I asked casually.

"The what?"

"You haven't seen the altar?" Claudette jumped in.

Stew frowned. "In the Pergamon Museum, you mean? That's the one everybody talks about."

"Listen," Claudette said, "forget it. If you haven't seen the Pergamon, you haven't seen anything."

"Yeah, I heard it's pretty amazing," he said. "You want to go find it with me?"

"Find it?" I tried to appear indignant. "It's the first place we went. You walk in and there's this white marble altar the size of a football field, it seems. Absolutely knock you out."

"I gotta see that," Stew agreed anxiously. "You know where it is?"

I consulted a little map showing the cluster of museums huddled close together in East Berlin.

"Let's see here," I nattered, trying to locate it.

"There," said Stew, looking over my shoulder. "It's just about a block away then, huh?"

"Right. Can't miss it." Claudette encouraged him.

"Well," he said, straightening up. "I gotta see that. Where are you gonna be? Maybe I'll catch up with you."

"We're going to hit the Old Museum after this," I told him, trying to sound organized, "and then the TV Tower."

"Say, I saw that outside," said Stew. "You going up in that?"

"Oh, sure," Claudette told him. "You have to."

"Yeah. Well . . ." He seemed to sway back and forth in his uncertainty and anxiety. "Well . . . maybe I'll catch up with you."

He hurried out, headed for the Pergamon Museum, which I understand truly is spectacular. If I ever get back to East Berlin, I certainly will have to take it in.

"Claudette," I hissed, and went to sit beside her on the wooden bench. "The damned thing's too high for you!"

The way we had planned it, she was going to lift *The Green Room* while I was the lookout. A closer look showed that the top of the painting was beyond her reach. I realized it was going to have to be the other way around.

"You have to be the lookout!" I told her.

She nodded and opened her purse, and I saw the paper bag inside containing the burglar's tools. I reached in and took the bag out.

"Okay, now," I reminded her, "if anybody comes, whistle. Right?" Her face registered panic as I looked into it. "What? That was going to be the signal. I was going to whistle if anybody came."

She spoke, but nothing came out. Then, "I can't whistle!"

"What? Anybody can whistle."

Her head wagged. "Not me. I never could."

Terrific. There we were in the middle of a multi-million-dollar caper inside Communist East Germany that might get us shot or cause an international incident or put us in a Soviet gulag, and the whole thing was about to explode because she couldn't whistle.

"What can you do?"

She searched her mind. "Uh . . . yell? No . . . stamp my feet?"

Great. A flamenco dance for a warning signal.

"Okay," I said. "Now, listen . . . once I start, you can't let them into this room."

"Yes."

"Once I start, if anybody comes this way, you have to lead them away. Knock a picture . . . scream . . . run . . . but away from this room. Right?"

"Yes."

"Okay. Get over there."

She got up and walked to the corridor that ran along the edge of the room and stood there glancing up and down. Then she gave me a look, took a breath, and nodded twice.

I stepped up to *The Green Room* and took out the razor. Once I started, there was no turning back, and I had to have two or three minutes without being interrupted. I glanced back at Claudette one last time, and she was staring intently at me.

I gestured to her to for god's sake watch the corridor and not me. She looked away.

Now. I raised the razor to the right edge of the painting, pressed it against the top right at the frame, and shoved in. A muffled scruff sound, like cutting wallpaper. Down along the edge of the frame with the razor, top to bottom on the right side.

The painting is two feet high and three feet wide. I hoped I wasn't cutting off much of the edge. I stood there sort of hypnotized as I looked at the razor cut, and something floated gently into my consciousness. Somebody was apparently annoyed at something and was tapping his or her foot.

Tapping her foot!

My head shot around to look at Claudette. She was stomping the stone floor and trying to look unconcerned at the same time.

Somebody was coming.

I stepped away from the painting and fought off an urge to run.

Two women and a little girl sauntered into the room, oblivious to the fact that they were walking into the midst of a grand art theft and were in imminent danger of sudden death at the hands of two desperate people.

The two women started studiously examining paintings and consulting a damned catalog as they moved from one to another. They were murmuring softly in some language that was neither English nor German. The little girl, who appeared to be about ten, glanced at me, then away.

I decided to get interested in some other paintings, and stepped away from *The Green Room*. As I did, I palmed the razor blade, and felt it slice into my skin.

The women and the child moved ever so snaillike around the room, heading gradually toward *The Green Room,* which was the second painting from the end on their circumnavigation of the room.

I looked covertly at the edge I had already sliced, and it was obviously a yawning chasm of a cut, visible from fifty yards away. No matter where I moved in the room, distancing myself from the three art lovers, I could see the immense canyon separating the frame from the right edge of the painting. They could not help but see it.

The little girl kept watching me from time to time, and it was perfectly clear that she knew everything. She noticed the slashed painting, all right. It was like that revolting little squirt in *The Third Man* who kept telling everybody in Vienna that Joseph Cotten had killed the porter. When they got to *The Green Room,* we would begin hearing the *eee-aaaah, eee-aaaah* of the Green Police coming for us.

They moved around the room, and so did I, in a sort of crazy geometrical dance, until they were in front of the painting and I was across the room staring blindly at Rodin's sculpture *The Thinker*. I don't know what the thinker was thinking, but I was thinking about how I wished I was back in New York being hassled by Ironhead.

They examined the slashed painting up and down, noting every inch of the barbaric depredation, and then walked away and out of the room. They hadn't even noticed.

I let out a breath I had held long enough to swim the English Channel underwater with, and glanced at Claudette. She was letting out a breath, too.

I walked over to her on shaky legs and we exchanged nervous looks from close up. I surveyed the end of the corridor without turning my head, using only peripheral vision. Two of the crone guards were there, chatting.

In my raincoat pocket, I felt something warm. Blood was oozing across my palm from where I had nicked myself with the damned razor blade.

"Two minutes," I promised Claudette and myself.

She nodded.

I walked quickly back to *The Green Room* and took out the razor. It was amazing how even a tiny cut disgorges blood on every damn thing. My palm was smeared with red. I took a handkerchief from my other pocket and wiped the blood off. More oozed up from the nick.

The razor was against the left edge of the picture frame, and I cut it in one long, even slice, holding the frame in my left hand to keep it from moving. Then the cut across the bottom, left to right. *La Chambre Verte* hung limply now, held only by a few threads on each side, and from the top. When I cut the top, it would be down on my head. There was no stopping now, anyway. Not even that little squirt kid could miss the mangling the painting had already undergone.

I reached up and made the last cut across the top, left to right, against the frame, and the whole thing went slack, but it still hung in the frame. I had to go around all four sides again, snipping threads, to get it out.

I shot a glance at Claudette, who stood there wide-eyed, about as calm as a jet passenger after the captain announces to prepare for an emergency landing over the Atlantic. She frantically scanned the corridor and looked back at me.

Shakily, I spread out the painting on the wooden bench and took off my London Fog. It took easily a million years to lift the lining enough to slip the painting up between the lining and the coat and to fasten the painting to the coat with safety pins. If anybody walked in now, it would be a ticket straight to the gulag. And then I realized I didn't have the copy of *The Green Room*. Claudette had it.

I walked over to her as calmly as I could and whispered to her to give me the copy. She slid it down out of her sleeve and handed it to me. By now I had the raincoat on again, with *The Green Room* shoved up between the lining and the back. The coat flared out in back as though I were auditioning for the role of *The Hunchback of Notre Dame*.

"Can you notice?" I asked Claudette.

She only stared as though Frankenstein's monster had asked if you could see the electrodes sticking out of his neck.

I went quickly to the vacant frame and kneaded putty into the edges, noting that more blood was oozing out of my palm and mixing with the putty. Then I shoved the copy of the painting into the frame edges, shoving it against the putty and getting more blood smears along the edge.

As soon as the painting would stay, I backed off for a look. It was a disaster! The damned thing hung there limply, with sags and billows and smudges of dirty blood along the edges. If anybody took a second look, sirens would go off from here to Moscow, but the thought of taking it back out and doing it over again filled me with terror.

I backed away and felt the painting inside my coat lining swaying around, like a sandwich board.

"Is it noticeable?" I said in the face of her look of consternation.

She blinked and swayed and said, "Oh, my God!"

∇

CHAPTER FOURTEEN

"**L**ET's get out of here."

I looked along the corridor through which we had come and saw the two frumpy guards at a bench, still talking. I led Claudette the other way, deeper into the museum, so we could make a circle of the first floor and come out without passing them.

"Walk behind me," I told her, hoping she could block out the rather peculiar looking backside of my coat. We walked along the corridor past another exhibition room and then another. We came to more statues, and a back exhibition room, and then a wall. There was only one way out. The way we had come in.

"Shit," I growled.

Back down the corridor to the room from which we had stolen *The Green Room.* I glanced at it briefly, and it was a dirty, bloody, smudged wound, which could now be retitled *The Green and Red Room.*

"Is it obvious there's something under my coat?" I said softly to Claudette.

She blanched and muttered, "Kind of."

"We have to get past those two women," I told her.

"Yes."

"Look, you have to get them to walk this way, past this room, into the next one. Then I can slip out."

She blinked at me.

"Now, for God's sake!"

"What can I say to them?" she fretted.

"I don't know. There's something you want explained. Anything."

Claudette moaned and moved off hesitantly toward the two beefy females. I stepped back into the exhibition room and tried to look interested in the Rodin again, standing there with my puffed-out backside toward the wall.

I heard the women talking, and then Claudette came along the corridor, passing the room. "I can't tell if it's Napoleon or Bismarck," she was saying. Behind her came one of the watchdogs. I waited for the second one. And waited.

Finally, I peeked down the corridor. The second one had not come with Claudette. She still barred my way out.

There was nothing to do but walk past her. I couldn't stay there with the painting up my coat, and I couldn't stay in that room with the gaping, smudged theft-wound glaring at anyone who came in.

Into the corridor and toward the second guard, walking straight toward her so she couldn't see behind me. Then, as I got to her and she was sort of smiling at me, or at least looking at me, I pretended to become fascinated with a Cezanne on the wall, and turned to back away from her. At the door to the lobby, I backed out, and then walked straight into the lobby and toward the wide marble steps.

Down the carpeted steps, counting every one. Fourteen steps. Ahead of me on the right was a counter behind which were two more women. As I got to the bottom of the stairs and passed in front of them, one woman got up and leaned over the counter, staring at me.

"*Entschuldigen Sie, bitte!*"

Panic seized me. I couldn't decide whether to bolt out the door or stop. I did neither, but kept moving slowly forward, turning to look at her.

"*Ja, ja?*"

"*Wo ist Ihre Freundin?*"

"What?"

"You came in with someone?"

I heard steps then, and turned my rounded back away from them to look back at the steps. There came Claudette, her face flushed and her eyes wide.

"She *kommt,*" I managed, and walked on out the door.

In a second, I was through the outer lobby, past the statues of ancient horses, out under the Friedrich statue and into the courtyard, and Claudette came running out behind me.

Across the little courtyard on Bodestrasse I could see Gerhardt the Dresdener, our lookout, standing there facing the museum. When he saw me, he immediately did an about-face, staring now at the Demokratische Volkskammer.

"Go ahead of me to the car," I ordered Claudette. "Open the trunk. Have you got the key?"

She nodded and walked in front of me, along the sidewalk skirting the courtyard, out to Bodestrasse, and disappeared behind the construction fence. I followed, going as fast as I dared without doing what I wanted to do, which was run like a maniac.

It was maybe a hundred feet to the street, but it seemed like a hundred miles. At any moment, I expected to hear alarm bells going off, police dogs barking, the clanging of

a Green Polizei siren, but nothing happened as I reached
Bodestrasse and turned right along the sidewalk to the
parked, cream-colored Opel with the red diplomatic license plates.

As I walked up in the afternoon darkness, Claudette
raised the trunk lid, and I quickly took off my raincoat to
extract the painting. In a moment, it was out of the lining
and into the trunk and the lid was shut.

I looked around, watching Gerhardt standing off from
us and glancing out of the corner of his eye.

We hurried straight along the street ahead of us, the one
that went by the Berliner Dom and dead-ended into the
Volkskammer at Unter den Linden. I could hear steps
behind us and glanced back to see Gerhardt following.

At Unter den Linden, I guided Claudette to the right,
toward Friedrichstrasse, fighting off a continuing urge to
run like a thief. Claudette walked quickly along beside
me, breathing hard and saying nothing.

Back along past Marx-Engels-Platz and over the bridge
across the River Spree. As we came to the museum of the
eternal flame honoring the victims of fascism and militarism, East German soldiers goose-stepped through the
changing of the guard, their faces immobile under their
salad-bowl helmets. It seemed odd to me that soldiers at
an anti-Nazi shrine still used the goose-step.

This was no time for reflection though. It was the time
for getting the hell out of East Berlin. I didn't slow my
steps until we were at Friedrichstrasse, and neither did
Claudette. For that matter, neither did Gerhardt the Dresdener.

At the corner, I stopped to light a Tiparillo and let
Gerhardt catch up. We stood there in the gloom, the whole
area half-dark, but seeming to me to be a floodlit prison
yard covered from all sides by machine guns.

"Well, Gerhardt," I said with nervous cheerfulness, "Thanks for everything."

I put out my hand to shake, and he expertly palmed the German marks.

"Ja, ja," he smiled. *"Auf wiederseh'n."*

"Wiederseh'n."

He strolled off across the intersection toward the Unter den Linden Hotel, and I watched him anxiously. Now that he had his money, it was time to turn us in if he planned to.

"Come on," I told Claudette, and struck off along Friedrichstrasse toward Checkpoint Charlie. She walked beside me quickly enough.

"Is it over?" she gasped.

"Not until we're through the checkpoint."

That quickened her step. We walked along in the dark, and other forms appeared, also walking, both toward us and with us, and everyone was KGB. I knew we were being watched, trailed, photographed, and ticketed for a Soviet prison. Across the street, about a block behind us, a tall man was walking in the same direction we were. I slowed down at an intersection, where an East German cop was directing traffic, wearing a belt around his middle studded with yellow flashing lights. The man across the street stopped a block behind us.

When we started walking again, he started, too. During the next two blocks, I glanced back again enough times to be sure of it. Once inside the checkpoint, if the man caught up with us, we could be in a trap with no way to even put up a struggle.

I stopped and lighted a Tiparillo, trying to think.

Claudette shuffled her feet anxiously. "Don't stop," she protested.

"Now, listen," I told her, grabbing her hand, which was limp as a dead cod at the Fulton Fish Market, "keep on walking to the checkpoint. Go through and don't look back, and don't wait for me."

Claudette's hand suddenly turned into a claw that gripped my hand. She stared wildly into my eyes.

"What?"

"Somebody's following us."

∇

CHAPTER FIFTEEN

"Fɪᴛᴢ . . . no!" She shot a look over my shoulder toward our shadow. "Let's keep going."

I shook my head. "Once inside the checkpoint, it'll be too late. Go on."

Suddenly, tears spurted from her eyes, and her grip became like iron. "Oh, Fitz," she cried, "oh, my God. What did I get you into?"

"Never mind," I snapped. "There's no time for that now. Get going. Don't look back."

"I won't leave you!" she insisted bravely.

I pried her hand off mine and shoved her. She walked a couple of steps and halted to look back, but I nodded my head in an order. She moved off toward the checkpoint.

I stood there waiting, smoking, glancing back across and up Friedrichstrasse toward my shadow. He had also stopped and was pretending to look at a map or something in his hands. I walked back toward Unter den Linden, back toward him.

For a moment, he stood still, studying his map, and then he also started moving. Now he was moving back up the street toward Unter den Linden also.

Now I was following him.

Moving along behind him, although across the street, I could make out his silhouette better, but it was dark enough that I couldn't make him out very well. All that was certain was that he was staying ahead of me, still about a block out of reach.

Again, I stopped. Maybe I had been imagining things. I turned around and headed along toward the checkpoint again. When I looked back, there he was coming along behind me as before. There was no doubt about it. The tall figure in the gloom of East Berlin was on my case—but apparently he didn't want to catch up with me or at least not out on the street. At the checkpoint, it would be different.

Oddly enough, the panic I had first experienced had gone away in the game of cat-and-mouse we were playing. Now I was intent upon closing with him, for better or worse, simply because I didn't know what else to do.

I stood still and peered at him, trying to get a better impression. Was he wearing a uniform? It didn't look like it. All I could make out was that he was pretty big, as a lot of cops are. I stood there a little longer, trying to look ahead to see if Claudette had reached the checkpoint, but she was out of sight in the gloom, too.

Finally, I stepped into a doorway in the ratty-looking, drab street. Toward the checkpoint, the East Germans were putting up what appeared to be apartment buildings, and there was a lot of construction equipment around.

I would wait until he came up to me and also give Claudette enough time to get through to West Berlin. From the doorway, I couldn't see him anymore. The street was deserted.

Then I left the doorway and walked again. There he was.

"Hey!" I shouted. "What do you want?"

He stopped.

"Was willen Sie?" I yelled.

A car came along Friedrichstrasse carrying several dark shapes. It came up to me, passed by, and kept going. When I looked again, the shadow was gone.

After that, I set sail for the checkpoint as fast as I could walk. I was far enough ahead of him, hopefully, that I could get to the checkpoint and through it before he got there.

I walked into the checkpoint and showed my passport, gave the East German guard the currency declaration slip I had filled out on the way in, and was ushered through without trouble.

When I came along the pavement and stepped through The Wall next to the American checkpoint building, Claudette rushed up to me and buried herself in my arms.

"What happened?" she cried.

"Damned if I know," I told her.

We were out safely, and the crazy caper had succeeded, I told myself in wonderment. It seemed to have been all too easy.

We hurried along Friedrichstrasse to the corner, passing the Checkpoint Charlie Bar at Kochstrasse, and hailed a taxi.

"Exil in Kreuzberg," I told the driver, and off he went.

Claudette plastered herself against me in the cab, clutching my arm tightly and floating on wings of euphoria, cooing and clucking that I was the most wonderful person in the world. Puzzled as I still was about my East Berlin shadow, her ecstatic endearments nevertheless filled me with a warm glow of expectation. My reward awaited under the *Plummel*.

As the cab rolled through Kreuzberg, I suddenly felt myself sweating and tensing. A knot was in my stomach and cramps in my legs, and sweat poured down my forehead. A reaction to the walk down Friedrichstrasse? Probably. I still wondered who that tall shadow was and what he was up to.

It was completely dark by the time the cab pulled up at the Exil, but I spotted the cream Opel with the diplomatic license plates in the parking area in front.

I paid the cabbie and we walked over to the front of the Exil to glance inside. In the back room beyond the food counter, I spotted Erik Grosse-Mund waiting at a table. Everything was progressing satisfactorily.

"There's Erik," I told Claudette. "Stay here."

She gave me the car key and I walked over to the Opel, which was backed in as ordered. Nobody was around, except Claudette at the front window of the Exil. I walked around and opened the trunk.

In the darkness, I couldn't see the painting right away. It seemed to have been covered with some kind of blanket or cloth or something. There was a pile of old clothes on top of it.

I reached in to move the old clothes or whatever it was and felt something solid. I moved my hand around over it and blood rushed to my head in fright. It wasn't old clothes.

Over the top of the car I could see Claudette at the front of the Exil, peering toward me and then into the bar. I couldn't stand there long with the trunk open. Frantically, I took out a book of matches, leaned into the trunk, and lighted a match.

The diplomat. Blood trickled from his mouth. This was the only possible time, I realized, to get the painting. I

nudged the body and reached under it for *The Green Room,*
but I guess I knew already that there was no painting there.

I closed the trunk and stood there frozen, unable to
think straight or even move. What would I tell Claudette?

"I'm sorry. Your painting's gone, but we do have a dead
diplomat."

∇

CHAPTER SIXTEEN

I SHOOK my head to come out of it. It was only then I noticed the shape, coming toward me from between the cars. A silhouette that I recognized as the shadow from Friedrichstrasse.

I stood there, momentarily paralyzed, unable to react or think of what to do. The tall silhouette was not paralyzed—it was moving toward me rapidly, with what intent I didn't know. It was time to run or fight or more likely be arrested for grand theft, international smuggling, and murder. There wasn't really a chance of flight, because he was practically on top of me. Being an ink-stained wretch has its drawbacks when you stick your nose into things other than writing news stories, because you don't carry a gun or any kind of weapon. If the tall, dark shape was armed, there wouldn't be much of a fight.

The face came into a patch of light from the Exil as he reached me. I looked into the face of big Stew Faulkner, the reporter from Wisconsin. Relief and confusion clashed head-on.

"Stew?" I blurted out.

"Everything go okay?" he asked in a flat voice. No more amiable Joe College manner. "Did you get it?"

"Did I get what?" I managed, trying to get plugged in to some kind of context.

"Did something happen?" he asked then, sensing my panic.

"What do you mean?" I stalled. "What are you doing out here? Want to have a drink?"

"Never mind that," he came back. "We don't have any time to waste. What happened?"

"I don't get you, Stew."

"Now, listen, Fitzgerald. I'm not Stew, and you're in big trouble if something went wrong."

My head spun at that. Not Stew Faulkner the reporter? Whoever he was, he now had about him a crisp, business-like manner that unnerved me, as though he knew things that I didn't.

"Was that you following me on Friedrichstrasse?"

"Yes, and that was some stupid stunt, yelling at me!"

"But who are you? Why were you following me?"

"Goddamnit, shut up," he spat harshly. "Open the trunk."

I hesitated. Who was this man? Somebody from the KGB? If so, it wouldn't do to open the trunk and give him the evidence he needed to haul me back through The Wall.

"It's not my car," I said, inventing desperately. "I was just back here taking a leak."

"Goddamnit, stop wasting time," he snapped. "Why'd you close the trunk?"

"I don't know what we're talking about here," I muttered.

"It blew up, didn't it!" he raged softly. "Goddamnit!"

"What blew up?" was all I could think of.

The time for stalling and pleasant chatting was past, though, because big Stew or whoever he was suddenly grabbed my right hand and got some kind of a pressure hold on my wrist, bending it down at a right angle so that a shot of electricity raced up my arm to the shoulder and I almost passed out. A noise burst out of me, a squeak of anguish, and I was helpless in the grip of whatever he was doing to my wrist.

His hand was in my coat pocket, digging for the car key.

Then I heard it in the distance somewhere, screaming in the dark and getting closer, the *eee-aaaah, eee-aaaah* wail of a German police vehicle. They were coming for us.

Stew Faulkner heard it, too, and cocked his head to listen, apparently surprised. The electric jolt in my arm lessened.

Something whizzed and went clunk, and Stew looked at me in stunned confusion for a second before he slid down and crumpled at my feet.

Claudette stood behind him, still holding a bottle, her eyes wide and crazy.

For a second we stood there, frozen, listening to the approaching *eee-aaaah, eee-aaaah*. She turned her head with a jerk, like a sparrow. I jumped over the clump at my feet, ignoring a low moan coming from it, and grabbed Claudette's hand.

"Come on!" I hissed at her.

"The painting . . . the painting," she howled. "Get it!"

I hauled her into a run through the darkness of the parking lot as she resisted and tried to squirm free.

"Fitz . . . what are you doing?" she cried frantically.

"It's not there!"

"What!"

"They're coming, damnit," I shouted at her, and dragged her onward, hearing *eee-aaaah* again.

Somebody shouted something.

I dragged Claudette faster.

"What happened?" she gasped.

"Not now!"

We went away from the Exil along a canal and through dark, deserted streets. There was a wooded park area ahead, and I dragged her into it, through trees and shrubs, and kept going. Ahead there were moving lights, which meant a street or road of some kind. We came through the small park and out into a wide avenue skirting the woods. A few cars were moving along, and then I spotted a double-decker bus moving away from us, too far away to catch.

I hurried along after the bus, dragging Claudette, watching for where the bus would stop. It finally did, several blocks further along the street. The walk to the bus stop took forever, and we both kept looking back for whoever was behind us.

The bus stop was a little metal shelter with a curved roof marked with the numbers of the buses that stopped there, and fortunately it was deserted. I slid onto the bench and lighted a Tiparillo, my head swirling and my right wrist still full of shooting sparks.

"What happened?" Claudette asked again.

I shook my head. "I don't know."

"Who was that man?"

"Stew Faulkner."

Claudette frowned. "The reporter?"

"He isn't a reporter."

"Who is he?"

"I don't know. He's the one who followed us in East Berlin."

"What did he want?" Claudette's voice was becoming strained.

"The key to the trunk."

"Oh, my God," she said softly. "Did you give it to him?"

Only then did I dig my hand into my coat pocket. It was empty. He had gotten it before Claudette coldcocked him.

I turned to look at her, still amazed at what she had done. "By the way, thanks," I said. "What did you hit him with?"

"A bottle . . . vodka, I think. I didn't know what to do."

"You did fine."

"I couldn't let him hurt you," she said. "There was a trash can there, and I saw the bottle, and . . ."

"He got the key."

She leaned back against the shelter in despair. "Oh, God! So he's got the painting!"

Lights glimmered down the roadway, coming along the park. I squinted at them, trying to make out the shape. It loomed up ponderously and assumed the form of a double-decker bus.

We climbed on and sat in the back, each lost in our own thoughts. I couldn't decide which would be the worst news for Claudette, but knew I had to tell her. It wasn't just a question of the painting anymore.

"The painting wasn't in the trunk," I finally said as the bus lumbered along through the dark streets.

"It wasn't?" She straightened up to study my face.

"No. The diplomat was in the trunk. Dead."

There was an intake of breath and her hand clutched my arm. She put a hand over her eyes and was shaking.

We rode along in silence after that, until we reached a large intersection where I saw taxicabs going by. We got off and hailed one, and rode back to the Kempi.

In the hotel bar, I ordered a Budweiser from Angelo and we sat in a sort of stupor, hardly knowing what to say or ask and yet boiling with craziness. Claudette had Scotch, straight.

"I think maybe we better get out of Berlin," I finally said.

"Oh, but Fitz . . ."

"I know, I know," I told her. "But we don't know what's going on here! It's probably crazy even to be sitting here, when Faulkner knows we're staying here."

"I just don't understand what happened," she moaned in dismay.

She wasn't alone there. I tried to think, but my overactive brain kept leaping back and forth. What happened to the painting? Who got the diplomat? What was Faulkner doing there, and who the hell was he?

"They can't pin anything on us, Fitz," she said hopefully. "As long as we don't go back to East Berlin."

Whistling in the dark. That might be true in New York, but who knew what the rules were in Berlin?

"Now, listen, Claudette, how do we explain that body in the trunk?"

"It's not our car," she came back.

I was playing devil's advocate, trying to show what a mess we were in, even though I couldn't really assess it.

"I had a key to that car," I said. "I was seen standing there with the trunk open."

"It was dark," she argued. "It's his word against yours."

I sipped my Budweiser. "What if Faulkner's dead, too?"

She shuddered. "I don't think he is. He was moaning."

I had to admit that was true. I didn't think Faulkner was dead. Not that that was all so wonderful, either, because that meant he would come looking for us. Christ, I didn't even know who he really was.

"He was the one following us in East Berlin," I told her. "I don't know if he's a Vopo or a West German cop or was after the painting or what. Whoever he is, he operates on both sides of The Wall."

"Fitz," she suddenly said, excitedly. "Maybe Erik got it!"

"Erik?"

"He was there! He's the only one who knew it was being delivered!"

I didn't know what to think about that. We hadn't given the art dealer any details, only that we would deliver the painting to him there. If Erik had *The Green Room,* did that mean he had killed the diplomat? I didn't know what to think about that, either.

"Maybe he's still there," said Claudette.

I looked at her. It was worth a chance. I got up and walked out into the lobby, to the pay phones near the registration desk. Claudette was right next to me and squeezed into the booth beside me. I looked up the telephone number and called the Exil.

"Ja, ja?" came a voice, with a lot of noise in the background.

"Bitte, Herr Grosse-Mund?"

"I can't hear you!" the man yelled in German.

I shouted Erik's name again, louder. The phone went clunk, and the noise in the background continued, a confused hubbub of voices and glasses clinking. I could hear somebody calling out.

"What?" Claudette nudged me. "What?"

"I'm waiting."

Then Erik was on the line. *"Ja?"*

"Erik?" I shouted.

"Ja! Wer ist da?"

"Erik, it's me . . . Fitz," I said. "What's going on out there?"

"Fitz?" he came back agitated. "Where are you? You didn't come."

"What's happening out there?"

"Schrecklich!" he yelled. "Somebody has been murdered! Police all over! What happened with you?"

"Erik, listen, did you get it?"

"What?"

"The painting . . . did you get it?"

Erik sounded totally lost. "Get it? What do you mean? Get it how?" Then he seemed to be talking to someone else. *"Bitte . . . bitte . . . nur einige Minuten . . ."*

"Erik . . . ?"

"They want the phone," he yelled. "The man who called the police."

"What?" I yelled. "Who called the police?"

"They want the phone," he said again. "Call me tomorrow. This is terrible here."

"Erik . . ."

But the line went dead. I called back frantically, but it was busy. I tried again and again, but it stayed busy. I could imagine the police had preempted the line.

We walked numbly back into the hotel bar.

I had the powerful feeling that we absolutely had to do something, but I had no idea what—except to beat it out of Berlin.

"We can't stay here," I said. "We're sitting ducks."

She only nodded grimly. "What shall we do?"

I pondered that. "Either catch a plane out of here right now, or go someplace else."

"We can't go yet!" she pleaded.

"Don't you realize we're sitting in the middle of a fire?"

As always, Claudette could think pretty straight when it came to her painting. She had whacked the bogus Stew Faulkner when he was trying to open the trunk to get what she thought was the painting, and now she was thinking pretty clearly again.

"Fitz, if Faulkner is a cop, he'd be here by now, wouldn't he?"

I didn't answer.

"If he found that body, and he has the key, he'd be here already. Or he would have sent somebody."

I liked her reasoning except that I hated it.

"Maybe he's an East German cop."

"Then he can't touch us, can he?" she came right back.

"Maybe not officially. But . . ."

That's how we sat there, in the bar of the best-known hotel in West Berlin, where we were known to be staying, like absolute idiots. The only reason I could think of that we weren't taken that night was because nobody could imagine we would be in such a public place drinking away like carefree tourists.

"So, did you have fun today?" Angelo the smiling Milanese bartender was standing behind the bar beaming at us.

"Oh, yes, Angelo," I said. "I've never had a day quite like this."

"Good," he smiled. "In Berlin, every day is just as good."

∇

CHAPTER SEVENTEEN

I REFUSED to let Claudette go up to her room to pick up anything and led her instead out the door of the Kempi and down the Ku-Damm to Rankestrasse to another hotel, the Steigenburger. We got a room and immediately collapsed into bed, mad for sleep and yet so jumpy we kept waking up and grabbing each other.

Under the *Plummel* where love awaited, there was no love that night, only terror and fear of the morning. I remember nothing about it except that it was endless. When I finally got up and checked my watch, it was only 7:00 A.M. I ordered coffee from room service and was drinking it when Claudette came abruptly awake and sat up, looking like Medea.

"Fitz!" she cried out, and then saw me.

"Have some coffee."

She got up and pulled on her clothes and came to the table.

Nothing had changed, but we were still uncaught.

Claudette sipped some coffee and peered appealingly over the rim of the cup at me, asking me to please make everything be all right. I lighted a Tiparillo and tried to think. Of course, the two big questions looming up in front of us were, who got the painting, and who killed the diplomat. Or vice versa. The answer to both seemed to be Stew Faulkner. Although that raised yet another question. Who *was* Faulkner? Claudette kept watching me intently, apparently imagining I was thinking deeply and had figured it all out.

"Well?" she asked expectantly.

"Well, what?" was my sparkling reply.

"Do you have any idea about what happened?"

I don't know why I was supposed to have any idea, since we had been together the whole time. She knew as much as I did. I tried to run over the loose ends. Okay, we put the painting in the trunk, and the nameless diplomat drove the car through The Wall and to the Exil. That much we knew.

Now, we're followed by Stew Faulkner as we leave East Berlin, but he doesn't stop us. When did he start following us? When Gerhardt the Dresdener left us? Are Faulkner and Gerhardt linked in some way? Were they letting us take the painting out of East Berlin for them, with the object of taking it from us once we were through The Wall? If that was true, did Faulkner get the painting before I opened the trunk?

"If Faulkner already had the painting, why would he ask me to open the trunk?" I said aloud.

Claudette thought that over. "To catch you with the . . . with that poor man?"

That was possible. But did Faulkner know what was in the car trunk? If he knew and he already had the painting, why would he hang around there?

"Maybe he wanted the painting and thought it was still in there," I suggested. "Somebody had beat him to it."

"Who?" asked Claudette.

I took a flyer. "Erik? He was sitting in the Exil."

Claudette frowned gloomily. The more we chewed on it, the more it turned to mush. We needed some hard answers to some of our questions. Who was that dead diplomat, for instance? Who was this Faulkner, for another instance? Where was *The Green Room?* And how the hell did I get out of this goddamn jam?

I dug into my jacket pocket for the Polaroid photo of the diplomat, standing in front of his cream-colored Opel accepting money from Claudette. The red diplomatic plate was clearly visible. It was a place to start, anyway.

"Who could identify this guy for us?" I wondered.

"The American Embassy?" Claudette offered.

I gave her a look. "Remember, this is a photo of you giving money to a murdered diplomat."

"Oh!"

Yes, oh! It would hardly do to show the photo around to official sources. It was our best lead and our insurance, all right, but it also linked Claudette to the murdered man and the car in which the body was found. The money changing hands would delight an interrogator, of course, and I had no doubt that as soon as Claudette was identified as the woman in the photograph, any cop on the Ku-Damm would be able to find out her quest in Berlin. That and the fact that *The Green Room* had disappeared from the National Gallery in East Berlin would be quite enough to banish the bloom from Claudette's comely cheeks for about twenty years.

"What shall we do?" she asked.

"Let's try to find out if anybody's looking for us," I said, and put in a call to the Kempi Hotel. I asked if there were any messages for us.

"Wer, bitte?"

"Herr Fitzgerald *oder* Fräulein Barry."

The operator went silent for a moment and then came back on to say that, no, there were no messages.

"Thanks," I told him, and hung up.

"What?" Claudette asked.

"Nothing," I told her. "No messages."

She stared at me blankly. Clearly, she had expected something. So had I. You would think since we had stolen a valuable painting from East Berlin, smuggled it through The Wall, and left a diplomat dead in a trunk, that somebody would be looking for us. It was eerie. I could sense that Claudette would almost welcome some kind of feedback, and I felt the same way. Had we dreamed the whole thing?

Eaten up with curiosity, I put in calls to both of our rooms at the Kempinski, but there were no answers.

"Well, there's nobody camped in our rooms," I said.

"Maybe they just aren't answering," Claudette suggested.

Great.

"I can't stand it!" she blurted out.

I sat at the table again, puffed on my Tiparillo, and gave her what I considered the best advice possible. "Let's get the next plane out of here!"

"Ohhhh," she moaned. "All right. I guess there's nothing else to do. But what about your story?"

I grabbed my ears and rocked my head. The story! God help me! If we stayed, though, I would be writing from Stalag 17. I willed the problem away.

"I'm going over to the Kempi and have a look," I told her. "If nothing happens, we can pack up and get out."

"Be careful," she said anxiously. "Shall I come along?"

"No."

"But if anything happens to you, I won't know."

"If you don't hear from me by noon, get out of Berlin," I told her.

She slumped at the table, her head in her hands, and was crying. "Why did I drag you into this?"

It didn't seem to me that that was going to help anything, so I left her and walked up to the Ku-Damm and down to the Kempi.

There was a new mob of tourists coming in as I got there, milling around in front, and I had to shove through them into the lobby.

"Ah, there you are!"

Hans Dieter had my arm as I came through the revolving door, and he led me over into the group of journalists, who were all standing around in the lobby. "You're just in time," he said. "We're going to the International Congress Center. I think you'll be very impressed."

"Congress Center?" I repeated stupidly.

I must have looked like something off skid row, with my unshaven face and wrinkled shirt, but Dieter nevertheless smiled expansively. Whatever mad events were taking place among his flock of journalists by night, Hans Dieter was there every morning carrying out the appointed tour, which I kept forgetting about.

I glanced nervously about the lobby, searching for I don't know what. Police, I guess. Nobody seemed to be noticing me, except as an American reporter.

Dieter was tugging my arm again, but this time he was more insistent, his hand tightening harder and harder as I stood there not moving. Finally, his grip was a vise, and I tried to yank my arm away, at the same time turning to tell him to stop it.

I glared into Hans Dieter's face and saw his tie. He was
a foot taller and his face was that of Stew Faulkner. His
hand was on my arm in a powerful grip that said he was
not kidding.

"Stew . . . uh . . . well . . ."

He threw his head toward the elevator, ordering me to
come with him. "Come on," he said gruffly.

"What do you want?" I resisted. The best place I could
think of being was right there in the middle of all those
reporters and next to Hans Dieter. "I'm not going anywhere."

Faulkner let my arm go. He leaned back and looked me
over a moment, and I tried to notice any kind of lump on
his head. Nothing was obvious.

"Listen," he said sharply, "we have to talk."

Again, I had that strange sensation about Faulkner. He
didn't act like a cop, that was for sure. All he had to do
was arrest me if that was the case. What and who the hell
was he?

"Where?" I finally said.

"Your room."

"Uh, uh. No way."

"You say then."

"Right here in the lobby," I said. "Right out in the
open."

"All right." He strolled away into the large sitting room
off the lobby, where there was a piano and tables and
chairs grouped together. I followed slowly and joined him
at a table.

He sat there staring at me, looking Joe College again in
his tweed jacket and striped tie. By now, though, I noticed
the eyes and knew about the strength in his arms.

He wagged his head at me in disgust. "What a couple
of goddamn idiots."

I decided to let that pass. "Who are you?"

"Anything I say to you is in confidence. You got that?"

"In confidence?" I was bewildered.

"You're a newspaper reporter, right? You might not believe in very much, but you do honor being told something in confidence, don't you?"

He had me there.

"I do, if I'm covering a story," I told him. "Is this about a news story?"

He sort of grunted in annoyance. "No goddamnit, it's about there *not* being a story."

I lighted a Tiparillo and relaxed a little. Whoever this mystery man was and whatever he wanted, it did not seem to be about arresting me or Claudette for murder or smuggling or theft. In fact, it was becoming clear to me that he didn't want anybody to know about the crazy night before any more than we did.

"I don't get it," I said.

"I know you don't," he said irritably. "You and that crazy broad shouldn't be let out without a keeper. That was some stunt you pulled."

I confessed that things had become slightly muddled.

A snort. "Muddled! You're lucky you're still alive."

"Do you know what happened?" I asked him.

He sank back in his chair and sort of revolved his head about, as though trying out one beginning or another and dismissing them all as inadequate.

"I don't even know how the hell to begin with you," came the reply.

"Why not begin by telling me who you are?" I suggested.

The mock reporter leaned forward again, glanced around the room to see that no one was nearby, and then said, "I work for McNamara. Is that enough?"

"McNamara? You mean . . ."

"Yes."

"You're an American agent?"

He shot me an annoyed glance. "We try to keep fools like you out of trouble."

"Let's see some ID."

"Jesus." He sighed, but he reached into his pocket, pulled out an official-looking ID, and showed it to me. The name listed was John Rhodes.

"Satisfied?"

I handed it back to him. "I guess so."

"Well, you'd better accept it, because that's all you get. And tell that crazy girlfriend of yours not to hit me with bottles anymore."

I'm afraid I blushed at that. "Well, hell, we didn't know who you were."

"All right," he said, and rubbed his head. "You're lucky I didn't shoot you both."

"You mean . . . you let us get away?"

"You can say that."

I measured big John Rhodes sitting there across from me and felt an expansive relief and confidence that this guy was on our side. Sort of. At least now, Claudette and I had somebody who could lead us through some of the blind spots in Berlin.

"Why were you following us around?" I asked him, realizing now that it was no accident that he kept turning up everywhere we went.

"I was trying to keep you from getting into something you couldn't get out of."

My God, I thought. A convoy and a bodyguard. In fact, a keeper.

"You knew what we were doing?"

"We suspected you'd be nutty enough to try."

"But you didn't stop us?"

"I tried to," he snapped. "Goddamnit, I *told* you not to go back to East Berlin."

"You mean at the Bürgermeister's luncheon?"

"Yes. And later, too."

"Later?" I tried to unravel that one. "*You* pegged those shots at us in the pedestrian tunnel?"

"I shot high."

Wonderful, I thought. No wonder our supposed executioner had missed. Rhodes wasn't a bad shot, he was a damned good one to come that close to us. So that had been he on the phone to our room, too.

The whole thing was impossible, Rhodes raged softly. The embassy couldn't sit by doing nothing when they knew Claudette and I were probably going to try to steal *The Green Room* out of East Berlin. They couldn't actually stop us, since the New York *Daily Press* had already threatened to blow up the story all across the United States that the embassy had become a dupe of the Communists. So Rhodes had been assigned to discourage us, and when that failed to try to keep us from getting shot or taken.

"Look," he finally said, "we don't mind you getting your painting back, but we can't be part of it."

"You watched us all the time?"

He nodded. "What a butchered mess! Dumb luck. Who was that guy helping you?" he wanted to know.

"What guy? Oh, you mean Gerhardt?" I told him about it.

He grunted. "So, you meet an East German in a bar and get him to help you steal a painting? You're beautiful."

"Is there a big stink about the painting being gone?" I asked.

He wagged his head. "I haven't heard anything."

"Nothing?"

"Not yet."

That was eerie, too. The painting had been gone for at least twenty-four hours by now.

"Do you know what happened at the Exil?" I asked him.

He stook his head. "What was supposed to happen?"

I filled him in on the plan.

He fiddled with a plastic drink stirrer for a few seconds, running it all around inside his head.

"You don't know who might have killed the driver of that car?"

A headshake from me. "Who is he?" I asked. "Or who was he?"

"No ID released yet," he said. "The story said he's a low-level Western diplomat."

"Story?" I asked, befuddled. "It's in the paper?"

"Well, hell, yes, it's in the papers. A dead diplomat is news in Berlin. I don't know about New York."

Oh, my God, I thought. "I haven't watched TV or seen a paper," I muttered. Not that I could have made it out very well in German if I had.

"What do the stories say?" I asked edgily.

"Not much. Mysterious murder of a minor diplomat." He studied my face. "He didn't give you a name?"

"No. You didn't recognize him?"

He grimaced. "How? From the ground? I never even got a look at him."

"What happened after we ran? Did you call the cops, by the way?"

No, he said, he didn't call anybody. When we were out of sight, and good riddance, he had walked off into the darkness just beyond the Exil parking area and watched. The Berlin police arrived and went right to the diplomat's car. Somebody had alerted them about it, all right.

Who would do that? I wondered. Somebody who had taken the painting and wanted to scare us off?

"Did you check the diplomatic plates on that car to get an ID?" I asked the putative CIA man.

Rhodes sat forward, fixed me with a hard glare, and said never mind about the license plates, because he wasn't there, and neither were we, and none of us knew a thing about it.

"You got that?" he declared. "You'd just better hope the police didn't pick up your art dealer Erik. If he tells them what he knows . . ."

I shuddered. "Yeah."

The image leaped into my consciousness and then out again. Someone in the lobby had stepped into the room and immediately pulled back out of sight.

A dark head reappeared, peeking out. I got up and waved her over to us. Claudette came hesitantly at first, and then halted dead when she recognized Stew as he turned to glance at her.

"It's all right," I called out.

She came on again, her eyes fixed upon Stew, her body language cautious and questioning.

"Miss Barry," he greeted her rather stiffly. She said nothing, but looked at me for help.

"John Rhodes," I said. "He works for McNamara. He was riding shotgun for us all the time."

Claudette sank into the chair beside me, and sighed with relief.

"We're not under arrest?" she asked meekly.

"Not so far," he said, which got our attention.

"What do you mean?" Claudette managed to get out.

What he meant, said Rhodes, was that the United States government was not going to arrest us, in spite of the fact that he had been whacked on the head.

"We know you took the painting, but McNamara says you have ownership papers for it, so we're ignoring that. We understand your problem, but cannot get involved officially. If you got the painting out, we would still know nothing."

"But I haven't got it," Claudette interjected.

"Miss Barry," Rhodes jumped back in, "please listen to me. I say, we know nothing officially about that painting. As for the diplomat, we know you didn't kill him, because I was on your tail the whole time. So, for the moment, as far as we are concerned, there are no charges against you and you are free to leave Berlin."

"Leave Berlin?" she said.

"Yes. If you do it now. Today! We are taking no action, but I can't speak for the East Germans, when they figure out what happened to that painting. Or the West Germans when they dig into the murder of that diplomat. When those things happen, you two had better be back in the States."

Claudette sank back in her chair and a look of uncertainty came into her face. It started with alarm, then shaded into doubt, and finally became a challenge.

"But I still don't have my painting."

"Listen, you've been had, see?" Rhodes told her. "Your bright little idea went kaflooey because somebody else had their own bright idea. This is Berlin, Miss Barry. Things happen in Berlin to people with bright ideas."

"What do you think happened?" I asked him.

"Officially, I don't have an idea," he said, sounding like

a certain late diplomat. "But my guess is whoever sent you that diplomat saw a way to get your painting out, and once it was out he didn't want the diplomat to be able to talk about it. Don't waste any time getting out of Berlin."

"But you said there are no charges against us," Claudette told him.

A red tide of frustration rose slowly out of Rhodes's collar and climbed up his face to his hair. He looked at Claudette the way one might glare at a three-year-old who wants to know why he should not play in the middle of the Grand Concourse.

"I'm telling you for your own good!"

"Is that an order?"

I thought John Rhodes was going to shout. Instead he let out a long breath and muttered something unintelligible.

"No," he said at last. "I wish it was."

Claudette sat forward. "I mean, now that you've been assigned to help us . . ."

She got no further. John Rhodes stood up and shot a murderous glance somewhere in the direction of Washington. He leaned over, with his face close to both of us.

"I'm telling you to get the hell out of Berlin now! Never mind your goddamn painting. This is a murder case now, and when they hook you two clowns into it, neither the State Department nor the goddamn Marines are going to be able to help you!"

And he sailed out of the Kempi.

$\triangledown$

CHAPTER EIGHTEEN

I WATCHED John Rhodes stalk out of the piano foyer into the front lobby where he was swallowed up by the journalists, who were filing out through the revolving door to the bus that would take them to the Congress Center.

I sighed and lighted a Tiparillo. I was supposed to be getting on that bus, too, but there I sat. I realized that I would never gather any kind of a Berlin travel story until I solved the problem of Claudette and her damned *Green Room*. But I could not figure out how to even start trying to find the painting when I kept worrying about Claudette all the time.

"Listen, Claudette," I said. "Rhodes is right. I want you out of Berlin today."

She looked up, alarmed. "But, Fitz . . ."

"Don't 'But, Fitz' me! Get a plane out today. I'll stay— I have to join that damned tour anyway—and I'll try to find out what happened."

She studied me, frowning, her eyes troubled.

"Damnit," I jumped in, "don't you realize it's only a matter of time till they grab you?"

"But what about you?"

I waved my hand. "I'm a reporter, they won't bother
me. It's not my painting. They want you. Get out! I'll be
all right."

"But, Fitz, we're so close now," she offered, which
struck me as one of the more preposterous pronounce-
ments I had ever heard.

"Close to what? A German dungeon? We don't know
what the hell we're doing."

That was true to a point, she conceded, but now we had
help. We had John Rhodes.

"Who wants us back in the States," I pointed out.

"I guess Rhodes is right," she said then, frowning. "It's
getting dangerous."

"*Getting* dangerous? Jesus!"

She sat there in a brown study, and then nodded as
though in answer to some inner decision. Finally, common sense had descended upon her pretty head. "All right,
Fitz. You go join your tour." She stood up.

Glad to hear that, I told her I would help her get packed
and checked out and get her to the airport before I joined
the tour.

"No, no, you go ahead," she insisted. I didn't entirely
like the way she said that. We walked into the front lobby.

"I want to see you safely onto the plane," I told her.

"Fitz, I am not a child," she snapped. "I've caused you
enough trouble. Now, go on! I can pack and check out,
for heaven's sake."

We stood there in the busy lobby, and all of a sudden it
was time to say good-bye. I had wanted to get rid of her
because all she had meant was trouble, and yet I stood
there feeling bereft and inadequate.

"I'll look into it," came weakly out of me.

"Please, Fitz, forget it," she said softly. "I shouldn't
have dragged you into this."

"Well, I guess I wasn't really dragged."

"You were," she said, looking away. "You pretend to be a cynical newspaperman and maybe you are a little, but . . . I could see you were attracted to me . . ."

I could think of no argument there.

". . . and, well, I got you to help me, Fitz."

She looked back at me again, her eyes level on mine. "I guess I sort of manipulated you. It was okay at first, but now it's gotten complicated. I know what kind of a person you are now, and I can't do it anymore. I'm a little ashamed."

"What the hell, Claudette," I muttered. "I guess I'd try to help anybody, if I could."

"That's just it," she said. "My God! What a character!"

Then she was in my arms, hugging me, until she backed off and kissed me. "Now, you go on," she commanded. "Maybe we'll see each other back in New York."

I looked at her a moment, and then turned to walk across the lobby and out through the revolving door. It was a long walk, I'm sorry to admit, and I found myself promising myself to do something about that painting. The thought of her going back home without it after all her struggle was a jab of pain behind my left ear, but at least she would be the hell out of Berlin, which I no longer considered a safe place for her. Or maybe for me, either.

I wish I could tell you that I pushed through that revolving door and hailed a taxi for the Congress Center, but the fact is that a revolving door *revolves,* going around in a circle, and if you don't get out at the sidewalk you go right back into the lobby again. If you then get out, you are back at the front desk standing behind Claudette Barry again, and you can hear her asking the striped pants, "What's the room number for Bibi Nelson?"

The striped pants smiled and gave it to her, and Claudette walked across the lobby to a house phone and dialed it. I was still right behind her when she dialed the phone and then put it down and turned around.

"What the hell are you doing?"

"Fitz!"

"Why are you calling that goddamn flake Bibi?"

"Go join your tour."

"Goddamnit, I thought you were leaving!"

"I am!"

"When?"

Well, there was no harm in at least contacting Bibi Nelson, she said, and finding out about that diplomat he sent us, and then there was Erik Grosse-Mund. What had happened? But she would not involve me in it any further, and I was to please stay out of her way.

"Now, you listen to me! If anybody's going to track down that boulevardier from Rio, I am! If anybody's going to find Erik, I am! You get out of Berlin!"

I'll say this for Claudette, she didn't back down. Oh, no, she stood right up to me, shoving herself against me and practically yelling that it was *her* painting, for God's sake, and that if I insisted on prying my way into her life she was at least not going to desert me.

Wonderful. I had to finally admit that nothing would get her out of there without *The Green Room,* and that I would never get a travel story until I put it into her hands.

"Bibi's out," she said. "With that tour, I guess. I'll call Erik." She dug the art dealer's card from her purse.

"Give me that," I said, and took the card and phoned Das Schloss Hotel. There was no answer in his room, either, so I called the front desk to leave a message for Herr Grosse-Mund to call us. The message clerk at Das Schloss reacted right away.

"Herr Grosse-Mund?" he chirped efficiently. "Wer sprechen? Herr Dahlem?"

"What?" I asked, confused.

"He will meet you in zee Alt Nürnberg *um vier Uhr, ja ja?*"

"*Wo ist das?*"

"*Hier. Im Keller des Europa Centers.*"

"*Danke.*"

"What was all that?" Claudette wanted to know.

I told her that Erik wasn't in, but that he had left a message for Herr Dahlem to meet him in the Old Nuremberg Restaurant in the basement of the Europa-Center at four o'clock.

"Dahlem?" she said. "Siggy Dahlem? That's the art dealer he was going to give the painting to for safekeeping! Fitz, Erik must have it. That's why they're meeting!"

I had to admit that it made some kind of sense, and that seemed to mean that we would be meeting Herr Erik Grosse-Mund again. Only half-an-hour before I thought I was out of the whole damned thing and now here we were again.

"Four o'clock," Claudette was saying. "God, Fitz, I didn't sleep a wink last night. We can take a nap till four." She blushed becomingly and looked away.

I grabbed a copy of *B.Z.* at the front desk, and tried to read it as we went up in the elevator.

"What does it say?" she asked, craning her neck to look even though she couldn't read a word of German.

My German wasn't so hot, either, but I could make out from the story that an unidentified Western diplomat had been found murdered in the trunk of a car in the Exil parking lot.

"Does it say anything about the painting?" Claudette asked.

"I don't see anything."

"Nothing?"

I studied the German words, but a lot of them were Greek to me. Still, it appeared to be a very sketchy story. Either the West German police didn't know very much, or they were holding back.

"See, they haven't linked us to it," she said hopefully.

"Not yet."

I walked with her to her room, expecting to find the KGB or the CIA or the French Sureté or the West German police or possibly Hermann Goering. But there was nobody there and the room appeared to be undisturbed.

She put her hand on my cheek and smiled at me. "Old Fitz," she said softly. "Trying to ditch me." Her kiss was gentle and inviting.

"Not really," I managed, but my arms were at my sides.

She pulled back and looked into my eyes. "What's the matter?"

"Nothing."

"This isn't manipulation anymore."

"I know. I'm just a little crazy at the moment."

"Sure. Come back for me at three-thirty?"

"I will," I told her, and left. It was wonderful, all right. Before she had been manipulating me and I didn't care, but now that she wasn't anymore I had backed off. What a prize sap you are, Fitzgerald.

I walked down the hall to my room and found it also as I had left it. What the hell was going on? Didn't anybody care that a couple of international killers and art thieves were on the loose in Berlin?

It was ten o'clock and how to exist until four in the afternoon without going mad, I couldn't imagine. I had hardly slept the night before, and yet I was so keyed up I could have run the New York Marathon.

Then I noticed the little red light on my phone beckoning for attention. Some one had left me a message.

I called the front desk and was told that a Mr. Matthews had called from New York City, *Vereinigen Staaten,* and that I was instructed to call him when I got the message. "At whatever hour," the front desk person said efficiently.

I sank onto the bed. "At whatever hour?" Ironhead wanted me "at whatever hour"? Visions of being pitched into the ninth circle of Dante's Inferno gripped me. It had to be about three in the morning in New York.

I got the operator and put through a call to the *Daily Press,* and got Glenn the night switchboard guy.

"Glenn? Fitz."

"Hey, Fitz," he said cheerily. "What's doing?"

"Look, I'm in Berlin. Ironhead wants me to call him."

"Berlin?" said Glenn. "Oh, you're the one."

I didn't like the sound of that. "What do you mean, 'I'm the one'?"

"Oh, he said a call might come from Germany, that's all. Wait a minute. Let me call him at home."

I waited, feeling a bear clawing up my spine, and then Ironhead's home phone was ringing. And ringing. I almost hung up, but then he came on the line.

"Hello . . . ?"

"Ironhead?"

A silence. Then, "Who is this?"

"Fitz. There was a message. . . ."

"Do you know what time it is, you goddamn hoople!"

"The message said . . ."

"It's three in the goddamn morning, you fuckin' idiot."

"But it said whenever I got the message."

"Now, you listen to me, when you call me, you make it three in the morning over there, not here! I can't goddamn understand anybody as crackbrained as you! What the hell do you want, and it better be good."

"I don't want anything, I'm returning your call."

There was a silence, and I heard a muttered command to somebody to go back to sleep. "It's that maniac Fitzgerald."

When he came back on the line, he had remembered why he called me. "Just what in the hell are you doing over there?" he demanded.

"What's the matter?" I managed.

"What the hell are you doing, drawing thirteen hundred dollars? We don't pay for your damned hookers!"

"No, no, that wasn't for . . ."

"Well, then, what's it for? Huh? What? Cat got your tongue, or is it some kraut floozy?"

I tried to think fast. Why hadn't I dreamed up some suitable emergency?

"Milligan was out at the city desk telling me you're drawing money like a Shriner! Now, what's going on?"

"See, there was this diplomat," I blurted out idiotically.

"Diplomat?"

"Uh . . . a murdered diplomat . . . and it could be a story, Ironhead."

There was a silence, and I had to imagine he was either lighting his cigar, or chewing it maniacally, or maybe he was strangling the phone.

"Murdered diplomat? In Berlin? We're not interested in stories about goddamn dead diplomats over there, you crackbrain! You'll account for every penny, you hear that?"

"Sure . . . sure."

"Drop the diplomat, goddamnit. Get that travel story.

Mrs. McFadden wants a birthday party story, and you'd
better bring it back here."

"You got it."

"And don't draw any more money."

"Right!"

"And if you ever call me again at this hour, don't bother
to come back!"

Blam! *Errrrrrrr* . . .

I hung up the phone, shaking like a leaf. Then it
occurred to me that drawing more money was exactly
what I had to do. I had used my own five hundred dollars
expense money, plus the thirteen hundred I had drawn,
plus the rest from Claudette, to give to that greedy diplomat, and I had almost nothing left. Why hadn't I gone
through the Raincoat's pockets when I was shoving his
body around?

I sank down onto the bed, and calculated that I had
already missed the first three days of the birthday celebration tour, and was getting nowhere fast concerning that
goddamn painting. The trouble was, of course, that I was
a fish out of water in Berlin.

It was not as though I were on my own turf in New
York City, where I had some vague idea of how to find
things out. Here in Berlin I was an *Auslander,* a stranger,
with no pipelines to the cops or officials. Of course, there
was John Rhodes, but he was more of a lead pipe than a
pipeline. He wanted us out of there.

The thing about being a reporter in a big city is that
after a while you develop a sort of a bug-in-a-rug status,
and you get to know the ins and outs as perhaps no other
person can. Here in Berlin, though, I didn't know anybody, didn't know my way around. I couldn't call some
detective and casually ask what was doing on that murder
at the Exil. Besides, I didn't think I wanted to know any

more. My insides were growling with frustration and hunger. I realized I hadn't eaten a thing since lunch the day before at the Opfern Cafe on the River Spree in East Berlin.

What I needed was some nice bratwurst and a decent contact.

I was going through the lobby when who did I spot but Franz Hoppenrath, the *B.Z.* reporter, looking for the touring journalists.

"You missed them," I told the portly reporter. "They went to the International Center."

"But not you?" He smiled.

"No," I admitted.

"Well, but are you seeing everthing you want?" he asked pleasantly.

"Oh, sure. Too much, maybe."

Franz allowed a laugh to rumble out of him, and suddenly I realized that standing there in front of me in the Kempi lobby was the answer to all my problems. Franz Hoppenrath would know the intestines of Berlin the way I knew New York.

"Listen, can I buy you a beer and some bratwurst?" I suggested.

Franz smiled. "Very good. You know a place?"

"No," I answered. "I don't know a damn thing here, and that's what I want to talk to you about."

He sort of grunted. "Well, Fitz, you know me. You don't need to know anybody else. Come on."

I checked my wallet and found twenty deutsche marks, or about ten bucks. There was simply no help for it. I told him to wait for me, and hurried up to the corner to the Ku-Damm and the Süddeutsche Bank, and drew another five hundred with a trembling hand. What I would tell Ironhead, I couldn't imagine. But what else could I do?

Back to the Kempi, and Franz led me a few blocks to Grolman-strasse, to a little place called Diener.

"It means . . . uh . . . The Servant," he explained when we were at a table in the back room.

We ordered two beers and some bratwurst. Then he took out his pipe and lighted up, and I lighted a Tiparillo. Finally, I had a handle on how to operate in Berlin. Give me one savvy reporter in a city, and I've got the place in my pocket.

"Look, Franz," I told him. "I need your help. You know Berlin, and I don't."

"Yes. Well, so how can I help?"

"You remember telling us we needed a diplomat?"

"Yes, yes. The painting."

"Well, we got both."

He looked at me questioningly, cocking his head as though he weren't sure he had heard correctly. "You got a diplomat . . . and you got the painting?" He seemed quite astonished.

I nodded, unable to help looking a little smug.

He hunched forward on his chair and leaned closer across the table, getting interested. "You got it from . . . from over zere?"

"Yes."

He smiled happily, and even sort of chuckled. "Ha, that's quite a good one! Right out of *Ostberlin?* Zis is *wunderbar!* But how did you do it?"

He was enjoying a big joke on the lousy Commies.

"Except that things got screwed up," I told him, "and somebody lifted the painting from us."

"What?" he frowned.

I filled him in on meeting Black Raincoat the diplomat and the Dresden engineer who wanted to exchange

money, and getting the diplomat to drive the painting to
West Berlin.

He lighted his pipe and studied me with interest. "But
you say something happened viz the painting?"

I told him about the incomprehensible events at the Exil
parking lot. "When I opened the trunk, the painting was
gone and the diplomat was in the trunk, dead."

Franz straightened up and fixed me with a startled look.

"But, say," he rumbled, "the diplomat at the Exil? The
one murdered? That was *your* diplomat?"

I nodded miserably.

"Ach!" He puffed his pipe. "We have a story, you
know."

"I know, but there's nothing about the painting, and
they don't even identify the diplomat."

Franz's eyes widened. "But we do! Maybe you saw an
early story. It's in the paper now. A British man."

"British?"

"*Ja*. Uh . . . Palmer . . . Palmer Enderly. Not so
important, you know. Except dead, of course."

Wonderful.

Palmer Enderly. It seemed odd to me. "He spoke perfect
German—so perfect I thought he *was* German," I said. "I
understood him perfectly."

"Ah," Franz smiled. "Maybe why you understood his
German was because it was very simple German."

I realized that was true. No wonder I could catch
everything he said. With a real German, all sorts of slang
and idiomatic expressions bounce in and you soon get
lost.

"And where did you meet this British man?" he wanted
to know.

"He called us. One of the reporters, Bibi Nelson from
Rio, sent him to us."

"Hmmm. And did you have to pay him?"

I admitted we gave him thirty-five hundred dollars, including money I'd drawn from the New York *Daily Press*.

"Zis is zumzing," he said, squirming around in his chair.

"I don't understand it," I confessed. "I thought the East Germans would be screaming by now."

"Huh!" he said, shaking his head. "And you don't know where is the painting?"

"No," I admitted. "Unless Erik got it."

"Who?"

"This art dealer. Erik Grosse-Mund. He was there waiting for us to bring it."

"He was zere . . . at the Exil?"

"Yeah. He saw whoever it was who called the cops on us. I haven't had a chance to talk to him. I haven't had a chance to talk to anybody. That's what's driving me crazy."

Franz nodded sympathetically. "Well, then, he is the one, yes?"

"He says not."

Franz nodded cynically. He was a newspaperman, all right. "What he says is one thing. But if he got it, what else would he say?"

I had to admit it sounded plausible. "I was wondering, Franz . . . you know Berlin. Could you ask around of the cops, quietly, you know, and try to find out what's going on?"

He grunted and halfway nodded. "This Erik, you say he saw somebody call the police?"

"That's what he said."

"Where is this man?"

"At the Schloss Hotel in the Europa-Center. I'm going to talk to him at four."

I wish I could tell you that it had occurred to me for even an instant that I was in Berlin talking to a reporter about a hot story that he was bound to cover. Why this most obvious of all realities didn't penetrate my brain—a reporter myself—I cannot account for.

Yet, back in New York, working for the *Daily Press,* I had met numerous politicians and burglars who spilled out every last detail while talking to me, once they got started. Part of it, of course, was that a reporter never considers himself to be of any news value, and this wasn't a story to me—it was a mess I had to get out of. It also was easy and comfortable to talk to a fellow ink-stained wretch who understood. Anyway, there I sat in the Diener eating bratwurst and *Bratkartofflen* telling a reporter for Berlin's biggest newspaper every damning detail of a hot story that could get me mangled into indistinguishable bits.

"You're not . . . covering this story yourself . . . are you?" I asked naively.

"I think now I have to!"

"But, you're not going to use what I just told you?"

Franz Hoppenrath's eyes opened wide. Was he hearing correctly? I had many times wondered how anybody could spill his guts to a reporter—to me—and then ask incredulously if I was going to print it. All of a sudden, I was on the other side of things, and I didn't like it.

"You didn't tell me anything in confidence," he purred. How many times had I said that into some panic-stricken face.

"But . . .

"It's all right," he soothed me. "I can ask the Geheimpolizei about it for you." He smiled like a fox, doing me a big favor.

"Do you have to mention Claudette and me?" I asked fearfully.

Franz Hoppenrath's face was a study in bewilderment. I realized what an idiotic question it was. Not use the names of the two Americans who had stolen a painting out of East Berlin and bribed a dead diplomat? I sat there frozen like a dope.

"Jesus," I muttered.

"Listen," he said, "the story won't be out until the morning. You have a little time, you know."

"Time for what?"

Franz examined my face soberly. "Well, Fitz, my friend, I zink you must get away out of Berlin. Don't you?"

∇

CHAPTER NINETEEN

I REMEMBER one time a millionaire politician stole another man's wife, leaving the cuckolded husband helpless and humiliated. He could not fight the immensely powerful millionaire, and so he simply climbed into a hole and spoke to no one. One night, Ironhead gave me his private home telephone number and I called him at two in the morning, and he answered it himself.

The poor bedeviled soul, surprised in his own home with a couple of drinks in him, poured out his lacerated guts for three hours to me, unable to stop, doing exactly what he had sworn he would not do. It is a curiosity of the human condition that under powerful stress, a person can undress himself to a reporter he doesn't know, when it is the last person he should even talk to.

Walking back to the Kempi alone after Franz Hoppenrath had escaped with his big scoop, I understood what had happened to that poor devil. Now, I had done it myself.

There was no way to prevent Franz from splashing that delicious story of madcap Americans into the columns of

B.Z. the next morning. I knew that as a reporter, I would have been unable to resist it.

I slunk into the Kempi hotel bar, kicking myself for being an idiot, and hoping Franz would be judicious in what he wrote. What a fool anybody is to hang out with self-serving, amoral, sensation-seeking yellow journalists!

Who did I find sitting at the bar but the very person I was looking for, Bibi Nelson, the boulevardier from Rio.

"Well, Bibi, I've been looking for you."

"Fitzgerald!" His video face smiled. "Say, what a town this is. I've got three interviews on tape already. Have a drink."

Angelo set up a Budweiser for me, and I studied the Phil Donohue of Rio for a moment. He certainly seemed quite relaxed as to why I wanted him.

"It's about that diplomat you sent us," I started.

Bibi's face flushed a little and he looked down into his yellow drink. "Oh, I'm sorry about that. I wasn't able to get you anybody."

"What?"

"You know how diplomats are. You can't pin them down. Bartol told me this morning he couldn't get you anybody."

I'm sorry to say I lowered my Tiparillo right into my amber glass of Budweiser.

"Look out," he chuckled.

"What did you say?" I finally asked him. "You didn't send us a diplomat?"

"What is the promise of one of these people worth?" He laughed contemptuously. "Wait until he wants to be on my show."

I was swaying around on my bar stool, trying to grasp what he had said.

"Are you sure of that?"

His eyes widened in surprise. "But, of course. Why?"

"But somebody came to us," I said.

"What?"

"Yes. Maybe your friend—Bartol, is it?—got somebody after all?"

He shook his head emphatically. "No, he did not. We had a yelling match about it."

I measured his ingenuous face. "He must have mentioned it to somebody," I insisted. "A Brit named Palmer Enderly called us."

Bibi shook his head. "Well, Bartol didn't send him."

I reached over and grabbed Nelson's shirt under his finely chiseled chin and jerked his head until we were nose to nose. His face went slack and pale in astonishment.

"Now, look, Nelson! You sent us Palmer Enderly and he's dead!"

Bibi's Technicolor face went from white to red, and his eyes rolled like a wooden doll's. He jerked free and stared at me in wide-eyed confusion.

"But, what do you mean? Dead? What? Good God! Fitzgerald, I tell you he didn't send anyone!" He suddenly got off the bar stool. "What do you think you're doing? I think you must be a crazy person!"

Before I could react, Bibi Nelson scurried out of the Kempi bar, darting a last, furious look at me before he vanished out of sight.

Bibi's wooden doll eyes and terrified reaction convinced me that he was telling the truth, and I was sorry I had grabbed him. Not that it did any good. By that time, all I wanted was to forget about the whole damned thing.

Then something happened that went a long way toward helping me forget. As though visiting from the land of the lotus-eaters, bringing soothing forgetfulness, a blond vision glided into the Kempi bar and climbed up onto the bar stool beside me.

Melanie of the shoulder-length blond hair and luminous eyes, the fetching Rheinmaiden who had flirted with me earlier, was back, with a provocative smile, arched eyes, a little tilt of her head, and the song of the Lorelei on her lips.

"Well, *Herr Schreiber,*" she cooed melodiously. "You are still here."

"Melanie," I breathed. "A sight for sore eyes."

"What does this mean?" she said softly.

"It means, have a drink, lovely creature."

A little laugh came from her throat. "I think you are a little crazy, *Herr Schreiber.* But nice. Are you getting everything you want in Berlin, Herr Fitz?" she asked, and crossed her legs.

Melanie the Valkyrie had a nice, heartwarming crush on the Irish reporter from New York. I was alone with a regular Marlene Dietrich in a friendly spa, with several free hours before me. I blotted out everything else.

Here, finally, was the Berlin of the lederhosen and oompah-pah about which Ironhead had railed. It was about time.

"And what are you up to?" I asked her.

She smiled. *"Mittagessen."*

The time had gotten away from me. It was the lunch hour.

When you're traveling in a foreign city, time has a way of getting fuzzy, and you don't measure things by the clock.

"You want to eat?" I invited.

She shrugged, sipped her drink, and smiled. You know

how it is when you're besieged by a host of unsolvable troubles and you have to immediately do forty-seven things or else, and it becomes so monumental that you don't do anything at all? That's the mood I was in as I sat there gazing luxuriously at Melanie, who didn't demand that I go out and get myself killed, or pester me about the labors of Hercules—who demanded nothing of me except fantasy.

So we sat there chatting away under the smiling eyes of the speak-no-evil, see-no-evil, hear-no-evil Angelo, who knew how to keep our glasses full, and Melanie gently turned more and more toward me until we were facing each other and her knees bumped mine ever so accidentally.

Ah, me, I felt I had reached the Happy Isles, or would pretty soon. I wish I could say that my mind was tormented with thoughts of disloyalty toward a certain sleeping mademoiselle from New Jersey, but all she meant was trouble, and all Melanie the swallow meant was invitation.

It's not too easy to kiss while sitting on bar stools in a public place during the lunch hour, but we managed. I forgot not only the time, but the place.

After a while, Melanie excused herself to go to the ladies' room, and came back smiling a secret smile.

"I have the rest of the afternoon off," she confided, and my mad head went into a swoon.

I asked her if she would like to go somewhere else for lunch. "Well, I don't know," she said prettily.

Then she asked me if I wanted to go see some sights, such as the Victory Column at Grosser Stern or maybe the Brandenburg Gate.

"Well, I don't know," I said.

Instead, we looked at each other from about two inches

away, and I, at least, savored a sight more fascinating than any tower or gate.

"How do you like Berlin?" she murmured.

"*Sehr gut.*"

"How do you like the hotel?"

"Lovely."

"And do you have a nice room?"

"*Wunderbar.*"

"What color are the walls of your room?"

A house was falling on me. "My room?" I finally intersected her train of thought. "Would you like to see it?"

"Oh!" she smiled demurely, as though wondering from where such an idea could possibly have come.

So, we had another drink and cooed at each other in the happy, drifting land-of-the-lotus-eaters afternoon, and then I signed my bar tab and we floated through the lobby to the elevators and rode up to my room. Once inside, she strolled around examining the typical hotel wall pictures with deep concentration for about a minute, and then was in my arms.

Ah, sweet Lorelei of the rocks, with her intoxicating mouth of lotus petals, and luminous eyes as deep as intergalactic space. She wrapped herself around me like the serpent around Laocoön, and I devoured her in a kind of swooning ecstasy. We slid onto the bed and turned into a spaghetti junction, until Ulysses came sailing along the Rhein and bumped onto the rocks, summoned by her siren. His boat thumped and whumped, and then the helmsman called out, "Fitz . . . Fitz."

I stirred from my pool of pleasure, trying to catch the call.

"Fitz?" A pounding.

I sat up. "What's that?"

Melanie gave me a cross glare and tried to pull me down to her again.

"Are you there, Fitz?"

I realized my time warp had righted itself, and that I was back in the present, and that Claudette was banging on my hotel room door.

"Tell them to go away," pouted Melanie the siren.

Bam, bam, bam! "It's time to get going!"

"Melanie, listen, could you hop into the bathroom for a minute while I . . ."

"What?"

"Well, you see . . ."

Melanie sat up. Her love-filled eyes clouded over and glimmered in annoyance.

"It's . . . somebody . . ."

"That pushy American Fräulein!" Melanie announced. She got up, though, and headed for the bathroom. Except that as she got to the foot of the bed, she seemed to be confused about the direction, because she turned right and headed straight for the hotel room door.

"Hey," I called out, "Not that door!"

Melanie either didn't hear me or didn't care. She stalked straight to the door and yanked it open. There she stood in front of Claudette with no shoes on and her clothes in rather provocative disarray.

"What do you want?" she demanded.

Claudette stepped into the room.

Melanie backed away enough to let her in, and then turned to begin flinging Teutonic insults in a rising shriek. This was not what I had had in mind. It was, in fact, a nightmare come true.

"What in the world . . . ?" from Claudette, who seemed

to speak with her mouth wide open. She gave Melanie a look that would have put a hole through the Siegfried line. Then she looked at me, and I was a fried smudge on molten steel.

"Excuse me," she said through icicles, "I thought we were going to find Erik."

"Brazen slut!" This was the pleasant comment from Melanie.

"I'm sorry I ruined your business," came back the French gendarme.

"*Heraus,* you stupid sow!"

"Berlin whore!"

"Wait a minute," came the feeble piping of a would-be mediator.

"You shut up!" Melanie snapped at me. "Throw this slut out the window!"

"Claudette, you see . . ."

"Don't speak to me! I don't want your help! Crawl back into your slime pit with Brünnhilde!"

She about-faced and stalked out, trailing clouds of outraged dignity and a whiff of innocence betrayed.

"Come back here!" screamed the Berlin whore, scrambling after Claudette. I struggled after Melanie, and the next thing I knew Melanie had leaped upon Claudette's back, and they were both down on the carpet in the corridor, halfway in my room, clawing and hair pulling and screaming the house down.

Jupiter Optimus Maximus!

"For God's sake," I cried, and tried to pull Melanie off Claudette. This allowed Claudette to get an arm free and to swing it wildly, catching me in the eye.

"Polizei!" howled Melanie.

"Wait a minute . . . !"

"Nice friends you have!" Claudette yelled, getting up.

I was holding Melanie from behind as she flailed away trying to punch or claw Claudette, yelling all the time like a berserk Circe.

"Shut up, will you?" I pleaded. "We'll have the whole staff down on us!"

"Yes!" screeched Melanie. "Get the police!"

Finally, Claudette got herself together and steamed away down the corridor, leaving me holding Melanie and wishing I was dead or in a madhouse.

"Look, I think we'd better do this some other time," I suggested to Melanie.

"Take your hands off me, American swine!" she suggested right back.

I let go of her and she flounced back into my room to gather her shoes and purse and straighten her dress. I trailed in after her, sat on the bed, and lighted a Tiparillo. It was quite a wonderful afternoon in Berlin, all right.

She stormed out without another word or any attempt to gouge my eyes out, and I got myself together to follow Claudette.

I caught up with her on the Ku-Damm, walking toward the Europa-Center and the Schloss Hotel. As I came alongside, she glanced swiftly at me and then straight ahead. She apparently had no words adequate for low creeping insects.

"I . . . uh . . . don't quite know how that happened," was the stumbling, hopeless apology from said insect.

"Hmmmmmph!" She marched on.

"She got a little . . . excited."

Well, that was certainly an amazingly perceptive, incisive, insightful, idiotic, revolting conclusion! A person with such analytic abilities belonged at the United

Nations, or possibly in The Wells underwater prison in Old Venice, where they kept traitorous dogs and vermin in sewer water up to their chins so they could be bitten by rabid blowfish!

She was annoyed.

We walked on in raging silence to the Europa-Center, which was just past the Tooth, and went downstairs into the huge, sprawling complex. It was like an American shopping mall, with shops, restaurants, and an immense water clock rising up two or three stories. Various containers and pods fill with water for each minute and hour, and at one o'clock and at six, everything empties out in a mad whoosh and it starts over.

We went by an English pub and an Italian restaurant and then saw it dead ahead—Alt Nürnberg—a Bavarian *Bierstube* with wooden booths and paintings of stags on the wall.

We gave the *Bierstube* a quick looking-over, and saw there was only one person there. A small man sat in a booth, watching the door.

I walked over to him. "Herr Dahlem?"

The small man in a black suit smiled eagerly at me. "*Ja?*"

I slid into the booth across from him, and Claudette sat beside me, although not close enough to touch me.

"You're waiting for Erik Grosse-Mund?" I asked.

Herr Dahlem registered surprise. "*Ja*. Did he send you?"

"We're here to meet him, too," said Claudette. "Tell me, are you meeting him about a painting?"

Herr Dahlem was again bemused, and looked from Claudette to me and back again. "Who are you?" he asked.

"Fräulein Barry," I said, indicating Claudette. "And Herr Fitzgerald."

"Does Erik want to sell you my painting?" Claudette jumped in. "*The Green Room?*"

Dahlem rocked back in the booth, and his face opened up. "So! Then, it was your painting? He was supposed to bring it to me last night, but he didn't come. When I called, he said to meet him here."

I lighted a Tiparillo. "You're the art dealer?"

Herr Dahlem nodded and produced a card. "I waited at the shop last night, but he didn't come."

"What did he say when he called you?" asked Claudette.

"Only to meet him. He said he didn't have the work yet, but hoped to get it."

We sat there for a while, drinking coffee, and then a fidgeting Claudette said, "Let's go to the hotel. He should have been here."

That was agreeable with Dahlem, so we walked through the Europa-Center to the Schloss Hotel, where Herr Dahlem asked the desk to ring Erik.

The desk clerk smilingly pointed out a house phone. Dahlem dialed the room, but there was no answer. "Not in," he said with a shrug.

"He must be," complained Claudette.

"Come on," I said, and led them to the elevator. We rode up into the hotel and went to Erik's room. I knocked on the door, and then noticed it was slightly ajar.

"It's open," I muttered, and called out, "Erik! Erik?"

I was also shoving at the door, which seemed to give grudgingly, as though something were blocking it. I shoved hard enough to get my head in to see what it was.

Behind the door, his chest a mass of bloody pulp, was the door stop. Herr Erik Grosse-Mund.

$\triangledown$

CHAPTER TWENTY

"WHAT's the matter?" Herr Dahlem was saying even as I pulled my head from behind the door. His eyes were staring, and he was backing away from us.

"It's all right," I said absurdly, intent upon calming him down. "It's . . . Erik . . ."

"What!" He backed away more, bumping against the wall.

Claudette stood there like a wooden totem pole. She seemed to sense that, whatever the case, it was certainly not all right.

"What's the matter?" she hissed, echoing the trembling Dahlem.

"Well . . . Jesus . . . I think he's dead."

That did it. Herr Dahlem got turned around and fled down the corridor like a kangaroo rat.

"Wait . . . !" I called to the already empty corridor.

"Is he—are you sure?" Claudette gasped in a tiny voice.

"Yes." There was no question about it. One look at a dead body is all you need. There is an absolute stillness and stiffness that is unmistakable. "We'd better get out of here."

She didn't protest, but followed me numbly along the corridor to the elevator, where I put my finger on the button and kept it there. Disconnected thoughts careened around in my head.

"He must have had it," popped out of Claudette, voicing one of my zigzagging thoughts.

When the elevator came, I pushed the button for the second floor and led Claudette out onto the balcony overlooking the lobby. I didn't know what might be happening. There was Herr Dahlem jabbering away to the desk clerk, who was himself jerking around like a puppet. Berlin was once more mobilizing to run down Public Enemies Numbers One and Two. I walked slowly down a staircase, with Claudette glued behind me against the wall, and slipped into a restaurant off the lobby. From there we reached Budapester Strasse and walked along in a state of ambling shock.

"My God." A barely perceptible blip from Claudette.

We hurried through the island around the Kaiser Wilhelm Memorial Church and then along the Ku-Damm, homing in toward the Kempinski Hotel like carrier pigeons driven by some unerring instinct. Once again, my only thought was zeroing in on the schedule of Pan Am's departing flights from the City by the Spree.

"We're getting out of here," I told her flatly.

"Yes."

We walked stiff-legged along the broad avenue, already getting dark and with some of the Ku-Damm hookers out and standing by the little glass advertising display cases that dot the avenue out in front of the stores. When we reached the hotel, I went straight through the lobby to the telephone booths and called Pan Am to book us on the next flight to Frankfurt, leaving at 8:00 P.M.

"Now, listen," I told Claudette when I came out of the phone booth, "pack right away. We're leaving this hotel in ten minutes."

She didn't say anything, but followed me to the elevator. Riding up, she stood in a corner like one hypnotized, and I wasn't much better, although I was twitching all over.

"What could have happened?" she muttered. "Dahlem said he never got it. Somebody got it from Erik!"

"I don't give a good goddamn!"

"No," she managed. "It's just . . . where is it now?"

I couldn't answer that. We got off the elevator and walked as fast as possible to her room, where she went in and started throwing things into her bag. I went down the hall and did the same, gathering up among other things stacks of unread brochures about Berlin and its anniversary. What the hell would I be able to write?

There was no time for worrying about tomorrow's problems when today's had me by the neck. I don't think I ever packed more riotously, although any bag I ever pack is hardly what you'd call organized.

We were soon back down in the lobby with our bags, and I had no intention of wasting any time checking out. Let them dun me at the *Daily Press* later. I motioned with my head to Claudette to follow me out the front door to get a cab. I had not counted on the excellent efficiency of the Kempinski, though. In such a first-class hotel, swarming with green-liveried bellboys, it's impossible to walk through the lobby carrying luggage.

"*Bitte!*" offered a polite young man, whisking my bag out of my hand. Another one had Claudette's. Before I could protest, the green bellboy with the pie-pan hat carried it to the desk, where a clerk smiled at us.

"Checking out?" he wanted to know.

"Yes," I glowered.

There was no way to find Hans Dieter at that precise moment to pay the hotel bill, so there was nothing to do but give the desk clerk my *Daily Press* credit card. This would further gladden the hearts of Jack Milligan and Ironhead Matthews.

"Passport, please."

"What?"

Of course, the hotel would need my passport if I was paying with a credit card, so I had to hand it over, as did Claudette. It's certainly wonderful to travel in a European city where they check your passport when you come in and when you leave, no doubt so that every move you make can be filed with the Gestapo.

We got our bill settled and rushed out to the street to get a cab, then went driving off through the night to Tegel Airport.

Claudette huddled against me, shaking, sobbing a little and then wiping her eyes. Then, she sighed. What a lovely departure from a lovely adventure. At the *Flughafen,* we wrestled our bags onto little green rolling carts and pushed through to the Pan Am ticket counter, where again they checked everything and looked at our passports.

I dragged a disconsolate Claudette into a bar in the international lounge and ordered two beers. She sat beside me in a dark blue funk.

"Oh, Fitz."

I tried not to listen.

"Oh, Fitz." Then several more of the same.

"Goddamnit, there's nothing else to do."

It was unfortunate that there was this waiting time before the Pan Am airbus could jet us out of that damned city to Frankfurt, our gateway to safety, because it allowed Claudette's active mind to start working all over again.

"Do you think Dahlem was in on it?"

"I haven't the faintest idea."

"He knew about *The Green Room*. Erik told him he expected to have the painting soon."

"Claudette . . ."

Of course, she understood that it meant very little to me. That was obvious. When the first little thing went wrong, there I was ready to throw in the towel and beat it.

"First little thing!"

I calculated dimly in my bedazzled brain that we had left a trail of bribery, international smuggling, theft from a foreign government, and two dead bodies. Not to mention a blank screen on my video display terminal back in the city room of the New York *Daily Press* when Mrs. McFadden the publisher's wife and Ironhead Matthews expected a concise history of the new Berlin from me.

She continued her wail of anguish until it was time to board the plane to Frankfurt, and I continued to turn a deaf ear. I more or less dragged her to the loading gate, where we could see the big jet outside the window and the Pan Am flight attendant at the little lectern-stall, checking tickets. I felt like Victor Laszlo and Ilsa about to get on the plane to Lisbon.

The Pan Am attendant was all smiles and courtesy as we got to her. She took our tickets and smiled, and then sort of flicked her head to the side.

"Ah, yes," she said. "Here we are."

Before I could think what that might mean, she signaled with her pretty head. I glanced around to see what she was signaling about.

The man wore a full-length black leather coat like Major Strasser, and his smile was fixed. He walked a few steps toward us and took the tickets from the Pan Am flight attendant. Then he gave us his professional scrutiny.

This time I knew it was no mistake. Our papers were not in order.

"You will come with me, please."

∇

CHAPTER TWENTY-ONE

THE insides of all police stations look pretty much the same.

We were ushered in by the leather-coated Major Strasser. There was a long, high desk, behind which a uniformed German officer stood with an impassive expression. We could have been in the 17th Precinct on the East Side of Manhattan, except for the Lion of Brandenburg Shield of Prussia on the wall.

We went into a room with a table and chairs, and there stood the little man in the black suit, Herr Dahlem.

He fixed a terrified look on us, raised his right hand to point at us, and said nothing. He didn't have to.

"Sit down," invited Major Strasser. "I am Lieutenant Wolfe. I must ask you a few questions."

The fat was in the fire this time, and no question. Claudette's hand found mine under the table and gripped it tightly.

"Okay," I said wearily.

Lieutenant Wolfe sat at the table across from us, slowly lighted a dark brown cigarette, and polished his rimless glasses.

"Is there anything you would like to tell me?" he began.
I felt a wild urge to tell him that it was all a huge
mistake, and that I was a mere American travel writer
visiting Berlin to write about bratwurst and Frederick the
Great.

"It's all because they stole my painting!" Claudette
suddenly announced.

I shook my head, trying to clear it, and lighted a
Tiparillo. It was inevitable.

"Painting?" asked the seemingly overpolite Lieutenant
Wolfe.

"Jupiter Optimus Maximus," escaped from me.

"*Bitte?*" he came back.

"Nothing. *Nichts.*"

"What is this painting?" said Wolfe. "Herr Dahlem also
mentions this."

"See, it was stolen from the Louvre," Claudette
launched in, "and . . ."

I'm not going to repeat the story Claudette told Lieutenant Wolfe, because I was by then totally sick of the
whole thing. The Berlin Geheimpolizist listened intently
to the whole elaborate travail of tears, though, and nodded
his head from time to time.

"*Entschuldigen Sie, bitte,*" he finally interrupted. "What
does this have to do with what happened this afternoon at
the Schloss Hotel?" His eyes were up and his head cocked
alertly.

I glanced at Herr Dahlem, who was sitting forward on
a chair in the corner.

"Oh, that," said Claudette.

"*Ja.*"

Claudette's hand tightened in mine, and she looked at
me, as though suggesting that the painting was her story,

but dead bodies were my department. Lieutenant Wolfe followed her eyes to me. He smiled at me expectantly.

I wish I could tell you that I had any idea whatever of how to talk our way out of this. I sat there and studied the detective face of Lieutenant Wolfe, and I figured he had to be much like any detective back in New York. I knew perfectly well that if I tried to invent something he would soon trip me up. The only possibility was to tell the truth, or as much of it as I knew.

I started by tossing my press card on the table. He examined it thoroughly, glancing up to compare my face with the hopeless photo on the press card, which made me look like a shoe clerk at Macy's.

"Hmmmm," he allowed, and put the press card down on the table. "Journalist."

"Right. Now, about Erik . . ."

"Erik Grosse-Mund, *ja?*"

"Yes."

"Who was murdered at the hotel this afternoon."

"I guess so . . ."

"Hmmmm."

A regular wooden-faced damned snoopy detective, all right. I told him that Erik was going to handle the sale of the painting for us, but that when we went to the Schloss Hotel, we found him dead.

"So," he commented drily, and waited.

"I don't know what else to tell you."

"Hmmmm." He was polishing his glasses again. "This painting you mention. Where is it?"

"That's what I'd like to know!" Claudette came back to life.

"They gave it to Herr Grosse-Mund, and he was supposed to bring it to me," came from Herr Dahlem in the corner.

"We did not," snapped Claudette. "It disappeared at the Exil."

I wanted to kick her under the table.

"The Exil?" asked Lieutenant Wolfe, and his eyes narrowed.

"Yes, after . . ." This time I did kick her. "Ahhh," she huffed.

Lieutenant Wolfe stood up, frowned at us for a long moment, and then turned to leave the room. "Herr Dahlem," he said, and motioned for that corner-commentator to go with him. They both walked out, leaving us at the table in a fine simmering stew.

"Fitz, what's going to happen?" she asked me, white faced.

"A German dungeon," I muttered blackly.

"I mean it!"

"So do I! How the hell do I know what's going to happen! If we lie, we're sunk. If we tell the truth, we're dog meat."

The enormity crashed down on Claudette. She cried. I wished I could. Why the hell hadn't we gotten out when we could?

After a while, Lieutenant Wolfe came back into the interrogation room with another man, who carried a little shoe-box-size metal machine with keys on it, which I recognized as a device for taking down testimony. Wolfe again sat across from us, and the man with the shoe box sat at the end of the table with the thing in front of him.

"You will please give us a statement about your activities in Berlin," said Lieutenant Wolfe. He nodded toward the shoe box man. "This is *ein Offizier* who will record it."

A statement? Christ, I thought.

"Then perhaps we can try to understand this perplexing situation," he added.

I strongly doubted they'd manage that.

"I don't know how to begin," I muttered.

"Begin at the beginning," our suave Major Strasser suggested in his oily way.

"You can't arrest us for stealing our own property!" declared the brainless half-wit sitting beside me. I glanced at her and saw a determined righteous face shining with sincerity. A sure ticket to the dungeon.

"Yes. And what is it that you stole?" Wolfe was all ears.

"Shit." I muttered. The shoe box man took it down, then gave me a disgusted look. He pushed some other keys apparently to erase it.

There was no longer a bridle on Claudette. Armored in her righteous cause, she let fly with the whole, awful story of our theft of *The Green Room* out of the National Gallery. Splat! The documentation papers were smacked onto the table for Lieutenant Wolfe.

"It's my property!"

Lieutenant Wolfe sat examining the documentation with considerable fascination, and I thought I detected a pleased smile flitting about his mouth.

"You . . . stole this painting out of the National Gallery in the D.D.R.?" he finally said with a grin.

"I liberated it!" Claudette corrected him.

"*Ja, ja.*" He chuckled.

Claudette nudged me under the table, obviously assuming we had solved our problems. Lieutenant Wolfe seemed by no means upset at our adventure into and out of East Berlin.

The German's policeman's affability vanished, however, as he heard about Palmer Enderly the British diplomat at the Exil, and then about Erik at the Schloss Hotel.

When she was finished, he sat there holding my press card and running his finger around and around its outer edge, frowning and shaking his head and then staring at the big shield of Berlin on the wall.

Finally, he put down the press card, slid *The Green Room* documentation back across the table to Claudette, and stood up.

"There is someone here to see you," he announced, and walked out, trailed by the man with the shoe box.

In walked John Rhodes, looking as though he wished he was back in Milwaukee. He walked to the table, halted, and stood there glaring at us. At last, he sank down into a chair.

"Beautiful!" he snorted.

"Hello, Rhodes," I said.

"My God, am I glad to see you," gushed Claudette.

"Why the hell didn't you get out of here?" he yelled. "Didn't I tell you to get out of Berlin?"

"What's going to happen?" Claudette asked.

John Rhodes hung his head and examined the tabletop intently, possibly hoping for inspiration. His head wagged back and forth. He ran his hand through his hair. There seemed no solution there, either.

"Damned if I know," he conceded. "The manual doesn't cover crazies." He looked up at us. "Am I to understand that they caught you with another dead body?"

"Caught us?" I complained. "We fell over him."

His head went up and down, as though bobbing for apples. "Yeah, sure. Just like you fell over the first one."

"There was a man with us," said Claudette. "He knows we didn't have anything to do with it."

"The man with you," Rhodes declared portentously,

"went straight to the police! You two wackos went straight to the airport!"

"You told us to leave Berlin," Claudette said sweetly.

"I wish you'd never come here!"

"Can't you explain what happened?" Claudette went on sweetly. "You know the whole thing. You know we didn't do anything."

Rhodes was outraged. "Didn't do anything!" He got up, turned around, and sat down again. "Goddamnit, you committed international grand larceny, bribery, and fourteen kinds of ordinary stupidity!"

"But we didn't kill those men," Claudette insisted.

Rhodes sighed. He had already told the Berlin police that we couldn't have killed the diplomat. That might somehow be gotten over, except there was the problem of the theft and the bribery, not to mention Erik.

We sat there blazing away at each other, to no great purpose, until Lieutenant Wolfe once more returned and sat next to Rhodes at the table.

"Well," said Wolfe, "we seem to have a situation here that is not quite clear. In fact, several situations."

Rhodes nodded his head but apparently didn't trust himself to speak.

"Herr Fitzgerald and Fräulein Barry discover a murdered man, but there is no evidence yet that they have killed him."

"Absolutely not!" declared Claudette.

"Hmmm," came from Lieutenant Wolfe. "And they are present when another man, a diplomat, is found also murdered. But Mr. Rhodes assures us that they did not participate in that crime, either."

Rhodes nodded his head. Grudgingly, it seemed to me.

But that was not the end of it. Lieutenant Wolfe went

on with maddening calm. Both of these situations, as he called them, were in some way connected to a missing painting.

Wolfe puffed on his brown stick. "But, you see, in order for us to examine a crime of a stolen painting, there must be a crime to examine. There is no such crime."

"What?" I asked, confused.

"No theft from the National Gallery in East Berlin has been reported," he said drily. "We have two murdered men to examine, but your story that it is because of a stolen painting is, I am afraid, fanciful."

"Lieutenant Wolfe, I told you we took it," pressed Claudette.

Wolfe shook his head. "We checked with the East German police. They deny any painting was stolen."

"They *deny* it?" I mumbled, dumbfounded.

"That's correct."

Claudette and I exchanged looks of astonishment. Rhodes shrugged and looked away.

"But we stole it!" I protested, sticking my neck further into the noose.

Lieutenant Wolfe was unperturbed. "The D.D.R. assures me that the painting is in the National Gallery, and that your story is a fabrication."

"It's a fake . . . a copy," said Claudette.

Smoke drifted from the brown cigarette. Lieutenant Wolfe's eyebrows elevated a trifle. He felt no need to say any more.

"But what does this mean?" I asked. "Where does that leave things?"

"Indeed," said Wolfe. "Where? With a murder investigation, involving you two."

"But you must find the painting," cried Claudette. "That will solve the murders."

"The painting is in the National Gallery in East Berlin," said Lieutenant Wolfe.

"It's not," spluttered Claudette. "That's a worthless copy."

Lieutenant Wolfe cocked his head slightly. "They could hardly be mistaken about a work of art valued at sixteen million deutsche marks."

"You mean you're not going to do anything about my painting?" Claudette complained weakly.

"Without a report of a theft, I cannot," he replied.

"All right, then," Claudette said brilliantly, "I report it stolen!"

"You?"

"Yes! It's my property. I want to file a report of a theft."

"Hmmm," said Wolfe. "Where and when?"

"Hermann Goering stole it from the Louvre in Paris in 1940."

Lieutenant Wolfe's wooden face registered this time, all right, but not pleasantly. It went from softwood to hardwood. Oak, maybe.

"I'm afraid that is out of my jurisdiction," he snapped, and stood up. "Mr. Rhodes, you will guarantee the availability of your fellow subjects in Berlin?"

Rhodes spat something vile. Then he nodded sourly.

To us, Lieutenant Wolfe said, "You will please not leave Berlin until this situation has been resolved!"

$\triangledown$

CHAPTER TWENTY-TWO

WE walked out of the Berlin police station in the disaffected custody of John Rhodes, whose entire manner shrieked that he wanted our company about as much as the Roman Emperor Valerian wanted the company of the Persians, who captured him and kept his straw-stuffed body in a temple for display.

He drove us back to the Hotel Kempinski, where we straggled in a hangdog manner over to the counter to check in again. The striped pants looked us over, frowned, hesitated, and asked uncertainly, "Are you together? One room or   "

"Separate rooms!" Claudette stood there stiffly. She obviously had not forgotten Melanie, the Berlin whore. The clerk gave us room keys, had our bags taken up, and we walked disconsolately into the hotel bar with John Rhodes, who ordered a double Scotch from our smiling cupbearer, Angelo.

Rhodes sipped his drink, shook his head in elaborate annoyance, and sputtered unhappily, "Don't leave Berlin!"

"Well, you might as well help us now," piped up Claudette. "It's the only way to get rid of us."

Rhodes grunted grotesquely. "Help you! My God! I'm going to be transferred to Beirut, I can see that."

I was on my own scent, though. "What the hell was that about denying the painting was stolen?" I asked.

"What did you expect?" he yelled. "You think the East Germans would admit anything like that?"

It was certainly wonderful. The East Germans refused to admit it was stolen, and the West Berlin police accepted it, leaving us hooked into two murders and still without *The Green Room*. I was as disgusted as Rhodes.

"Under the circumstances," I tried reasoning, "why don't you tell us what you know that we don't?"

Rhodes snorted. "That would take five years."

"Try us."

Rhodes proceeded to rather furiously pour out what he knew about the distressing imbroglio. Palmer Enderly, he said, was a third-level British air attaché in the West Berlin British Embassy, and had a checkered history of drunkenness and philandering in several embassies around the world. This post in West Berlin was about his last chance. Which it proved to be.

"How did you find him?" Rhodes wanted to know.

"I don't know," I sighed, which didn't please John Rhodes, but there it was.

I lighted a Tiparillo and tried to think. I realized my last hope of dropping the whole thing had vanished with Lieutenant Wolfe's pronouncement that we were not to leave Berlin until this mess was "resolved." Wonderful word. How could we resolve anything when we didn't understand what the hell had happened?

"Did the cops tell you how Enderly got it?" I asked.

Rhodes related rather soberly that Enderly the diplomat was hit with something hard, maybe a lug wrench, and then practically disemboweled by the sharp end of the wrench, which was driven up under his ribs.

Claudette's face drained to something like the color of white paper.

"How about Erik?"

That was more efficient, said Rhodes. He was also hit on the head with something, probably to stun him, and then gutted with a long, sharp object, probably a knife.

Claudette excused herself to go to the ladies' room.

"Does Wolfe think it was the same person?"

Rhodes nodded. "Looks like it. Similar procedures."

I tried to make sense of it. Two men more or less butchered. Two murders without a gun, and done thoroughly by somebody with strength and experience at close combat.

"Sounds like somebody who's been a soldier," I ventured. "Somebody who saw some tough hand-to-hand combat."

Rhodes grunted, and gave me a look. "Yeah." His eyes narrowed. "You cover murders back in New York?"

"Some."

He sipped his Scotch. "That's about the way I figured it, too."

So what had happened at the Exil? Enderly showed up with *The Green Room* and was met by somebody, and that somebody killed him and took the painting.

"That's the part I don't understand," Rhodes muttered.

"What?"

"Why Enderly delivered the painting to the Exil. He had it and he was in West Berlin. He was home free."

I decided it was time to show him that Polaroid photograph of Claudette bribing Enderly in front of his car, and pulled it out of my pocket. "This is why." I tossed it in front of Rhodes.

"Jesus," Rhodes breathed, frowning at it. "Has anybody seen this?"

"Only you."

Rhodes shoved it back to me. "Not me, either. That's all Wolfe would need, or anybody."

I put the photo back in my pocket, and tried to reconstruct that bizarre incident in the Exil parking lot. I certainly agreed with Rhodes that Enderly would have disappeared with *The Green Room* if he could have. My photo had apparently ruined that idea and forced him to go through with the deal.

"Somebody else was in on this," I told Rhodes, thinking out loud. "Whoever sent us the diplomat. What must have happened was that they were after the painting, and when Enderly actually delivered it to us, or tried to, there was a difference of opinion."

"Yeah," the big agent agreed wearily. "The other guy wanted the painting."

I pondered the situation. There was Palmer Enderly, shaky low-level diplomat, with an eight-million-dollar treasure in his hands but unable to keep it because we had his photo. He must have decided the thirty-five hundred dollars would do, but his partner would have none of that and took the painting.

I could imagine the nondescript little Brit pleading that his "whole career" would be ruined, until the lug wrench from the car trunk came down on his head.

"That would explain the lug wrench," I suggested. "The guy hadn't planned it. It was the only thing handy."

Rhodes nodded slowly. "The second time, he was prepared."

Then Claudette and I had showed up, followed soon by John Rhodes.

"Wait a minute," I said, remembering something else. "By the time you walked up to me, I could already hear sirens. The cops were already on the way. And you said they went right to the car."

"That's right."

What did that mean, I wondered? Somebody had already called the Green Polizei before the body was discovered. The killer was going to tie things up neatly by having Claudette and me arrested for Enderly's murder.

Then I remembered what Erik Grosse-Mund had shouted over the phone, when we had called him later at the Exil. Somebody who had called the police earlier wanted the phone.

Poor Erik Grosse-Mund. He had seen the killer but didn't know it. He knew when the call for the police had been made. That's why he had been knifed in his room. That time, the killer was prepared.

Well, there was a scenario, a problematical one to be sure, of what might have happened. Whoever had sent us Palmer Enderly the diplomat must have killed Enderly and Erik, and now had *The Green Room*.

I was back to square one. Who sent us the diplomat?

Claudette came back, and we decided there wasn't much more we could do just then. Rhodes left, and we walked to the elevators.

Once again we were in separate rooms on the same floor, separated by a long carpeted corridor. I didn't care, though. In fact, I was glad, because this time I was absolutely through with the whole benighted business. I would rejoin the journalists for the last two days, get my story, and avoid the Typhoid Mary of Postimpressionism like the plague. I unpacked in my disorderly way, took a shower, and plunged into the oblivion of the bed. For once, I slept like a stone in the Berlin Wall.

The next morning, while I was drinking coffee and digging out the itinerary for the birthday tour, the phone rang. It was you-know-who.

"Listen, Claudette," I told her firmly, "I'm bailing out on this thing. It's all yours."

"Fitz, you don't understand!"

"I understand, and I'm sick of walking through a mine field."

"We're in the paper!"

"That's too bad—we're in what?"

"*B.Z.!* I can't make it out, but our names are in it! My God, did you talk to a reporter?"

The smug face of portly Franz Hoppenrath grilling me at the Diener crashed into my mind.

"What does it say?"

"I can't read it," she said. "Come and tell me."

I walked down the hall to her room, went in, and there she sat in that tantalizing green robe with the white, silky teddy underneath, and I wished I could get my hands on Mother Nature for about two minutes. Or maybe I wished I could get my hands on one of her more fetching creations.

Claudette shoved the copy of *B.Z.* into my hands.

"The room service man brought it," she said, "and there's some kind of a story by Franz! I didn't know he was covering this."

I mumbled something and took the tabloid sheet. There was the terrifying story, all right, all about the *B.Z.* reporter's interview with American reporter Edward Fitzgerald and his ingenuous outpourings of crime and mayhem.

"Jesus," I muttered.

"What?"

The gaudy story was a regular artillery barrage about Claudette and me careening around Berlin, bribing Palmer Enderly the British diplomat and then being present at the Exil when he was murdered.

"Damn!"

"What?" howled Claudette.

"It's all there," I finally caved in. "Jesus! I'm sorry. While you were napping yesterday, I had lunch with Franz and asked for his help."

"Help?" Claudette's voice climbed the Matterhorn. She got up and stomped around. "Help? Why, he's eviscerated us!"

"There was no way he could avoid the story," I pleaded.

"He? What about you? Why did you shoot your mouth off?"

It seemed odd to me that she was now accusing me of what I had been accusing her of, up until then. We were both a couple of bumbling madcaps.

"What does he say about the painting?" she asked, coming to sit beside me again.

I scanned the German words, but could find no mention of it. No *Gemälde* or *Grüne Zimmer*. Well, Franz had tried to be decent about it by not dragging that in, anyway.

"I told you he was a colleague," I said triumphantly. "He didn't even mention it."

"What?" She seemed bewildered.

"I asked him to take it easy."

Claudette's eyes opened wide at that. I had handed Franz a story with which he had blown us to smithereens, and that was taking it easy on us?

I lighted a Tiparillo and explained to the foolish amateur that a reporter couldn't ignore a story about a dead diplomat and that he had been decent enough not to drag in the

damned international smuggling theft, which might force
the East Berlin government to officially recognize
that there was a theft and to come after us. She wasn't
buying it.

"Goddamnit, do you want a public story that we stole
a painting out of East Berlin?" I demanded.

"But how can I ever get it back if nobody admits it's
even missing?" she wailed.

"Listen, at this point all I want is to get out of here in
one piece," I railed at her.

"Oh! So you think these murders can be cleared up
without anything coming out about the painting?" she
sneered. "Why were those men murdered, if it wasn't for
the painting? Answer me that!"

I puffed on my Tiparillo. It was a perfectly absurd
question. There was the first murder case, and another
one, and then there was the theft, and there was no
connection. Anybody could see that. Just because we had
bribed Enderly to bring it out, and he got killed, and just
because Erik was going to sell it for us, and he got killed,
didn't mean . . .

"Shit," I ran down.

"What does that mean?"

It meant she was right, of course, but I couldn't say it.
Instead, I tried to figure out what we could do. Where in
the world could we even begin? There was no trail that
didn't lead to a disemboweled body.

"Okay," I finally decided, "we have to follow that
diplomat's footsteps."

Claudette threw her hands up. "How? He's dead! He
isn't making any footsteps."

"We have to go the other way," I said, not quite sure of
what I was thinking. "From the Exil backward."

"Backward?"

"What else? Where did he come from? Who sent him?"

"But I don't see how . . ."

I didn't see how either, right away, but the more I ran it around in my head, the more my thoughts led backward to the only place where we had met him.

"Across from the Tooth," I blurted out. "Cafe Möhring."

It was a possibility, I realized even as I said it. Enderly had picked the place, and later he had told us he would be there every morning at ten o'clock until we made contact again.

"It was just a meeting place," she protested.

"Got any better ideas?"

She flounced into the bathroom to dress, and I reached into my pocket and found the Polaroid photo I had snapped of Enderly.

We walked up to the Ku-Damm and down along it to the staid Cafe Möhring of the Prussian *Gemütlikeit,* where we sat at our old table against the side wall. Outside across the broad avenue, we could see the blackened Tooth.

After a few minutes, because they don't hurry you in the Cafe Möhring, a blond waitress in a black dress and pink apron came to take our order. When she brought two pots of tea, I smiled at her.

"Bitte," I tried. "We are looking for a friend."

"Ja?" She smiled distantly.

I dug out the photo and showed it to her.

"Here he is. Palmer Enderly."

The waitress took the photo, looked closely, and nodded her head.

"Ja, that is Pökel." She smiled and handed it back. "He does not come here anymore."

"Who . . . Pökel?"

The waitress frowned, looking for an English word.
"Yes, you say . . . um . . . pickle."

"Pickle?" I asked.

She grinned. "*Ja.* Pickle! That is what they call him. I
have not seen him so much since his friend left."

"What friend?" I pressed her.

"She used to work here, you know. Melanie."

I froze. "Melanie?"

"*Ja.* She worked here, *und* Pickle would come for her.
She called him . . . um . . . Pickledilly." She giggled.

"Pickledilly?" I tried to get it right. "Could it have been
. . . Piccadilly?"

"*Ja.* That's what I said."

I glanced at Claudette, whose face was flushed and stiff
at the mention of the whore of Berlin. I was quite keyed
up at the idea that Melanie knew Palmer Enderly, who
was apparently from around Piccadilly in London.

I thanked the waitress, and she walked away.

"Enderly and Melanie knew each other," I babbled.
"For God's sake."

Suddenly I realized that the delicious Melanie might not
have been hanging around me entirely because of my
raffish charm. This didn't sit too well with me, but there
it was.

"She must have been . . . sicced on me," I managed,
my neck reddening. "What did I tell her? *She* must have
sent us Enderly!"

"She was with you yesterday, too," Claudette remembered.

"Yeah."

"When Erik was . . ."

I shuddered. Was that what happened? Melanie was

keeping me occupied to make sure I wouldn't go find Erik when somebody else needed to find him alone, in order to steal the painting and kill him? My head was spinning as I sat in the Cafe Möhring sipping tea and realizing that things that had happened around us had not been what they had seemed.

I tried to remember what had happened the first time, when I was at the Kempi bar with Claudette, and Melanie came in.

When the waitress came by again, I motioned her over.

"*Ja?*"

"*Bitte*. You said Pickle used to pick up Melanie here. Did he meet other people here, too?"

"*Oh, ja. Hier war Pökel so gut wie zu Hause.* Cafe Möhring was like his office."

"Do you know who else he met here?"

She rolled her blond head. "*Oh, nein. Es gibt zu viele Leuten.* Many people. I don't know."

"Do you know where Pickle and Melanie went?"

"Oh, *ja*. Dancing. Melanie loves to dance."

"Dancing? Where?"

"Cafe Keese," she smiled. "Oh, Melanie was doing all right. Pickle sat at his table meeting people—*er war ein* ambassador, you know, and then off they would go." She sighed. "Berlin couldn't hold Melanie."

"She wants to leave Berlin?" I asked.

"Oh, yes. And she will, too. I know Melanie."

"Where does she want to go?"

"Oh, of course, Paris. Pickle promised her Paris. That's the only reason she would go with him."

$\triangledown$

CHAPTER TWENTY-THREE

THERE would be nobody dancing at Cafe Keese yet, so I told Claudette I was going to catch up with the Berlin birthday party tour and get some notes. I had missed almost all of it, and every time I thought about it I felt a deep rumbling in my belly. Eventually, I would have to walk back into the New York *Daily Press* city room and face Ironhead, and if I came back with excuses instead of a travel story, there would be a scene rife with outrage and flying expletives.

"What?" I could imagine Ironhead spluttering. "You spent five thousand dollars on goddamn Berlin tarts and you didn't even see the Brandenburg Gate?"

"See, there was this murdered diplomat . . ."

"Goddamnit, didn't I tell you to forget that?"

"I did, but then I found Erik sliced up like a suckling pig . . ."

"Erik? Who the hell's Erik?"

"Then the Berlin cops got me . . ,"

"Cops . . ."

"And there was a story . . ."

"Story . . . !"

Bad as that imagined fusillade was, there was another droning in my ear.

"But we have to keep on this," Claudette demanded.

"Now, you listen to me," I told her, finally making my own Declaration of Independence, "I am here on assignment for the New York *Daily Press*. If I don't get some kind of a story while I'm here, I'm going to be drawn and quartered when I get back to New York. If I get back."

"But we have a lead, now!"

"I'll tell you what—follow it, then! But I'm going to join that birthday tour today, and that's final!"

"Yes, Fitz," she said softly, her dark eyelashes fluttering.

"I mean, this whole thing is idiotic," I went on, through the soft fluttering.

"I'm sorry, Eddie," she murmured. "I know I've been a terrible pest."

"Besides," I went on, the ink on the Declaration beginning to run, "the Cafe Keese won't be open until tonight."

She brightened at that. "Sure! You can spend the day getting your story, so that will be all okay, and then tonight . . ."

"Tonight, I'm going to go out and get drunk!" I spat viciously.

"Oh."

"I haven't seen or done a damned thing in Berlin," I ranted. "This is supposed to be an exciting city! You haven't, either."

"Oh, I know it," she mourned. "Fitz, I'd like to get drunk, too! Why don't we both make a night of it and forget all this craziness. That is, if you want me to come along."

The ink ran into smudges, and the paper itself shredded into confetti. The confetti wrapped itself around my hand on the table, and its touch was electric. I squeezed her hand back, making a Devil's compact with Benedict Arnold.

"I'll tell you what," she smiled prettily. "You do your tour and I'll take in Ka-De-We."

"What's that?"

"But, Fitz, it's the biggest department store in Europe! It's supposed to be terrific, like Harrod's in London. I haven't done a lick of shopping, you know."

Shopping? I let that go. We agreed to meet later, and I hurried out of the Cafe Möhring and down the Ku-Damm to the Kempinski, where, according to the program tour, the bus would be leaving at 11:00 A.M.

I walked into the lobby among all the journalists, and right away I felt a soothing sensation of belonging creeping through me. Just being one reporter among forty touring Berlin, gathering bland and harmless information about conventioneering and trade and other boring statistics, became the most pleasing prospect I could imagine. Let me disappear into this herd, and be unnoticed.

"So, where are we going today?" I cheerfully asked a tall reporter whom I seemed to remember was from Australia.

"How's that, mate?" he asked, measuring me with a journalistic eye.

"What's on the schedule?" I repeated.

The tall Australian squinted a little. "Well, I don't know who you're looking for, mate. This is a group of reporters."

"I know. Ed Fitzgerald, New York *Daily Press.*"

His eyes widened. "Funny, don't remember seeing you before," he tossed off, and turned back to chat with a guy from Singapore.

Then who did I spot standing among them, chatting amiably with an Indian woman with a red dot on her forehead, but the treacherous Berlin Bear from *B.Z.* As soon as he saw me, his face plunged into an expression of deep concern that would have done justice to a crocodile. He walked right over to me, the shameless creep, and I wanted to knee him in the groin.

"Fitz!" He gasped. "I thought you had left Berlin!"

"Not yet," I told him coolly.

"But you must be crazy to stay here," he blurted.

"Did you find out anything from the Polizei for me?" I asked.

Franz said he had talked with Lieutenant Wolfe, and that I could be arrested at any minute.

"For what?" I asked. "Did he say?"

"Not exactly. They are looking into currency smuggling. Didn't you exchange money with somebody over there? They think Enderly was taking deutsche marks over there." He shook his head.

"Did he mention the painting?" I asked. "And by the way, thanks for leaving that out of the story."

His face flushed at that. "Herr Fitzgerald," he declared rather pompously, *"Dies Gemälde . . .* why do you tell me such a thing? Zee Geheimpolizist say there is no painting. Nothing was stolen."

"Franz, I'm telling you—we stole it."

His face went stubborn. "Lieutenant Wolfe says no. Ostberlin says no. I cannot print what I cannot make true."

Terrific.

"I tell you, Fitz, get out! Enderly was murdered over money changing, and that is serious business in Berlin. I give you fair warning."

I strolled away. It was certainly a continuing refrain from everybody, first one side of the record and then the other. Either we were warned to get out of Berlin, or not to leave.

Pretty soon, here came the efficient Hans Dieter, shooing everyone onto the cream and red bus. He paused to give me a surprised look.

"Fitzpatrick . . . Philadelphia?" he said uncertainly.

"Right," I told him.

"Ja!" he smiled at his feat of memory. "I thought you had left."

The bus rolled out through Berlin to the Grunewald, the green forest of Berlin, and to a charming wooden chalet on the Wannsee called Blockhaus Nikolskoe, which we were informed was built by King Friedrich Wilhelm III for his daughter Charlotte when she married the future Tsar Nicholas I. From the shore, you look across the Wannsee at Peacock Island and Potsdam.

That's where I was standing, waiting to go into the chalet for lunch and to hear some minister or other, when I realized someone was standing beside me at the rail.

"So, finally I catch up with you."

I glanced and saw the little mustache and the pinched face of Michel Granger, the French Sureté man.

"Granger?" I said uncertainly.

"Where is Mademoiselle Barry?"

"Why?" I asked guardedly.

"Come, come," he snarled rather menacingly. "We know you have it."

"Have what?"

He turned to light a cigarette and gazed nonchalantly at the Blockhaus and the other reporters.

"We know you have the painting, and you will hand it over. It is the property of the French government."

"Sorry to disappoint you," I said, "but Mademoiselle Barry doesn't agree."

"I have not the slightest interest in whether she agrees or not! I claim it. Now, where is it? This is no longer a little game. This painting is claimed by France as a national treasure and will be returned to Paris. Those documentation papers are worthless."

I glanced at him and suddenly realized who had searched Claudette's room and what they were looking for. "If they're worthless, why did you send somebody after them?"

Granger gestured and snorted, dismissing the subject.

I looked out across the lake at Potsdam, and wondered if Harry Truman had had as complicated a mess on his hands when they were dividing up Europe.

"How'd you find me?"

"You were supposed to be following this tour. Perhaps you will tell me what you've been doing instead? But never mind. I know. This is the last possibility before official action is taken."

I looked at him. "What official action?"

"Never mind! Where is *La Chambre Verte?*"

"In East Berlin."

He glared at me.

"It's in the National Gallery. If you don't believe me, ask."

He looked me up and down one last time and strolled off between Blockhaus Nikolskoe and the chalet to his car, parked beyond our bus. So much for my feeling of safety by hiding out on the Berlin tour. If I stayed with it, it would be simple for anybody to find me, including Lieutenant Wolfe.

I sat through a lunch at Blockhaus Nikolskoe, during

which a Berlin minister told us much about the wonders of the City by the Spree, and then we all rode by the Olympic Stadium, which somehow survived the Allied bombing in World War II.

Hans Dieter walked along the aisle of the bus and announced that tomorrow would be a special treat, to which he knew we had all been looking forward.

"We go to East Berlin," he said. "Please remember to bring your passports."

Well, I could forget about that. There was no way I could go back to East Berlin now. When we got back to the Kempinski Hotel, I checked to see if I had any messages. As usual, the striped pants at the desk smiled as he handed me a thick sheaf of slips. I was getting popular.

The first one said, "Call Mr. Matthews." The hair rose on my neck. Ironhead wanted me again? Then I remembered I had drawn more money. Wonderful.

The second one said, "Call Mr. Matthews."

The third, fourth, fifth, and sixth said the same.

I sighed and considered ignoring all of them, and then realized it might be better, at that, to talk to the ICBM of the *Daily Press* at the remove of a few thousand miles. I rode up to my room, trying to think of some excuse or other, but finally accepted it and picked up the phone.

A knock on the door.

I put down the phone, grateful for any interruption, and went to open it. There stood the Geheimpolizist and another gentleman who looked like an insurance man.

"Lieutenant Wolfe," I managed.

They stepped in, both smiling official smiles. "Herr Fitzgerald," said the oily German *Offizier*. "And how are you finding Berlin?"

I wanted to say "crowded," but got out a noncommit-

tal, "Fine, fine. Come in." They were already in. Lieutenant Wolfe closed the door and stood there polishing his
glasses. Official, all right.

"This is Herr Poole of the British Embassy," said Wolfe,
nodding to the insurance salesman. Wonderful, I thought.
That made it complete. I was being crowded by the French
Sureté, the West German *Polizei,* and now the Brits. The
whole goddamn Allied presence in Berlin was after me,
except for the Soviets. They surely couldn't be far behind.

$\bigtriangledown$

CHAPTER TWENTY-FOUR

P OOLE of the British Embassy made a little bow and showed a set of yellowing teeth under a bushy mustache.

"How d'ya do?" he chopped.

Lieutenant Wolfe sat at the desk. "Mr. Poole wants a little talk with you."

Poole straightened up. "All informal, please," he said. "Thought it might be just as well done here."

I sat in the chair, which left Poole either to stand or sit on the bed. He stood.

"It's about Enderly," he got out, looking away. "Rather one of those things, you might say."

"Yes," I agreed.

"Well, it needs some clarification, don't you know?" said Poole, shifting his weight from one foot to the other. "Sort of murky, now."

Lieutenant Wolfe allowed himself one of his brown cigarettes. "There is a published story that Herr Enderly was paid money," he explained. "The story used the word . . . *bribe*." Lieutenant Wolfe put on a face that wasn't a smile but wasn't completely deadpan, either.

"Quite," said Poole. "Rather a thing. Not according to practice, of course, and . . . well, you do see?"

I told him I understood there was a problem, but I certainly didn't "see."

"There was no money on Enderly," came back Poole, and he didn't sound like an insurance man anymore. "Naturally, therefore, there's a matter of credibility."

"Somebody got the money?" I asked, interested.

"Rather, the question is whether poor Enderly got the money to begin with, wouldn't you say, Mr. Fitzgerald?" He sounded like a barrister in the Old Bailey now. "The story alleged that you and, I believe, Miss Barry, uh . . . paid Enderly to . . . uh . . . transport something or other."

"A painting," I helped. "That's correct."

Mr. Poole of Whitehall or wherever he was from was now moving around in little steps, sort of swaying back and forth, as though addressing a jury.

"But you will note that no money was discovered, leading to problem one. Are you with me?"

I studied him. He was perspiring rather freely. I suddenly got the idea that I was not of the jury, but the one on trial.

"Mr. Poole," I told him, "I don't know what you're getting at. I guess whoever killed him got the money."

"If there was any!" he declared stiffly. "It is mere supposition, and it is, in fact, our position that the entire transaction is and was quite spurious."

"What?" came out of me. "Could you say that in English?"

Lieutenant Wolfe let out smoke. "Herr Fitzgerald, you understand that we have here a British diplomat accused of something that he cannot defend."

"Exactly!" from the barrister. "One would not like to

put something unsubstantiated on one's record. Simply will not do."

I lighted a Tiparillo and looked them over. "Look, what do you want from me? I told you what I know, and I wouldn't lie in such a mess. All I want is to get out of this."

Poole's yellow-toothed mouth broke into what was almost a smile. "Of course! So would we all! And you see, we can."

I was starting to like what they were saying, but that made me nervous since I didn't know what they were saying.

Lieutenant Wolfe stood up. "Let us consider for a moment, for the sake of argument only, your story that you . . . uh . . . engaged Enderly to complete a certain task." He paused and his eyebrows went up questioningly. Did I understand? I nodded.

"Now, this task that you mentioned, for which money supposedly changed hands, this bribe, so-called," said Lieutenant Wolfe, picking his way through a mine field, "concerns something that did not happen. *Ja?*"

"How do you mean?"

Poole the barrister was back in the Old Bailey. "Why, simply put, the East Germans say no painting was stolen. So, you see, there could have been no bribe. So much for problem two."

I puffed on my Tiparillo. "Well . . . ?"

"Well, but don't you see?" Poole dashed on, pacing around like a bee on a hive, "that clears up all difficulties. No painting, no bribe!" He smiled.

I marveled at them. "The whole thing never happened?" I asked.

Well, said Poole, there was the unfortunate demise of

poor Enderly, that was true, but it was not likely to be cleared up in a city like Berlin. He had died, poor Enderly, in the service of the Crown, and that was all.

Franz Hoppenrath's story in *B.Z.* flipped into my mind. I had been quoted about paying Enderly a bribe.

"What about that story in the paper?"

Poole impatiently waved that away. "A newspaper story is just that, a story," he snapped. "We need take no official cognizance of that. Journalists deal in unfounded speculation, something with which I'm sure you're familiar." He smiled smugly.

Then I finally got it. Back in New York, it's called disposing of a case. Enderly's reputation was resurrected in death, and the Foreign Office would close its books on the matter. It did not want to discover that poor Enderly had been bribed to help steal anything out of East Berlin.

Out came a typed paper from Poole's insurance-man suit. In his other hand he held a pen.

"If you sign this statement, I'm sure we will have gotten round all problems and difficulties."

I glanced at the statement, worded in British legalese, which declared that I had had only normal journalistic dealings with Enderly and certainly had not offered him a bribe, nor had he accepted one. It was a tricky situation. I was being let off one hook—any involvement in Enderly's murder—but being put on another. Perjury, because Lieutenant Wolfe already had our statement about bribing Enderly. It was another Devil's bargain.

"Does this mean we're not wanted anymore?" I asked.

"Not by us," declared Poole. "Clearing Enderly of bribe taking clears you of bribe giving. *Quid pro quo.* And it's only for our files."

I picked up the pen. "Mr. Poole, why would a diplomat

need extra money?" I held the pen above the paper, waiting.

Poole shuffled his feet. "Why, uh, sometimes diplomats have wives and children at home, don't you see. And sometimes one stretches oneself too thin." He looked at his feet.

I signed the paper, which Poole whisked away into his pocket.

"Well, yes, there. I think that concludes our transaction," he said. "This matter is, of course, confidential," he added. "Not for publication." His face was a question mark awaiting my confirmation. Here was another official who wanted to say something was off the record after he had said it.

I smiled and said nothing, which seemed to satisfy him. He took his paper and left.

Lieutenant Wolfe lingered, however, giving me a thin smile.

"I have a cousin in Pennsylvania," he said. "Pottstown. Do you know the place?"

"Not exactly."

He stood there. "So, Herr Fitzgerald, the Enderly matter is . . . um . . . taken care of. As for the killing of Erik Grosse-Mund, you and Herr Dahlem were together when that happened. So you are once again free to leave Berlin."

He reached into his tunic pocket. "Allow me to return your tickets." He handed me the Pan Am tickets he had relieved us of at Tegel. "I have taken the liberty of changing the reservation to eight o'clock tomorrow evening."

I took the tickets. Once more, the red carpet treatment for us to get the hell out. I lighted another Tiparillo and offered him a drink of schnapps from the little minibar in the refrigerator in the hotel room. He took it, and sat.

"Listen, Lieutenant Wolfe," I said, trying to get past that impenetrable railway clerk's smile of his, "why don't we level with each other and talk turkey?"

"Turkey?"

"I realize that you can't officially admit a painting was stolen, but you know damned well it was."

"I know you say so."

"Enderly is dead. Erik is dead. Isn't that enough for you to want to help us find that painting? It's the only way you'll ever really clear this up."

The railway clerk smile was intact. "Herr Fitzgerald, since we are sitting here alone and neither of us is a fool, let us say that, yes, I accept what you say. You have stolen a painting from East Berlin, and two men are dead because of it. If I was to help you find this painting, what would I do then? Embarrass the D.D.R. by announcing we have recovered a painting stolen from their National Gallery which they deny is missing?"

"Why would you have to announce anything?"

"Ah! But if, as you say, the finding of this painting was to solve murders, then what? Not announce that, either?"

"Don't you want to clear up the murders?"

"This is Berlin, Herr Fitzgerald. Things are not always so . . . tidy . . . as in New York, perhaps."

Tidy in New York? He sounded just like a Big Apple politician. Things in Berlin and New York were equally untidy, but I didn't bother to tell him that.

"Herr Poole is satisfied as to Enderly. We have no case as yet concerning Herr Grosse-Mund. But let us say that we find the painting and solve both murders. What do we have?"

"I don't know . . . justice?"

He mangled the word in his mouth. "Justice." He

nodded his head. "What we will have is the British un-happy because of a bribed diplomat. The East Germans unhappy because of a stolen painting. And finally, Herr Fitzgerald, a story about something stolen by the Third Reich almost fifty years ago, an event we do not wish to dwell on unnecessarily now. Please, go home."

Now I was pacing around in a tight little circle like Poole.

"Not without the painting," came out of me, and I realized that I had insisted to Claudette only that morning that I was through, through, through with the damned thing. Now, though, since I was being told officially to forget about it, some bizarre perversity was in me.

Lieutenant Wolfe put down his schnapps and stood up. "I cannot help you. I advise you to be on that plane tomorrow." He walked to the door, but paused and looked back.

"You seem to forget something, Herr Fitzgerald. You want to find that painting. Everyone who has found it so far seems to be dead."

"Except the person who has it now," I corrected him.

"I do not want you to find the painting," he said sharply. "I do not want a dead American reporter on my hands."

CHAPTER TWENTY-FIVE

I CAN'T say that Lieutenant Wolfe's words didn't make an impression on me. When the cops say they're not going to help you and in fact are working against you and tell you to get out, you have to pay attention. It was true, also, that *The Green Room* seemed to carry with it some kind of a King Tut curse. I didn't want him to have a dead American reporter on his hands, either.

As far as I was concerned, I was ready to get a plane out that night, never mind waiting until 8:00 P.M. the next day. I even considered packing up and getting the hell away before Claudette came back from Ka-De-We.

Of course, I didn't, and pretty soon it was too late because she called me to her room and showed me her purchases. This involved a sort of fashion show, with her ducking in and out of the bathroom to try on new clothes, including Lederhosen, which are cute little leather shorts with suspenders.

"What do you think?" she asked, standing there with her hands on her hips, looking sideways at me.

"Breathtaking," I said, and I didn't mean the Lederhosen.

"Really?"

I don't have to tell you what happened to the Lederhosen, or to us, either. I forgot about Lieutenant Wolfe and *The Green Room* and even that we were in Berlin. We sailed around on an outer planet, and when we got back I filled her in on what had happened with Poole. She snorted in outrage that she would go directly to the United States Embassy and complain.

"They won't officially admit anything, either," I reminded her. "We're on our own."

"But if we have to leave tomorrow . . . ?"

"Yes. We have to go dancing at Cafe Keese tonight."

"Well," she said brightly, "at least I have something to wear."

I went back to my room to shower and shave, and tried to think about Enderly and Melanie. The British diplomat apparently had a wife and family back home and had found a Lorelei in Berlin. Okay, so he needed money. I tried to remember if Melanie had been around us when we were talking about trying to find a diplomat, but couldn't get it clear. Had she been at the Exil that night? If so, I hadn't seen her.

Something was missing, all right, my head included— but it occurred to me that the reason Melanie and Pickle wanted to go to Paris was to deliver *The Green Room* to the French for a fat reward.

Cafe Keese on Bismarckstrasse turned out to be a sort of West Berlin version of Roseland, a fairly large, sprawling dance hall with a dance floor in the middle and tables all around it. There was a stand-up bar when you first came in, another one back in a corner, and a noisy orchestra blasting away. Claudette and I walked in not knowing quite how we would find Melanie.

"My God, it's so big," gasped Claudette, surveying the crowded dance floor and tables clustered with people on all sides.

"Yeah."

I led her to the stand-up bar, ordered two beers, and shoved our Polaroid photo of Enderly at the bartender when he picked up my money.

"Do you know this man?" I asked him in German.

"What?" He squinted at it.

"They call him Pickle."

He scrutinized the photo in the less than perfect light behind the bar and slowly shook his head.

"Do you know a Melanie?" I tried again.

"Melanie . . . ?" His shoulder went up and down. "Melanie who?"

We walked further into the place, past the bandstand where the orchestra was blaring away on "New York, New York," of all things, and tried the back corner bar.

Two more beers ordered and the photo shoved under the eyes of the busy, distracted bartender, and we were still without a clue.

I sank onto a bar stool and decided to at least have a sip of this beer. Claudette leaned against the bar beside me and looked out over the big dance hall. Our best chance would be to spot Melanie, she seemed to think, since showing around the photo of the dead diplomat wasn't working.

"There must be a thousand people here," she said hopelessly.

"Yeah."

She sank onto a bar stool beside me, dismay written on her lovely face, and let out a defeated sigh. "It's impossible."

I looked out over the place. There were tiers of tables all around the dance floor, and back from there to the walls. Waiters scurried between the tables, people strolled around table-hopping, the dance floor pulsed with bodies.

"Maybe if we got closer," I offered. "A table on the edge of the dance floor. That waitress at the Möhring said she loved to dance."

Claudette was on her feet at once. "Yes . . . can you get us one?"

I led her down from the corner bar, among the tables packed tightly along the edge of the big, crowded dance floor and found a waiter charging hurriedly between them.

"*Bitte* . . . can we get a table?"

The waiter halted abruptly and looked at me as though I had suggested a tryst behind the bear cages in the Tiergarten. *"What!"* He waved his arms.

I dragged Claudette on along the edge of the dance floor. The tables up close were apparently choice locations, and one didn't simply walk in at the last minute and find one unoccupied. The thing is, when you're in a foreign city, you have the idea that the customs are madly different and that saying or doing the most innocent thing might be the equivalent of profaning the Kaiser. When that thought flitted through my head, I realized that it was nonsense. I realized that Cafe Keese in Berlin was probably no different from Roseland. We needed a ringside table. What would I do in New York?

The highly charged waiter came headlong past us again, and this time I got in front of him.

"Herr Ober," I said urgently into his face. "Rudolph sent me."

Ober the waiter stared at me, momentarily fazed. "Who?"

"We want a table," I said, and reached for my wallet. He started to wave his arms again, and then he saw the wallet.

"*Bitte* . . . wait."

Off he went with a tray holding little dark bottles topped with gold paper.

"Who's Rudolph?" Claudette hissed.

"The person who gets you tables," I said.

"But," she said, looking around doubtfully, "they're all taken."

"He said wait." I knew from New York that all tables are never taken, no matter how things might look. Sure enough, there came *Ober* back again, carrying a round table over his head.

We followed him around the side of the floor, where he shoved his way between other tables and stood there barking out orders to people sitting there. There's something quite intimidating about a waiter ordering you around while he holds a table over your head. The girls at the two tables on both sides were squealing and looking at the floating wooden thing over their heads. Everybody got up, and one man turned to confront *Herr Ober*. When they all got up, *Herr Ober* ignored everybody and immediately shoved the tables apart. Then he dropped our manhole cover-size table between them and marched off, leaving the displaced groups to scurry around, clucking and muttering, to get their chairs rearranged.

We stood there at the little table, outcasts, without chairs, until the waiter came back carrying two chairs over his head and again terrifying everybody.

We sat. *Herr Ober* smiled. "So!"

Of course, I had to order individual bottles of champagne, and they came with accompanying shots of schnapps, and I had to slip him a fifty mark bill, but we had our table.

We also had looks from the people at the tables on both sides, including a large Wagnerian diva who looked as though she had just stepped out of *Die Walküre* at Bayreuth. I thought she was going to pull a spear from under the table, and then I realized her seemingly ferocious mug of hatred was really a smile.

Claudette sipped champagne and let her eyes rove intently over the mass of swaying couples. I tried to look, too, but had that eerie sensation of being watched. I peeked again, and Brünnhilde was still grinning at me. She seized the moment of eye contact to speak up.

"*Kommen Sie!*" she yodeled. "*Wir tanzen!*"

"What?"

Claudette looked around. "What's the matter?"

"This woman asked me to dance," I muttered sheepishly, expecting her large, stout escort to get up and take issue with me. The man beside her only beamed.

"Thanks, but no thanks," I managed. We had no time for idiotic distractions if we were going to find the elusive Melanie.

Brünnhilde's mouth popped open in astonishment. She jabbered animatedly to her large escort, who gave me a hard look. *Now* he seemed inclined to take issue, it seemed.

I looked away and tried to figure out how to proceed. Then a tall, imperious gentleman was standing before me. "*Amerikaner?*" he asked pleasantly. Startled, I looked up and admitted it.

"*Ach!*" he said. "So this is your first time at Cafe Keese?"

I admitted that, too.

The man, who appeared to be the headwaiter, leaned down a little to bring his face closer. "You see, here we have what we call a ball-paradox." He grinned, as though that explained his presence. "You understand?"

"Not really."

"Here at Cafe Keese, it is the women who ask the men to dance."

"Ohhhh!" I smiled. Well, that was quaint. "I see."

"Tell him we're not here to dance," hissed Claudette, but I decided against that. Silence should do as well.

"Thank you," I said, and he backed off a step.

Then the diva at the next table got up and walked to our table, smiling that ax-faced look that really needed a helmet of horns to round it out.

"Please tell the lady I'd rather not," I whispered to the headwaiter as the Wagnerian heroine radiated happiness.

The headwaiter leaned closer again. "You cannot refuse a lady's invitation at Cafe Keese, *Mein Herr*. To do so means we must ask you to leave." He smiled.

"Oh."

Ax-face took my hand and was leading me onto the floor.

"Fitz!" came from Claudette.

"Rules of the house," I flung at her, and my partner and I were swallowed up in a sea of jostling bodies. For a great sow, Brünnhilde was surprisingly light on her feet, clearly an experienced dancer, while I was a stumbling embarrassment.

"Chicago?" she asked with a twinkle.

"New York," I said.

She threw her head back and laughed. "I knew it."

We careened around the floor, as must happen when the lady is the dancer but the man is trying to lead. I tried to look through the bobbing heads to our table. When I finally got a look, Claudette was gone. I jerked my head around, on the verge of panic.

Then I noticed Claudette bumping through the dancers in the arms of Brünnhilde's large escort.

"Do you see her?" she asked as she sailed past.

I tried to look for Melanie, but it was difficult to do that and concentrate on trying to lead Brünnhilde when I didn't know what the hell I was doing.

When we were finally back at the table together, I lighted a Tiparillo. "Ball-paradox," I said to Claudette and shook my head.

"If we both dance with others, we can cover more of the floor," she said efficiently.

I sipped some champagne, which is something I almost never drink, and even touched the schnapps, which is rarer. I was beginning to feel a buzz, and then slid into a hallucination—because there in front of me was Melanie. She walked right up to the table and asked me to dance.

Claudette recognized her, and froze.

I got up and went onto the dance floor with Melanie. She was in a yellow, low-cut dress, and gold teardrops dangled from her dainty ears.

"Well, *Herr Schreiber*," she cooed. "What brings you here?"

"Pickle," I said, and watched her blue eyes. They blinked.

"Who?"

"Palmer Enderly," I said. "We have to talk."

My attempts to lead her from the floor met with resistance. She kept me dancing—and in Cafe Keese, the lady is always right.

"Listen, Melanie, Pickle's dead. You know that, I guess. And they're going to come looking for you. Maybe I can help, if you help me."

She swayed gracefully in my arms and glanced up into my face again. "I don't understand what you mean. I knew Pickle, yes. What of it?"

"What of it is that somebody killed him," I said. "Why were you spying on me?"

"Spying . . . ?" Marvelous bewilderment.

"Hanging around me."

"But I like you, Fitz." She snuggled closer into my arms.

I sighed. It would be nice to think so, but I knew better. "Where's the painting?"

This time she stopped dancing. "You are a fool, Herr Fitz! I told you to get out of Berlin!"

"Now, you listen to me," I told her. "Unless you stole the painting yourself, you're in more trouble than I am. Pickle's dead, and so is that art dealer."

Her lovely face paled at that. "What?" She pulled away and stumbled her way through the dancers, with me following. She walked to a table off the floor and collapsed into a chair, apparently half-fainting. She lighted a cigarette and gasped something to a man who leaned over to hear. He looked up at me with a hard expression.

In a moment, Melanie and the man gathered up their things and hurried away through the tables toward the front door. I followed and realized in a second that Claudette was running up behind me.

"What did she say?" she gasped.

Melanie and her escort kept going, however, and I pushed after her out the front door onto Bismarckstrasse. Claudette grabbed my arm and was trying to hold me back, and when I turned toward her it wasn't Claudette.

"Let's go!" Michel Granger of the French Sureté had me by the arm, and there was a man with him who looked like somebody in charge of the tumbrils during the French Revolution.

"What?" I said in confusion. "Let me go!"

"We have business that can't wait," he snapped.

I glanced at Claudette, who shoved up next to me, and saw we were between a rock and a hard place. Melanie was disappearing down Bismarckstrasse, and we had only that night to find her and *The Green Room*.

I had to hope it would work. Looking at Granger, I threw a blind punch as hard as I could at the midsection of the Quasimodo with him. Quasimodo went *oof* and sat down on the sidewalk, and when Granger turned to look at him, I let fly again at the pride of the Sureté.

I barely brushed his head, but he backed off anyway. I grabbed Claudette's hand and fled down the street after the disappearing Melanie. Granger was screaming vile French invectives.

We turned a corner, and there went Melanie and her friend, half a block ahead of us. I didn't know how we could catch them, except that just then a taxi pulled alongside of us as we ran, and the driver waved us in.

"*Kommen Sie!*" he cried out. A Good Samaritan in Berlin.

I shoved Claudette to the taxi and we jumped in on the run, tumbling into the backseat. I got myself righted to look ahead and noticed there was already somebody in the taxi.

He sat against the other window wrapped in a trench coat, staring at us.

I started to say something, but then noticed the gun in his hand.

Some Good Samaritan.

$\triangledown$

CHAPTER TWENTY-SIX

"PLEASE be calm."

Fat chance.

We sat there immobilized, but hardly calm, as the taxi rolled along, gaining speed. We passed Melanie and her friend, who were looking back, apparently pleasantly surprised that they had lost us.

I turned my attention back to the trench coat. A sturdy-looking individual with steady eyes and a quiet air of authority. In other words, a cop or official of some kind.

"Where are we going?" I asked him, and felt Claudette's hand clutching mine as she huddled behind me, looking over my shoulder.

"Someone wishes to speak to you," he explained. His manner and delivery suggested he was used to giving orders, instead of clearing up situations. "I advise you to remain calm."

Claudette's hand dug into mine.

The car moved through darkened Berlin, and I soon realized that it wasn't a taxi at all, as I had thought. It was a fairly large black thing, the kind favored for official use.

It stayed off the Ku-Damm and went along side streets,

along a canal, and through Kreuzberg, from what I could
gather. It wasn't until the car turned onto Friedrichstrasse
that I realized we were heading for Checkpoint Charlie
and East Berlin.

"Fitz!" Claudette had also realized it.

The trench coat's eyes and steady hand did not waver.

"I'm an American newspaperman," I announced threat-
eningly in my best "Do you know who you're dealing
with!" voice.

I think he smiled.

The car rolled on, past Kochstrasse, into the checkpoint.
Plans whirled through my head. When we were checked
out, I would yell or bolt out of the car. I considered
making a try at the trench coat, but thought better of it
immediately. He was ready for anything like that.

When the car reached the checkpoint, I tensed myself
for the moment when the door would open. I squeezed
Claudette's hand, trying to alert her to be ready. The car
rolled through without stopping. No doors opened.

"They didn't stop," gasped Claudette.

I sat back and lighted a Tiparillo. No check. No stop. It
could only mean one thing. We were in an official vehicle:
a diplomat's car, or a police vehicle of the Kommandatura,
the four-power commission that administers Berlin.

We were on the other side of The Wall in East Berlin in
the hands of the Communist East German Government.

"Who wants us?" I finally got out. The car was moving
along Friedrichstrasse toward Unter den Linden.

"You will see," said blabbermouth.

I puffed somberly on my Tiparillo. I had finally done
it, all right, gotten myself into the Deutsche Demokratische Republik just like Nicholas Daniloff. The doors
of Lubiyanka Prison yawned before us, or some remote
gulag in Siberia from which no traveler returns.

We went along Unter den Linden across the River Spree and past Marx-Engels-Platz, glimpsing the Altes Museum and the National Gallery out the car window over our host's shoulder. Then through Alexanderplatz with the Television Tower rising above it, and down Karl-Marx-Allee. After a while, we turned left and I was lost. More turns, and the car rolled through iron gates into a courtyard, under an arch and into an inner courtyard paved with cobblestones. There we stopped.

The trench coat opened the door behind him and stepped out backward. Only then did the gun disappear into his pocket. We got out, and he indicated a door in the stone building.

We walked in, followed by our escort, and were in a marble-floored lobby with gray walls and a worn blue carpet. A comforting photo of Lenin stared down at us.

The driver came in behind us, also, and we were shown to a wooden bench in the lobby.

"Wait," the trench coat commanded, and walked in through a door, leaving us under the watchful scrutiny of the driver. He had the same steady eyes and calm manner of the trench coat.

Through the door at the end of the lobby, I could see the trench coat standing at a desk making a phone call. He stood there watching us, and then when he started speaking softly, he turned his back to us. We couldn't make out what he was saying. When he finished listening, he was turned around, staring at us again. He nodded, hung up the phone, and walked back out to us.

"This way."

Another door off the lobby was opened by the driver, and we walked along a hallway ahead of them, Claudette clutching my hand in a vise, until we came to a dead end.

There, the trench coat opened a door and indicated we should go in. We did.

I was trying to figure out what to say to whoever awaited us inside the room at the end of this hall. Protestations of innocence fled through my excited brain, along with denunciations and demands to see the U.S. Ambassador.

"I am an American newspaperman!" formed indignantly in my mouth. "Get me the White House."

Inside the room there was a bare wooden table and two chairs, and a wooden bench along the wall. While we were giving it a quick look, the door closed behind us. Claudette fled into my arms. She was shivering and crying.

"Fitz! My God! Where are we?"

"I don't know," I admitted, and held her until she stopped trembling.

I surveyed the room, but it didn't take long. It was barren except for the few pieces of furniture and a fluorescent light in the ceiling which cast a pale glow at best. There was one window, but I could see from where I stood that it was guarded by an artistically twirled iron grating.

When Claudette finally let me go, I walked over and looked closer at the twirled iron bars, which ran from top to bottom. Artistically fashioned, yes, but definitely bars. Beyond it, in the darkness, I seemed to make out a wall.

"What are we going to say?" I asked rhetorically, and immediately wondered if the room was bugged.

"But they can't do this!" Claudette decided.

"I know," I agreed. "Except they have."

"I'm not telling them anything," Claudette declared. "They can go to hell."

"Okay," I said.

"But we *have* to say something to get out of here!" she switched.

"Right."

Well, that was the wrong thing to say. Was I going to just stand there talking like a babbling dummy? Didn't I realize that we were in some awful, hopeless mess that required a plan, a strategy, *something,* to get us out? Was I going to stand there like a goddamn pillar and agree with her when she didn't have the faintest idea of what to do?

I sat in one of the wooden chairs and lighted a Tiparillo. She sat in the other one and leaned across the table at me, apparently assuming that this dressing-down had sparked some plan of salvation.

"Look," I told her, "somebody will be in here in a minute, and we'd better figure out what we're going to say. I suggest we identify ourselves and that's it."

"But what good will that do?"

"So what else do you want to tell them?"

In slow motion, her head lowered forward to the top of the table, and she sat like that, hunched over, head resting on the tabletop and said nothing.

I puffed on my Tiparillo. Once again, my speeches ran around in my head, and all came out to the same thing. To wit: they had no right to do this. Except that they were doing it. I decided I would call McNamara, except that I didn't have a telephone. I would threaten international sanctions, except that we had stolen a painting and if I explained that, things might get worse. Although I didn't know how.

Around and around in my head I went, but nobody came in to listen to any of my harangues. I checked my watch. It was almost eleven at night, and pitch-black outside the window.

After a while, the hunched-over statue came back to
life, stood up, and walked around the room to look out
through the grate. Then she came back to the table.

"When are they coming?" she wanted to know.

"Good question."

We sat there silently, listening for footsteps in the hall,
my Tiparillo sending up swirls of smoke to the pale
fluorescent tube in the ceiling.

When I checked my watch again, it was almost midnight. Claudette was by now staring fixedly at me, her
face growing more and more grim.

I went to the door through which we had come, and
knocked on it. "Hey!" I knocked again. Then I pounded
and yelled, "Hey out there!" Silence.

I went to the window and tried the iron bars, but that
was quite absurd.

All sorts of little fears started up inside my head,
gradually growing more and more ominous. I had read of
the silent treatment and of isolation as a calculated way of
breaking down the will of any prisoner. Was that what we
faced in this barren room with no way to contact anyone?

"Fitz?" she whimpered, "why doesn't somebody
come?"

"Well, it's late," I suggested. "Maybe . . ."

Her eyes widened. "You don't think they're going to
keep us here all night!"

I wanted to say that I hoped it would be *only* all night.

By two-thirty, I realized that it would be definitely all
night. I looked around for a switch for the light, but
couldn't find one.

"Listen," I suggested, "why don't we try to sleep. In
the morning . . ."

"In the morning?" Her voice went up the scale to
somewhere close to high C on "morning."

"Well . . ."

"They can't do this," she murmured a few more times, before putting her head on the table again.

I stretched out on the floor under the table to shield my eyes from the half-light of the fluorescent tube. Well, we had done it. We had managed to find ourselves a barren cell behind the Iron Curtain, and the Allied Powers in Berlin had washed their hands of us.

∇

CHAPTER TWENTY-SEVEN

UNDER the earth somewhere, possibly buried in Chateau D'If with the Count of Monte Cristo. Above me, a heavy door that is closed. Or is it not a door but a great weight slowly pressing down on me? I am one with Vercingetorix the Gaul in a Roman dungeon awaiting the executioner with his bowstring, or perhaps that door opens into the Coliseum where the Emperor Nero sits waiting. Another condemned speaks from his cell next to mine: "Remember this maxim on every occasion that tempts you to vexation: 'This is not a misfortune; and to bear it nobly is good fortune.'" Somehow, the wise Roman Emperor Marcus Aurelius is imprisoned with me and is still spouting his idiotic Stoic piffle in the face of disaster.

A thump! The guillotine is being tested. Another thump. A clatter. Chains are coming off the door, and I'm to be led out into the Circus Maximus to be drawn and quartered among centurions' chariots.

I sit up, and a Roman Legionnaire brings his club down on my head to teach me manners.

"Fitz!" somebody cries from the catacombs. "Fitz!"

I came clawing awake under the table, upon which I hit

my head while sitting up abruptly, and realized that somebody was knocking on the door to our little prison. The lock was turning.

I crawled out from beneath the table, rubbing my head, trying to clear my mind as to where I was and what was going on. Ah, yes, we were in the room with the barred window in East Berlin.

The door opened, and there stood the trench coat from the night before, now wearing a gray suit. No doubt he had had a good night's sleep.

"He will see you now," announced the gray suit, and then turned to walk down the hall. We followed, and I checked my watch as we walked along—9:00 A.M.

As we walked into the lobby with Lenin still on guard duty on the wall, the gray suit walked ahead of us to a huge, varnished door topped by a Gothic arch. He knocked and opened the door, and stood aside for us to enter.

Inside, we were in a large, almost rococo room with a high ceiling, with walls covered in red damask, crowded with paintings of Old Berlin, and a finely polished Biedermeier desk, behind which stood an imposing Kommissar with riotous dark hair, an expansive chest, and a full, red face like Peter the Great, Tsar of all the Russias. He stood up behind his desk, his arms behind him, and measured us with dark eyes under bushy eyebrows. Then he nodded his head a few times and pointed to two chairs in front of his desk.

"Please be seated," he said smoothly, in only faintly accented English. "Miss Barry and . . . Mr. Fitzgerald? Yes?"

"That's right," I managed to get out. "What's this all about?"

The large, beetle-browed Kommissar or whatever he was sat down at his desk and leaned forward with his hands folded in front of him.

"We know what it's about, surely," he said rather gruffly. "I am Maximilian Messer, Vice-Kommissar of Fine Arts of the Deutsche Demokratische Republik."

"And we are American citizens," I tossed out, "and somebody's going to hear about this!"

Kommissar Messer snorted, and spun his chair around to give us his back. He muttered something, then spun around again.

"Let us maintain our composure," he said. "After all, we have something in common. We both have a deep interest in fine art."

I glanced at Claudette, whose face was getting paler by the moment.

"Is that why we were arrested?" I asked.

The full-faced Kommissar leaned back in his chair and threw his arms wide. "Arrested? Am I a Vopo? Is this a prison? I have invited you to my office. To reach an understanding." He smiled rather ferociously.

"About what?"

Messer opened a little ceramic box on his desk, lifting off the cover by putting two fingers on either side of the head of a figurine seated on it. The Empress Maria Theresa, maybe, or Lola Montez.

He removed a brown cigarette, lighted it with a gold lighter, and stared at us. A collector and maybe even a connoisseur of artistic baubles, was our Kommissar.

He let out smoke. "Let us state the case. I want that painting."

Claudette's hand squeezed mine tightly, and a little squeak squeezed out of her.

"I don't know what you mean," I spluttered, not knowing what else to say.

The Kommissar laughed. Deep, loud, like the immense organ at Radio City Music Hall. Then he stopped laughing, stood up, and yelled like a Brooklyn longshoreman.

"You are a couple of children to steal a work of art that is the property of the U.S.S.R.! Do not think your cowardly State Department will help you! Or the West Berliners! You will deal with me!"

Messer had stated the situation succinctly, all right. I took out a Tiparillo and lighted it, trying to keep my hands from shaking. I have faced people in my life as a newspaper reporter who mean business, who know what they are talking about, and who cannot be flummoxed. Such a person sat behind his Biedermeier desk, now, glaring out from beneath his Joseph Stalin eyebrows.

"But we haven't got it," somebody said, and I realized that Claudette had never been a reporter. She was sitting forward, and her voice was beseeching. A winsome seal pup trying to charm a hungry polar bear.

The hulking polar bear gave her a contemptuous glance and his chest heaved with a sarcastic snort.

"Vladimir!"

The huge varnished door immediately opened, and the gray suit stepped in.

"Search them."

Vladimir the gray suit walked to us, motioning in a hands up fashion for us to stand. We stood. We went through our pockets and dumped everything on the desk in front of Kommissar Messer—wallet, notebook, cigars, press card, pen, and passport. Claudette's purse, with everything she owned in it, also.

Messer went through them while Vladimir stood behind

us, which made me very uncomfortable. I couldn't see him, but I knew he was there.

"Well, well," said the Kommissar, after unfolding papers and scanning Claudette's documentation for *The Green Room*. He laid it on the desk in front of him.

"Where did you get this forged documentation?" he asked.

Claudette's beseeching posture vanished. She stood to try to peek at the paper until Vladimir's hand on her shoulder sat her down again.

"It's not a forgery," she snapped. "The painting is my property! It was stolen from the Louvre . . ."

"Shut up!" Messer waved a hand and studied the paper. "So, you claim to be related to Claude Gramont. Clever. Ridiculous, but clever." He pushed the paper aside.

"Where is it?" he snapped, his eyes fixed on Claudette. She remained mute, so the siege gun swiveled to get me in his sights. "Well?"

"She told you the truth. We haven't got it. Besides, I'm told it wasn't stolen."

The Kommissar waved his hand. That was not worth discussing, it seemed.

"As Vice-Kommissar of Fine Arts for the D.D.R., I am responsible for this painting," he boomed at us. "Do you understand?"

"I understand," I managed, and realized what he meant. The painting was the property of the U.S.S.R., not of East Germany or even East Berlin, and it had been lifted while in his custody. Kommissar Messer was in trouble with his Moscow masters. No wonder he had denied it was missing.

"You . . . woman . . . come here," he commanded.

Claudette rose on wobbly legs and hesitantly stepped to his desk. "Yes, sir?"

He scribbled something on the Louvre catalogue and shoved it in front of her. "Sign this."

Claudette leaned over, trying to see what he had written.

"What does it say?"

"Sign it!"

"But . . . I don't know what . . ."

The great polar bear rose to his feet, towering over her, and shoved the pen at her. "You will sign this documentation over to us. That is all. No discussion."

Claudette glanced back at me, terrified and bewildered. I nodded for her to sign. There was nothing else to do. She signed, and Messer put the paper in the desk drawer.

"Sit down," he commanded. Claudette sat beside me again.

"So much for your ridiculous documentation," he said. "So, you don't have it? In that case, I don't know what use you are to us."

I didn't like the sound of that.

"I might be able to find it," I said. "We'd have to go back to West Berlin."

The Kommissar leaned back and smiled. Then he laughed. Then he sat forward again. "Yes. You will do that. And we will help you."

I didn't like the sound of that much better. Clearly, we were in a situation. I had the idea that the only way we could get out of it was to return the painting. Us for *La Chambre Verte*. The damned painting became considerably more valuable in my eyes.

"You will take us back to West Berlin, and we'll help you find it, then we'll turn it over to you?" I suggested hopefully.

"Very good," smiled Messer. He got up, delicately lifted

off the cover of his ceramic cigarette box by Maria Theresa's head, and lighted another cigarette. He strolled around the office, which was decorated with oil paintings and a marble bust of somebody on a slim pedestal. It looked like the head of Goethe. Under the tunic of this gross cossack beat the heart of an aesthete.

"You must understand that we do not view fine works of art as capitalistic boodle," he lyricized. "The Gramont belongs to all of the people of the Soviet Union. For your personal greed, you would rob millions. This will not be allowed."

He paused to admire Goethe, then spun to face us.

"You will return to West Berlin, Herr Fitzgerald, and bring the painting back to us. Fräulein Barry will remain with us until then."

Claudette slumped against me and emitted a stifled cry.

My original assessment of Kommissar Messer had been correct, all right. He was not to be flummoxed.

You know how it is when you're in a spot that can't be fixed, or squirmed out of, or finessed? When you face a dentist or a speeding moving van or maybe Ironhead Matthews in a towering rage? Instinct takes over. Thinking goes into overdrive, and you have to act.

Even as I realized this, my instinct made rapid calculations. There was no way I could leave Claudette there, for one thing. For another, Kommissar Messer was so worried about the missing painting that he had brought us to his office, instead of to a prison. Like the comrades in West Berlin, he also had to operate unofficially. Finally, the gray suit with the gun in his pocket was in the room with us.

"All right," I said, which caused Claudette to shoot a look of despair and betrayal at me. I stood up and moved toward the Kommissar's desk, reaching for my box of Tiparillos. "Mind?"

"No, help yourself," he said, maintaining a careful temper. He also had to be cautious until he got back the painting. The thumbscrews could come later.

I glanced out the large windows that rose almost to the ceiling of the high room and saw the inner courtyard through which we had come. Lifting the dainty cover of Maria Theresa from the cigarette box, I saw that it was an exquisite work of art.

I lighted a Tiparillo and put my right hand over the cigarette box again.

"There is a condition, however," I said, and flung the ceramic Maria Theresa cigarette box high into the air, across the room, over the head of Vladimir.

"Ahhhhhh!" screamed the Kommissar. "Vladimir!"

I had aimed the precious and breakable box high enough over Vladimir's head so that he had to raise his arms and run to catch it, and out of the Kommissar's reach.

As the startled Vladimir moved to catch the flying Maria Theresa, I darted around the desk and kicked the slim pedestal holding Goethe's head as I went by the frozen Kommissar, so that the bust tottered and the pedestal toppled. I had to hope Messer would catch Goethe's head while I went for the man with the gun.

Vladimir caught Maria Theresa over his head at the same time I blindsided him from behind. I drove him as hard as I could, dead-end into the wall, while his hands were frantically clutching the Kommissar's little treasure.

"Woof," came out of him, and I'm sorry to say I kicked him in the face, hoping to stun him.

I yelled wildly at Claudette to break something to distract the frantic Kommissar, who had caught Goethe's head in both hands. She rose to the occasion, all right, grabbing an immense painting of the Elector of Brandenburg off the wall and coming down on Messer's head with it, destroying the painting and momentarily imprisoning the bedazzled aesthete in the frame. He lowered Goethe's head onto his desk.

I dug into Vladimir's trench coat for our key to getting out of there and came up with the black 9mm. pistol. He got his hand on my wrist, though, and we rolled on the floor with my hand on the pistol but still in his coat pocket.

"Claudette," I yelled.

Goethe's stone head came crashing down on Vladimir's as he rolled on top of me. He sighed, let go of my wrist, and flopped on his back on the floor, having gotten Goethe's message.

I scrambled up and turned the 9mm. on the Kommissar, who was stepping out of the tangle of the Elector. His face was a symphony of distress. It was as though the Goths had desecrated the temple of Capitoline Jupiter.

I waved the gun at him. "Let's go."

He glared at me, but said nothing. I motioned him toward the high, varnished door and prodded him ahead of us. He opened the door and looked out.

I stuck the gun in his back. "We've got nothing to lose, Kommissar," I said softly. "Move."

He walked out into the inner courtyard, with us as close behind as possible. I kept the gun in my pocket as we walked through into the outer courtyard and to the street. There he halted.

"Don't be ridiculous," he muttered without looking back.

I bumped him into a corner by the front gate, and

swung the gun up under his arm, and hit him in the face
with it. He slumped down like a pile of rags.

In a moment, we were on the *Strasse,* walking hurriedly
along, not knowing where the hell we were, lost in East
Berlin. Then I realized we had forgotten our passports,
not to mention Claudette's precious documentation papers.

"My papers," she cried. "We have to go back."

I waved the gun. "Shut up, goddamnit! Move!"

She moved, but the look on her face was like that of a
soldier going before a firing squad.

∇

CHAPTER TWENTY-EIGHT

W E walked quickly along, and the only reference point I had was the immense East Berlin Television Tower, which can be seen from anywhere and which I knew was at Alexanderplatz. From there, I knew our way back to Checkpoint Charlie. As we walked, I knew I had to think fast, but at the same time there was no time for thinking.

How to escape over The Wall without passports? A thousand news stories welled up in my recollection. People had gone through in hollowed-out parts of cars, but we had no car. People had shot arrows over with cables attached and slid down the cables, but we had no bow, no arrow, and no cable. People had tunneled their way under The Wall, but we had no time to dig a tunnel or any way to do it. People had crashed through in cars and trucks, but the gates had been reinforced and narrowed to stop that, and besides, we had no truck.

Most troublesome was that we had no time. The Kommissar and Vladimir would both be awake and back in action very quickly.

"Why did you make me sign that paper?" Claudette whimpered, and I wanted to give her such a kick in the patoot that she might sail over The Wall without further assistance.

"There was no choice, goddamnit," I flung out.

"But now they own it!" She was inconsolable and had completely forgotten that my heroic though probably foolhardy action had saved her ungrateful life.

"Where are we going?" she asked anxiously.

"Head for the TV Tower," I told her.

So we did, walking along strange side streets but angling always towards the looming, graceful, slim needle with the onion bulb sight-seeing capsule toward the top.

"How are we going to get out?" she insisted upon asking.

"I don't know."

"Oh, Fitz," she keened, "I'm so sorry for complaining. I knew you wouldn't leave me . . . and . . . oh, Fitz . . . I am such an unthinking fool."

"Shut up," I muttered. "Keep walking. There's no time for that. Think of how to get us out of here before the goddamn Vopos catch up with us."

As on our earlier visit to East Berlin, nobody paid any attention to us as we hurried along through the streets. When we got to the TV Tower and then moved onto the main drag of Unter den Linden, it might be different, but I knew of no other way to go except toward that tower.

"Rhodes," I muttered.

"What?"

"John Rhodes! If we could reach him."

"Do you have a number?"

We walked on. Of course I didn't have a number for him. He always just came up out of the woodwork whenever he could cause the most trouble.

"If we could get to the embassy," Claudette said, on

the same track. That seemed our best chance to me, also.
McNamara could hardly turn us away under the circumstances. Once inside the U.S. Embassy in East Berlin, we
would be safe. It might take the State Department to get
us out of there and back to New York, but we would be
safe there, anyway.

We reached Karl-Marx-Allee and turned right, the great
red-and-white Television Tower a beacon ahead of us.
Finally, we reached Alexanderplatz at the tower, and I saw
a visitor's bureau on the ground floor.

"Come on," I told her, and led her inside to a counter
where East Berlin tourist officials handed out maps and
brochures.

"Telephone?" I asked.

The smiling Fräulein pointed to a pay phone. We dug
through our pockets and found enough East German
marks for the phone, and I called the embassy.

"United States Embassy," somebody answered, and I
asked for John Rhodes.

"Who, please?"

"Sometimes he calls himself Stew Faulkner," I hurried
on.

"Faulkner?"

"Listen, is McNamara there? This is an emergency!"

The phone did some click-clacking and then Mc-
Namara's Duke University voice poured through the
phone.

"May I help you?"

"McNamara, it's Fitzgerald!"

"Who?"

"The reporter. Claudette and I are in a little jam here."

Silence. "That painting woman?" He sounded considerably alarmed and distressed. "Where are you?"

"Is this phone safe?" I blurted idiotically.

"Are you in East Berlin?" he asked rather edgily, apparently hoping we were calling from Dubuque, Iowa.

"Yes! Can you send somebody to bring us in?"

"Bring you *in?*" He cleared his throat. "You mean *here?*"

"We're at the TV Tower, and they're after us!"

"Oh, my God!" he moaned. "Look, can you get here? We have no jurisdiction out there. You're in a foreign country."

Foreign country? We were a few blocks away.

"Please come straight here!"

"How?"

"Right down Unter den Linden."

I noticed the East German tourist girl was watching my rather animated conversation and realized we were doing the one thing we didn't want to do—get ourselves noticed.

"We have to go," I said softly. "We'll be there."

I hung up the phone and led Claudette outside into the Platz again.

"What did he say?" she nagged me.

"Go there."

"What? How? Is he crazy?"

Then I spotted our salvation. Two U.S. Army officers were strolling along, patches on their shoulders and America written all over their faces and manner.

They were crossing Unter den Linden, and I fell in step with them.

"Excuse me," I muttered. "Americans?"

The one closest to me smiled and nodded. "Yep. How ya doin'?"

"Listen," I said softly, "we're Americans, too. This is Claudette."

"How do, ma'am," he said in what sounded like a southern drawl. All American soldiers in Berlin seemed to be from Louisana or Alabama.

"Hey," I said urgently, "can you help us? We're in trouble."

The American lieutenant sort of moved a step further off as we walked and measured me more closely with his eyes.

"What's that, pal?"

"We've got to get to the American Embassy."

He stopped walking as we reached the sidewalk on the other side of Unter den Linden and examined us carefully. Then he pointed down the broad avenue. "Why, it's just on down there by Friedrichstrasse, I think," he said helpfully.

"Could you walk us there?" I asked anxiously.

"What?" He stepped back, and his pal moved closer beside him. "What's the matter, Herb?" the friend asked levelly.

"Why, I don't know, Em. These people here . . . we're just sightseeing, you know, pal," he told me. "What's the trouble?"

I looked at Claudette, and she pushed up closer to them.

"See, the police are after us," she said in a rush, "because they stole my painting, and we stole it back, and . . ."

A wary look came over Herb and Em from Alabama or wherever they were from.

"Well, gee, we ain't stationed here," Herb said, backing off. "We're not supposed to get mixed up with . . . you'd better go to the embassy."

"Goddamnit," I spluttered, "if we're stopped . . ."

"They took our passports!" Claudette railed.

"Come on, Herb," the one called Em said, pulling his buddy away from us. "We can't get involved in this. They'll have our ass, man."

Wonderful. The more we tried to importune them, the more they moved off. Finally, Herb turned on us.

"Get away from us," he commanded. "How the hell do we know who you are? The captain told us to watch our butts here. Get away from here."

They turned and hurried smartly down Unter den Linden toward Marx-Engels-Platz.

We followed them, since we were going in the same direction, and tried to pretend we were with them, but they turned off at the Berliner Dom and headed toward the National Gallery. There was no way we could follow them there.

Onward, across the River Spree. Then I heard it: The *eee-aaaah* of a German police vehicle. Claudette stopped on the bridge and shot a look backward. I dragged her along and shoved her into the next building we came to. We were in the Zeughaus, the Arsenal Museum. We wandered around, waiting for the *eee-aaaah* to die down, and I found myself gazing at medieval drawings of weapons on the wall. There was a detailed sketch of a Roman catapult, which threw immense stones at the walls of fortified cities.

"Claudette, look," I told her. "A catapult. It could throw us over The Wall."

Claudette didn't bother to look at the drawing. She looked at me, and her eyes were wide. Was I totally crazy? I was, all right. A catapult? How in the world could we build one, even if we wanted to? I was beginning to fantasize.

"Come on!" she ordered.

We kept going down Unter den Linden and reached

Friedrichstrasse, not far from the East Berlin American Embassy. We were going to make it, after all.

When we got to the block on which the embassy is located, Neustadische Kirchstrasse, however, I spotted Vopos in green uniforms at both intersections, above and below the embassy. They were waiting for us. This was where we had been stopped by a Vopo the first time, and this time we had no passports. The American flag fluttered over the embassy, but it was in a no-man's-land we couldn't reach.

I pulled Claudette away, and we strolled aimlessly along, bereft of a destination or idea.

We were around embassy row, and dead ahead I saw the Brandenburg Gate, with West Berlin enticingly just beyond. There it stood, beckoning, with The Wall beyond it, the whole area around it a clear grassy field. I had been told it was loaded with mines. In the distance I could see the Grosser Stern with the Victory Column in the middle. I experienced the poignant misery East Berliners who wanted out must live with daily, gazing across no more than a hundred yards to the west.

We stood at the iron gate in front of the Brandenburg Gate arch, and there was nothing we could do. Without passports, we could not go through any checkpoint. To run across the grassy field before us and try to scale The Wall was an act of madness.

Once again, I wondered what internal flaw resided inside my deranged persona that got me into such bizarre situations. How in the world had I allowed Claudette Barry to lure me beyond the pale of civilization into this twilight world of East Berlin, which was on the surface so benign but from which there was no exit for people who did not possess a simple little piece of stamped cardboard called a U.S. passport?

Why couldn't we simply hail a taxi, as on Seventh Avenue in Manhattan, say, "Kempinski Hotel, please," and go flitting off back to West Berlin? Why couldn't we just hop on the red-and-cream bus that was rolling along slowly past the Brandenburg Gate, its windows filled with tourists looking out and snapping photos as it moved?

So hallucinatory was I that I not only noticed the tourists and their cameras in the windows of the bus, but I recognized some of them. There was the Australian reporter who had not believed I was one of the touring journalists. There was an Indian woman reporter with a red dot on her forehead.

"Claudette!"

"What?" she asked.

"It's the goddamn reporters' bus!"

She spun around and zeroed in on it.

There it was, the Berlin Tour journalists' bus moving along right past us, and I remembered that today was going to be the trip into East Berlin, the trip I couldn't take.

"Wait!" I screamed at the bus, but it kept moving along very slowly. I waved my arms wildly at the journalists, and a couple of them pointed at me and smiled and waved back, but the damned thing wouldn't stop.

It completed a snaillike circle at the Brandenburg Gate and turned to roll back up Unter den Linden.

"Come on!" I yelled, and we ran up the street after it.

At Friedrichstrasse, it stopped for a red light, and we caught up with it and began banging on the side.

"Hey! Open the door!"

A window slid open, and Hans Dieter looked out, bewildered.

"Wiedersehen," he threw out. "Is that you?"

"Yes! For God's sake, open the door!"

He seemed confused. "Fitzpatrick . . . Philadelphia?"

"Open the door!"

He turned away a moment and then stuck his head out again.

"But, it is forbidden to stop . . . or open the doors," he called out. "We'll be at the hotel later."

I wanted to try to climb into the window, but it slid shut, and the damned bus moved off along Friedrichstrasse toward Checkpoint Charlie, leaving us standing on the corner.

"Stop them!" Claudette shrieked in frustration.

"He says the bus can't stop," I said idiotically.

"And you call yourself a reporter!" Claudette howled indignantly.

I grabbed her hand and ran along Friedrichstrasse after the bus. Somehow, it had to get us out of there.

Of course, the journalists' bus soon outdistanced us, gaining a block on us, and then two, as it made the lights and we fell behind. We had to catch it before it went through the checkpoint.

I spotted a florist shop, with bicycles in front. I grabbed one, and Claudette needed no prompting to grab another. Off we went, pedaling down Friedrichstrasse after the bus, with shouts in our ears. Then I heard another noise, more ominous, the *eee-aaah, eee-aaaah* of the Vopo.

I can't tell you how demented we were, bicycling along Friedrichstrasse through traffic, with a Vopo car screeching after us. We were saved by the fact that on any major avenue anywhere in the world a bicycle can make better time than any car or any bus. We careened through intersections, past traffic stuck in lanes, and finally caught the damned bus as it stood on the sloping road that leads to the checkpoint. When we caught up to it, I shoved my bike close to the back of the bus and told Claudette to climb onto my shoulders and onto the roof.

"The what?"

"Goddamnit, get up there!"

Well, she scrambled up onto the handlebars, then onto my shoulders, and grabbed the edge of the roof, and pulled herself up. I propped the bike against the rear and tried to climb up, too, but then the bus started up.

I hung onto the back, my feet on the rear fender, my hands holding onto the rim of the back window, and rode the damn thing along like a kid clinging to the back of a bus on the Grand Concourse in the Bronx. It was a very stealthy way to get out of East Berlin, with Claudette flattened out on the roof of a bus and me plastered to the rear end.

Nevertheless, the bus rolled down the sloping pavement of Friedrichstrasse and into the checkpoint, where it slid past one gate and halted in front of another.

I peeked around the side of the bus and saw two green-uniformed Grezenpolizisten walk to the front door. It opened and they got aboard. A head poked over the top of the rear of the bus and looked down at me.

"For God's sake!" Claudette hissed at me.

Do not ask me how I climbed up the back side of that bus onto the roof, but I did. Claudette crouched there on the roof on hands and knees, looking absolutely hysterical, pointing at the glass windows of the East German offices of the checkpoint. Grezenpolizei were looking out at the bus and us on the roof. The Vopos inside the bus apparently didn't know we were up there, and there was no time to think or laugh or go crazy if we wanted to do any of those things while still alive.

I grabbed Claudette's hand and ran across the roof of
the bus toward the front, clump, clump, clump, with her
behind me. I launched off the front of the bus into mid-
air, in unthinking terror—and splanched madly onto the
concrete in front of it. I landed and my chin went right
down onto my feet, and Claudette was on top of me in a
pile.

Ahead was the border, with the low Checkpoint Charlie
American shed in the middle, and people walking back
and forth with protest signs as usual.

We hit the pavement and scrambled dead ahead in a
frenzied dash, right into the people walking back and
forth. It was about twenty-five yards, and our only hope
was that the Grenzenpolizei wouldn't be able to shoot at
us from behind, because if they did they would hit people
ahead of us on the other side of the line.

I sprinted dead ahead and shrieked something at Claudette which was, I'm afraid, "Run, you goddamn bitch!"

We ran as though demented, which we were at the
moment, and the two East German border guards standing
in front of us with their backs to us, watching the West
Berlin side, didn't get alerted and turn around to see us
until we were on top of them. They were unslinging their
AK-47 rifles when she bowled one over and I bowled over
the other. We both skidded over and through them and
over the line into West Berlin in a rolling slide like Mookie
Wilson taking out the shortstop to break up a double play
at Shea Stadium.

CHAPTER TWENTY-NINE

W HEN I gave John Rhodes Vladimir's gun later, he told us that the East German border guards could not understand what had happened, and that people had tried to escape riding under buses, but never on top in full view, and that because we ran straight into the crowd of people on the West Berlin side and at their own border guards, they couldn't shoot us down like the capitalistic dogs we were.

"They put this whole thing down as a fluke that can't possibly happen again," he told us.

I didn't care. There was no way I intended to ever go through The Wall again.

That was the end of the Berlin story, as far as I was concerned. We were booked on the 8:00 P.M. flight to Frankfurt and New York, courtesy of Lieutenant Wolfe, and I planned to be on that plane, no matter what. We rode a taxi silently back to the Kempinski Hotel, Claudette having sunk into quiet resignation. She had signed *The Green Room* over to the East Berlin Kommissar, and that, finally, was that.

We dragged ourselves up into the hotel on the elevator,

and I left Claudette at her room door. There seemed nothing more to say.

Inside my room, I collapsed on the bed and tried to think of nothing at all. A blank screen was what I yearned for, but of course impressions flitted across my restless consciousness. Ironhead Matthews popped up and screamed at me, which caused me to realize once again that I had to write a story about Berlin when I got home.

I willed that impression away, and it was replaced by an accusatory Claudette Barry staring reproachfully at me. Others followed. Palmer Enderly with his raincoat and mustache, Erik Grosse-Mund, and finally Franz Hoppenrath the *B.Z.* reporter.

Loose ends were unraveling through my agitated mind. Somehow they would be cleared up, eventually. Maybe. And yet, with us gone, they might never be tied up, because there were people who didn't want them to be.

And I knew then what was bothering me. An unfinished story that had left two men dead, and Claudette and me frazzled. Somebody had succeeded in stealing that painting from us, and we didn't even know who.

I wiped the screen clear and grumpily sat up to light a Tiparillo. All right, so it was a total mess, but I couldn't help it. We had to leave, didn't we? We had tried. What more could I do?

Then it occurred to me that I could, at least, turn the story over to somebody else, somebody who would remain in Berlin and perhaps could work it better than I had.

Franz was the obvious choice. Sure, I had been furious with him for writing us up, but any reporter would have done the same, including me. In fact, Franz had sat on part of the story, which he hadn't had to do, and probably shouldn't have done.

I put in a call to the *B.Z.* for Franz, but he wasn't in. I left a message to call me, and forgot about it. Maybe Clotho, the Roman god who spins our thread of fate, had decreed that this was not to be.

I took a shower and started packing.

Then the phone rang, and it was Franz Hoppenrath.

"Fitzgerald?" he said. "Hallo! Franz here."

"Wie geht's?" I said. "Listen, we're leaving tonight."

"Ahhh," he grunted. "Well . . ."

"I just wanted to tell you I understand that you had to use that story. I would have done the same."

"Sure," he agreed eagerly. "What else could I do?"

"Anyway, how about a beer? I suggested. "Why don't I fill you in on anything I've picked up that you don't know? The damned story isn't over yet, but I won't be here to cover it."

"But what have you found out?"

I sighed. "Meet me for a beer. The key to the damned mess is a girl named Melanie."

"Melanie? Melanie who?"

"That's what you're going to have to find out," I told him.

He finally suggested we meet across the Ku Damm, and we met at the bar about half-an-hour later.

"What is this about Melanie?" Franz asked abruptly, as soon as we were settled in with our beers.

I filled him in about what I knew.

"She must have sent Pickle to us," I said. "She might know who killed him. She might have the painting, too."

Franz appeared to be plunged deep in thought. "Hmmm," he muttered. "But you don't know who this Melanie is or where to find her?"

"No, but I know where to find Lieutenant Wolfe."

I told him about Cafe Keese, and being chased by the French Sureté man into the arms of the KGB.

"She and her boyfriend got away," I grumbled, still annoyed at the way it had happened.

"They were at the Cafe Keese together when they ran away like that?" he asked me.

"Yeah."

"Well," he said. "And this man you saw at Cafe Keese, what did he look like?"

I had only a vague shape in my head. "Tall, dark face, sort of square. A little balding in front on top of his head."

Franz grunted shortly, and I thought I heard him say something muffled that sounded a little like "Otto."

"Why?" I asked. "Does it ring a bell somewhere?"

"Yes, in a way. It is very confusing, *ja?*"

"*Ja,*" I agreed. "But I'm pretty sure Melanie is planning to skip out of Berlin with the painting and head for Paris."

Franz either dropped his pipe on the bar or knocked it against the wood. "Paris? How do you know this?"

I told him about the waitress at Cafe Möhring.

"You have been digging into things," he said, rather subdued.

I sipped my beer and looked out the window of the *Kneipe*. People strolled or hurried by, some wrapped in *Mantels*, for it was gradually getting colder in Berlin, and I wished I could be one of them, just a tourist wandering around harmlessly, enjoying oom-pah-pah and leather pants as Ironhead Matthews had ranted. Instead, I stood there lighting a Tiparillo and going over things in my mind because Franz Hoppenrath rightly called the whole mess a Flying Dutchman in a fog bank.

That's the trouble with stories with holes in them. You can have a lot of information without being able to understand it if the major piece is still missing. That misty, uncertain shape in the fog tantalizes as it shifts and wavers and changes its outline. The problem is, sometimes the instant the Titanic realizes that that shape up ahead is an iceberg is the same moment it realizes it cannot avoid hitting it.

"There's some speculation," I told Franz, "but putting together what I know will give you a pretty good picture. If you follow things up, the whole damned story should fall in your lap pretty soon."

I went over it again for him and for my own satisfaction. First, of course, there was Palmer Enderly, who drove the painting out of East Berlin for us.

"This Melanie worked at the Cafe Möhring once, and she knew Enderly," I said. "So, she and Enderly were in this together, presumably to steal the painting from us."

"Ummm," went Franz.

"So, you have to find Melanie," I went on. "I don't know her last name or where she lives or where she works, if she works."

He was wagging his head and frowning. "I do not get this at all. Nobody will find this woman. Not now. You must get your plane and go home and forget about this whole thing."

I was a little irritated. "Franz, will you listen to me? This is a helluva story for you."

He was still frowning. "I don't cover things like that, usually, you see. I cover political stories, international affairs, you know."

"You covered me," I stuck in with some annoyance.

"Ja, well, but you shoved it in my face that time."

That was true. Well, I was shoving it in his face again.

"Just bear with me," I continued. "I guarantee this

whole thing is ready to fall apart. Somebody's going to
break this story. It might as well be you."

Franz raised his face to stare intently at me. "You think
so?"

"Absolutely! If you don't want it, I'll call the Associated
Press and give it to them."

He seemed to relax then, and apparently decided that,
like the Wedding Guest transfixed with the glittery eye of
the Ancient Mariner, he was forced to hear me out.

Melanie, I told him, was certain to be found. She was
known at Cafe Möhring and Cafe Keese. I had a photo of
Enderly that a waitress at the Möhring identified as her
boyfriend.

"A photo?"

I dug out the Polaroid of Palmer standing at his car and
showed it to him. "They must know there where she
lives," I said. "That links her to Enderly, and there's
another guy involved."

He put the photo down on the round table at which we
were standing.

"At the Exil," I went on, "somebody was waiting for
him. Somebody who must have been in on it."

"Melanie?" he asked reflectively.

"Maybe. But a man, also. The one who killed him and
took the painting. See, maybe Enderly and Melanie had
set this guy up."

"Hmmm," rumbled Franz.

"This guy, whoever he was, called the police from the
Exil, and Erik Grosse-Mund heard and saw him do it. So
he had to kill Erik, and Melanie kept me busy that same
afternoon. So that links the killer, Enderly, and Melanie."

"You have quite a lot of information. Do the police
know all this?"

"Not yet. But if you work with Wolfe, you can't miss."

"Go on."

"The killer showed proficiency that indicates he has been in close combat. A soldier, Rhodes and I think."

"Rhodes? The American agent? He knows these things?"

"Some of them. Then I found Melanie at Cafe Keese and she was with this square-jawed guy. He's got to be the killer."

"I see. Well, well." Franz seemed impressed at last. "This square-jaw—Otto, you called him—can you identify him any better?"

"All I know is she was very much with him, if you know what I mean, and they beat it together. He's got to be the other man, and they're headed for Paris together with our painting."

Franz put away his pipe, gave a knock on the tabletop with his right fist, and then said, "Well, I see what you mean about all this. You are right. It's ready to come all apart. I think I have an idea of what to do."

He tossed some money on the table and walked out, motioning with his head for me to follow. Outside, he walked me to a car, and we drove off rather quickly with me sitting beside him.

I was still wrapped up in my own attempt at identifying the shape in the fog, pleased that I had at last gotten Franz Hoppenrath's reportorial motors working. I had apparently finally convinced him that with what I knew, Melanie would be found. Part of the fogbound monolith assumed a solid outline. The tip of something, perhaps.

"We know almost everything," I told him, "except who the killer actually is."

"Hmmmm," he said, and drove on quickly, apparently sure of his destination.

"Where are we going?" I asked. "Lieutenant Wolfe?"

"I think I know where to find Melanie."

"What do you mean?"

He said nothing more, but kept driving. I noticed that he was on the alert, though, watching me out of the corner of his eyes.

It was as though I'd heard the sound of a loud crack out there in the fog.

"Helluva story," I said then, rather idiotically.

"Yes. One that can't be stopped now," he said with a grimace.

The foggy shape loomed more distinct. Patches swirled away, revealing fleeting glimpses. That crack I had heard, I suddenly realized, was the scales dropping from my eyes. Being myself a reporter, I understood with a shock that Franz had not been acting like a reporter. I had to talk him into a hot story that was right under his nose on his own turf.

Once the thought gripped me, I considered other things. Why hadn't Franz printed the story of the stolen painting? The West Berlin police had a reason to keep it quiet, and so did the East Berlin Kommissar, but what was Franz's reason? No reporter would sit on a story like that.

He had told me he didn't print anything about *The Green Room* because the police wouldn't confirm the theft, but the story he did print made me and Claudette murder suspects. That story was likely to chase us out of Berlin.

I tried to look ahead through the windshield, but I was watching Franz out of the corner of my eye, too.

Maybe Franz Hoppenrath wasn't just a *B.Z.* reporter! After all, John Rhodes had pretended to be one when he wasn't. In fact, being a reporter is a favorite cover for all kinds of shady officials. If Franz was an East German agent, or even somebody working for the French Sureté, it would make sense.

Then a kind of newspaperman's instinct took over. I went onto automatic pilot. I had the sensation that we were heading for a showdown that couldn't be far off— and my instinct told me that Franz was a reporter, all right. That was certain.

If he was a reporter, though, then why didn't he print the story about *The Green Room?*

I lighted a Tiparillo and let my instinct wander through the fog some more, measuring that shape. Did he sit on that story because he had an interest in the painting? Did he want it to disappear, and then want us to disappear?

I puffed, and the name "Otto" jumped into my mind. Franz had said I had identified Melanie's friend as Otto, but it was he who had supplied the name.

I heard another crack and detected what it was. Ice breaking. Dead ahead, I finally identified that shape in the fog. An iceberg, all right, and I was on the Titanic with Franz, who had once served on the Eastern Front.

▽

CHAPTER THIRTY

THE red Rabbit turned off into a residential street and Franz guided it into a driveway and behind a house. He parked, set the brake, said, "Well, come on," and waited until I opened the door before he got out, too.

"What's this?" I asked guardedly.

"Well, let's see," he said, and indicated I should walk ahead of him. He did this with a sort of body language that suggested command, with one hand in the pocket of his coat.

I walked ahead of him to the back door of the house, a gray-walled residence with blue shutters, and it was as though there were no further necessity for conversation. Clearly, we were no longer newspaper colleagues working together on a hot story.

Up a few steps to the back door, where I glanced back over my shoulder. Franz nodded me into the house. I opened the door and walked inside.

We were in an ordinary Berlin kitchen, except that it was a frightful mess, with dishes in the sink, open cereal boxes standing around, and an open jelly jar on the sink.

It looked something like my place on East Eighty-second Street back in Manhattan, and I understood why right away. This was the home of a bachelor.

Franz stepped in behind me, and I kept a few steps ahead of him, because I was being ushered along where he could see me. Neither of us had said anything, but we both understood the situation.

"Who lives here?" I ventured.

He sort of waved his hand to send me further into the house, through the kitchen and into a living room. There I stopped once more and turned to face him. There was a suitcase open on the sofa, and another one on the floor, closed up.

Franz let out a disgusted grunt, shook his head, and leaned back against the archway leading into the room.

"*Ach, Gott,*" he sighed.

"Listen, Franz," I started, but got no farther.

"Shut up."

He walked to the closed bag on the floor and nudged it with his foot. Then he backed away and told me to open it.

I lifted the bag onto the top of the open suitcase, undid a strap over the top, and unzipped it. I laid the cover back and saw a cardboard tube packed on top of clothes. I had no doubt it held *La Chambre Verte*.

Franz came close enough to look at it, keeping a table between us, and then wiped his face with his left hand. His right hand was still in the pocket of his coat.

"So," he said with immense disgust, and sort of chuckled wanly as he looked at me. It was supposed to explain everything, apparently.

Well, in a way, it did. Here was the stolen painting packed in a bag, with another bag beside it. All ready for a prompt departure.

We had thumped into the iceberg in the fog, all right, and I could hear cries echoing off the ice.

"Melanie!" I heard, and it was a soft cry of anguish from Franz, who stood leaning against the archway, drained and miserable.

I tried to think fast. This was not the house of a woman, I had already concluded. It must be Otto's place, and if Franz had come here looking for Melanie, then what did that mean?

Then I heard something else. Water rushing. Actually, it was the end of water rushing. Somewhere in the house, somebody had turned off a shower. Franz heard it, too, and straightened up.

"You know Otto?" I tossed out.

"*Stille!*" he snapped. Silence.

"You know Melanie, too, don't you?"

Franz shot me a look, and his right hand came out of his pocket. He held the gun down at his side and watched me, listening to the sounds of movement on the floor above.

"I'm sorry, Fitz," he said then. "You should have gotten out of Berlin. This is not a good town for amateurs."

Melanie and Franz! It rushed together in my confused head. Melanie and Franz and Pickle! What could that mean? But I didn't have to really ask. Franz wrote political stories, he had said, which in Berlin meant he covered foreign affairs. Franz had sent Palmer Enderly to us, and Melanie was in on it, too. Franz had to be the killer.

That had hardly sunk in when a soft cry came down the stairs.

"Otto? *Bist du da?*"

Melanie's musical voice floated down and assailed Franz's ears. His face went red. She had used *"du"* for

Otto, which is a form of address in German used for lovers.

Light steps on the stairs, several in a row. Then another call, "Otto?" A few more quick steps, and she looked into the room—and froze.

"Ahh!"

"Come in," Franz told her in a voice that was both lifeless and full of dread.

She stepped in hesitantly, wrapped in a blue terry cloth robe, looking vulnerable and fetchingly beautiful. Her glance flicked over me, and then to Franz, and what she was thinking I don't know. My thoughts were that there was treachery in that room, and that explosive, murderous fury was just below the surface, and that somebody was going to die. I wished I still had Vladimir's 9mm pistol.

Franz let his gaze roam to Melanie's suitcase, and then back to her.

"You are going somewhere?"

Thoughts of self-preservation slid over the blanched face of the lovely Melanie. "Franz . . ."

He watched her. "Yes?"

I was in an ammunition dump, which could go off with the tiniest spark. Melanie and Otto, it seemed, were about to leave Franz in the lurch. I wasn't entirely clear as to what they were saying, because they spoke in German, naturally, but I was able to pick up enough of it to be properly terrified.

"Where's Otto?" Franz now demanded.

Melanie twitched, and started to speak, but fell silent. Finally, almost inaudibly, "I don't know . . . what do you mean? Franz, what's the matter?"

It was no good, that was obvious. Melanie in a blue terry cloth robe freshly out of the shower in Otto's house,

with *The Green Room* packed in a suitcase, could not be
explained away. She couldn't even seem to think of how to
try.

"We were going to meet you," finally escaped from her
desperately. "I tried to call you . . ."

Franz sort of grunted, a sarcastic little laugh.

"And why did you bring this fool reporter here?" she
scolded, attempting to slide the conversation into some
other channel.

"I wondered where you had gone," Franz said slowly.
"I never thought of Otto Nollendorf." He laughed, but
without mirth. "I should have, of course, Mr. Dancefloor."

"But I was trying to reach you! It's only . . . Otto
doesn't matter. Only to help us get out."

"Too old, huh?" he said to her. "That's what you said
about Pökel, that he was too old, and you wanted me,
fool that I was. I am older than Pökel. We grow too soon
oldt, and too late schmart." He laughed.

"Franz," she wheedled, "we mustn't . . . we don't have
to do this. Let's get away now, you and me. Yes? But what
are we to do about him?" She tossed her pretty head in
my direction.

I was extremely interested in the answer to that question, as well. I had the feeling that I had no time left, that
this momentary fulcrum in time was almost past, and that
a spasm of rage or despair would tilt the balance one way
or another, toward reconciliation and flight by the two of
them, or toward a final reckoning. Either way, my presence would become expendable.

I slowly reached into my shirt pocket and took out a
Tiparillo, watched languidly by the pale eyes of Franz, and
cautiously lighted it.

Franz turned his eyes back toward Melanie, who was gradually gaining a slim hope due to Franz's hesitation.

I lowered my left hand with the burning match in it to my side, and then let it fall into the open luggage.

"We have it all now," Melanie was cooing seductively. "I didn't want Paris . . . never mind that. Rome! That's what you wanted! Come, come, Franz . . ."

A flicker of flame shot up from the luggage, and with a start Melanie whipped her head toward it. Franz looked, too, and I went over the table in a desperate dive, into Franz, grabbing his arms to hold them against his body so he couldn't raise the gun.

Melanie shrieked, but worked on the fire.

"Ach!" escaped from Franz.

My knee went up and into Franz. When he doubled over, I came down on his head with a right that I hoped would knock him into cuckoo-clock land, but Franz had been in combat before—maybe a long time ago, and he knew more about it than I did. He went down, all right, but didn't let go of the gun.

I kicked his hand. I think he laughed grimly.

Beyond Melanie was the front door, and what I wanted was to reach it and get the hell out. He was stunned a little, curled up on the floor on his side, but the gun was still in his hand and his eyes were still open.

I scrambled toward Melanie and the door.

A red-hot poker went through my leg and the smell of gunpowder panicked me—and Melanie, in front of me, looked blankly into my face, her mouth open. A chopped, violent "Uhh!" spit out of her. As if in slow motion, she slid down to the floor before me, and I saw a tiny speck of blood on her left breast, where her blue terry cloth robe had fallen away.

"Melanie!"

Panicky and bewildered, I rolled to the side, my leg all but useless, and saw Franz sitting up, his eyes fixed on Melanie in terror. He scrambled across the floor toward her, and bent over her, oblivious to everything else.

Franz cradled her in his arms and rocked her, keening her name. I could see she was dead. Franz's shot from the floor had gone through my leg, without a pause, and had crashed into Melanie's breast, right at her heart.

I crawled toward the back door and saw the suitcase on the sofa, a singed blouse crumpled up where Melanie had smothered the fire. I grabbed *The Green Room* in its cardboard tube from the top, and managed to half-limp, half-crawl back out through the kitchen and to Franz's car.

I couldn't start the damned thing, though, without a key, and decided to get away from there any way I could. I went along the side of the house, leaning against it, holding the cardboard tube, and came to the street.

Providence! A taxi rolled up—and who got out but Mr. Dancefloor himself, Otto Nollendorf of the bald spot on the front of his head. Not that I could see it. Otto wore a spiffy French beret and a glorious new overcoat, a lovely outfit for a trip.

As he paid the driver, I dragged myself to the cab and opened the door.

Otto glanced curiously at me, seemingly trying to place me, or maybe noticing my odd movements. I got in and told the driver to take me to the Kempi. Otto took a step toward the house.

I heard a muffled, sharp crack from inside the house and knew what it was. Otto jerked his head toward the house, but the cabbie didn't seem to notice at all.

We rolled away, and I sank back on the seat, which was already turning a dull red.

$\triangledown$

CHAPTER THIRTY-ONE

I HARDLY remember that ride. My right trouser leg filled with warm, sticky crimson as blood oozed out in front and back. The cloth against my leg seemed to grow thick with it. It hurt like the devil, and I must have groaned aloud because the cabbie turned and asked what I said.

"Nothing . . . *nichts*," I managed. "Hurry."

"*Was sagen Sie?*"

"*Schnell!*"

He sort of glared at me through the mirror. Here was an imperious rich American tourist ordering him around. He speeded up, though.

I must have fainted at one point, because when I came to my head was lolled back against the seat. I tried to feel the wound, but oddly, I couldn't locate it. Only coagulating blood pulping around the wound, which seemed to be all over my right thigh just above the knee. It was sort of numb, and I imagined a great, raw, gouged-out, fleshy crater the size of a cherry tart.

Light-headed and giddy, I saw trees drifting past the cab window, swaying gracefully in slow motion. Cars and lumbering psychedelic double-decker buses lazed along, oblivious to one mangled, foolish New York reporter.

The Berlin taxi began to float, to elongate, the driver slipped away from me down a long corridor, and became the Cafe Möhring, with the blasted Kaiser Wilhelm Gedächtniskirche out the window, just beyond the wings. Barren rocks sailed by beneath us, and the Berlin taxi-Cafe Möhring–Lufthansa jet throbbed on aimlessly over a limitless ocean. A flaxen-haired, buxom flight attendant came close and smiled at me from an inch away, her face smearing out of focus, and then she reached out to me and kept demanding my ticket.

"What?"

"*Drei Mark fünfzig,*" said the face, and it was the Berlin cabbie, looking back over the seat at me quizzically.

"*Ja.*" I dug into my pocket and came out with my wallet, smeared with blood. I counted out the money to him in a half-dreamlike state, and he watched me as one in a trance himself.

"*Gott in Himmel,*" he blurted.

Then I opened the taxi door and fell out onto the sidewalk in front of the Kempinski Hotel.

Slanting green East Berlin border police, kneeling and shouting. Round pie pans on their heads. Somebody in a blue jacket and striped pants kneeling over me. I am moved, dragged, somehow carried stumblingly into a great carpeted space. People back off and look at me oddly, murmuring to each other.

"Herr Fitzgerald!"

A lovely, terrified face comes down to me—black hair around a delicate face, now twisted in a cry.

"Fitz! My God, get a doctor!"

I am lifted and become weightless, float away into the fog and then I know no more.

A white field of snow or ice, flat. Then three lines leading away from each other from a point, in geometric proportion. Follow the line that goes down, and it is the corner of a room. A voice murmurs something. I look up.

"Where am I?"

"Fitz!" Claudette hovers over me, her face tear-stained, and strokes my face. "Thank God!"

The bed is hard, and a white log is lying in it with me. I try to move my leg and my leg is the white log.

"Jesus!"

"How do you feel?" Claudette fussed over me, stroking my forehead, her face wreathed in concern.

"Christ," I said, and looked around at the room, apparently in a hospital somewhere.

Then John Rhodes stood up from a chair and came over to the side of the bed. He looked me over.

"Are you all right?" he said with ill-concealed annoyance.

"I don't know. How's my leg?"

"Somebody put a bullet through it," said Rhodes.

"Yeah," I said, and it all came swarming back. "How bad is it?"

"Bad enough," said Rhodes. "But it went right through."

"Is something broken?" I asked, looking down at the white cast again.

"What the hell happened?" asked Rhodes in reply.

I tried to figure out how to answer that.

"I don't know," I mumbled. "Everything. Claudette . . . have you got . . ."

She leaned down and kissed me. "Yes! My God, how did you get it?"

More questions. How much did they know? I was dizzy

from trying to get a handle on things. I felt maddeningly floaty, disembodied, drifting somewhere up on the ceiling by the geometric point and looking down on us, me included.

"Oh, Fitz," Claudette gushed, falling over me, kissing me, and crying at the same time. "I love you so much! I was so scared! Oh, my God, Fitz!" She wept on my chest.

"Listen, we've got to get going here," Rhodes snapped irritably, and pulled Claudette off me. "The damned plane is leaving in half-an-hour."

"Plane?"

"Yes, goddamnit," Rhodes complained. "You're getting the hell out of here!"

"He's right," said Claudette, looking calmer.

She handed me a glass of orange juice, and then Rhodes poured a shot of something into it. I gulped it down, feeling the tart orange juice and the bite of the schnapps.

Rhodes helped me put my plaster leg over the side of the bed, and brought me a crutch. The cast went from above my knee down to my ankle, so I was a stiff-legged hump of a mess, tottering across the floor until I grabbed the wall.

"Beautiful," I muttered crossly. What an exit I would make from the City by the Spree.

I realized I was in the same clothes I had been wearing, with the pants leg slit and still bloodstained. I managed to pull on my jacket with Rhodes's help, and then Claudette helped me into my London Fog. I would hardly pass muster as a Port Authority Terminal derelict, but there was no help for it, and I wanted out of there in the worst way.

Claudette helped me as I hobbled stiff-legged out into a corridor and then along it to a door to the outside. Rhodes hurried ahead of us. Outside, we struggled into a car, with me in the backseat, and off we went. I tried to make sense out of things. A million loose ends dangled before me.

"Rhodes," I said, "listen, I'm in a helluva mess."

"You don't say," he growled, with a lamentable lack of sympathy for my pitiable condition. He snapped something vile.

"You heard about it?"

"No," he fairly screamed. "No, goddamnit, I don't know a thing! All I know is, I'm getting a goddamn insane pest onto a plane and the hell out of here."

I had to think that he did know at least something.

"What?" Claudette suddenly piped up. "He won't tell me anything! What happened?"

I told her what had happened, as best as I could remember.

Claudette, sitting in the front seat and leaning back over it to listen, went pale when I got to the part about Melanie.

"The same shot?"

"I only heard one," I said. "You say the one that hit me went right through my leg?"

Claudette nodded. "That's what the doctor said."

A clean shot, a powerful slug that went right through me and killed Melanie. I could still see Franz curled up on the floor, the gun in his hand.

"Rhodes," I went on, "when I was outside, I heard another shot. Was it Franz?"

Silence.

"Did Franz shoot himself?"

A hunch of the shoulders, a twist, as though to throw off and evade an answer.

"Forget it," he finally said.

"What about Otto?"

"Otto?" he came back. "What Otto?"

"The guy Melanie ditched Franz for," I said.

Rhodes gulped something extraordinarily disgusting. He went into a spluttering gargle, and I couldn't make out much, except something like, "Holy good–fucking–god–damn–shit! Not another one!"

The car went around a corner with tires squealing.

We came rolling finally into the Tegel Flughafen, where we struggled through the airport with Claudette trying to help me and me thumping along. Rhodes came behind us with our bags to the boarding area, and then shoved emergency passports into our hands.

I looked at him. "Hey, listen, thanks, big guy."

I think he winced a little. "Sure, always happy to help out. Now, get on that damned bird!"

"Did you check us out?" I asked Claudette.

"Yes. Hurry."

I tottered along, still in a dream state, and we got through the loading gate and into the big rolling canopy that connected to the Pan Am jet. As we struggled through the corrugated tunnel, I suddenly turned to Claudette and asked what had happened to the painting.

"It's all right," she said. "Keep going."

"But we have to go through customs," I complained. "How the hell are we going to get it out?"

"It's all right, Fitz. We did the only thing we could."

"You mean we haven't got it?"

"We've got it," she smiled, and winked at me. I stumped along, trying to figure out where the hell it could be.

Whump! went my plaster leg against the floor, and I felt an itch inside the cast.

"Oh, for crissake!" I muttered.

$\triangledown$

CHAPTER THIRTY-TWO

About the only people I know who are more arrogant and nosey than city editors are doctors, if you want my opinion. They seem to have the idea that their licenses are the most sacred documents in the world, and they fly into a tizzy over the slightest things.

At least that's the way it was with Dr. Richard Griffiths on Lexington Avenue when Claudette and I went there to get my leg cast cut off. Mike Santangelo, who has covered a few murders and stranglings in his years at the *Daily Press,* sent me to this guy, and the first thing he wanted to know was why Claudette insisted on being in the room while he removed the cast.

I'll admit it was distracting, her hopping around telling him to for God's sake be careful where he was cutting.

"Excuse me, miss," Dr. Griffiths said rather frostily, "but just what is the problem?"

"There's something in the cast," Claudette explained.

"Inside?"

"Yes. And you musn't touch it."

Dr. Griffiths glanced at me. Then at Claudette. "What

is it? I can't be mixed up in . . . contraband. Not drugs, I hope?"

He had taken his hands off the cast as though it were radioactive, apparently assuming that the white plaster was all cocaine.

"No, no," said Claudette. "Just something."

"It's a stolen painting," I told him, and enjoyed the look of surprised dismay on Claudette's lovely puss. She had done it to me enough times. "It's a painting we brought out of Europe, but she owns it."

Dr. Griffiths clunked his plaster cutting shears on my cast and pursed his lips. "If it's hers, why is it hidden inside a cast?"

"It's a long story," I sighed.

"You can ask the State Department if you wish," said Claudette. "But don't cut *The Green Room*."

Dr. Griffiths grumbled a little, and I think he actually asked his nurse to call the State Department, but he did manage to snip the cast off a little bit at a time, instead of cutting it off in one long slice. Every thump hurt, and my only consolation was that once *The Green Room* was out of my leg, Claudette would be out of my life.

Then he discovered that the problem under the cast was a gunshot wound.

"I have to report gunshot wounds to the police," he said stiffly.

"It happened in Berlin," I explained. "But go ahead. Call the FBI! I've been chased by the KGB and the French Sureté. What the hell do I care now?"

Dr. Griffiths was fairly well flustered by the whole thing, and we left him to puzzle it out any way he wished. Claudette slid *The Green Room* into a cardboard tube and we left.

When I hobbled into the New York *Daily Press* city room on my cane the next day, Ironhead Matthews spotted me from the city desk, and watched me all the way across the room. He slowly took out a fresh cigar about the size of the Goodyear blimp, unwrapped it as carefully as if it were a stick of dynamite, and then lighted it, staring at me through clouds of stench.

He looked me up and down, not neglecting a sneeringly puzzled examination of the prop on which I leaned.

"Well," he finally declaimed, "what the hell do we have here? The goddamn second coming of Long John Silver?"

"I'm back," I said rather absurdly.

A disconcerting expression of incredulity mixed with distaste slid over his face, and he bit into his cigar like a lion sinking his teeth into the neck of a wildebeest.

"The toy department sends him off to a goddamn beer party and he comes back looking like pig vomit!"

"Now, wait a minute, Ironhead . . ."

"He gets a cushy travel job that any cub quiff from Vassar could write while having her toenails painted, and here he is a beslimed hoople with a goddamn cane! What the hell did you do to yourself, fall out of a cathouse?"

"Well, see . . ."

But Ironhead didn't really care, because he grabbed a sheaf of papers off his desk and started waving them around. "What the hell did you spend all this money on, entertaining the German General Staff?"

Oh, that.

"It was because of the painting in East Berlin."

"Painting? You bought a painting?" He frowned in confusion.

"No, it was to grease this diplomat."

"Diplomat? Is this the murdered diplomat I told you to drop like a hot potato? Is that it, huh?"

"That was later."

"Later?" He twirled his cigar, chewing each side so that it became a slimy, unmentionable affront.

He snatched the sheaf of papers up again and darted his index finger accusingly at some figures.

"Here! What the goddamn hell is this? Thirteen hundred dollars! Do you think you work for the fuckin' City of New York?"

"But we had to get the painting out, and this diplomat had to have thirty-five hundred . . ."

"Thirty-five . . . !"

"But I only put up part, and we'll get it back when the painting is sold."

Ironhead swiveled around in his chair, apparently having developed a crick in his neck. He glared at me from an angle, as though he couldn't stand watching me head-on.

"Painting? Diplomat? I sent you over there to write a piddling travel piece that nobody will even read, except yuppies and other weirdos. Now, what happened?"

It was difficult to tell a basically improbable story to somebody with the niggling mind of a bookkeeper.

"Ironhead, the damned CIA and the French Sureté were chasing us, and then we got shanghaied into East Berlin, and . . ."

"CIA?"

"How was I to know that a Berlin reporter was behind it? But then he shot me, so I had to believe it."

"Shot you!"

"And then they threw us out with *The Green Room* around my leg, and basically that's it."

Ironhead's head jerked. He seemed to examine the ceiling for a second. Then he picked up the sheaf of offending financial swindle sheets, and sort of gestured emptily. Red faced, he shoved the stack of papers aside and fixed me with a bedazzled expression.

"You will explain this goddamn swill to Jack Milligan," he commanded. "You got that? I am not going to sit here and listen to some pisswillie talking in tongues!"

"Right."

"Now, let's have a look at your Berlin story."

He calmed down a little then, because reading copy was something he could cope with.

"Uh, well, I'm not quite finished."

"Well, goddamnit, give me what you've written so far. Mrs. McFadden's been on my butt about it."

"I'll get going on it right now."

"You'll . . . get . . . !"

"It's all here in my head, Ironhead."

"Holy good-goddamn Mother of Jesus!" he gargled miserably. "Get away from me."

"But, it won't take long . . ."

Ironhead shot straight up to his feet, and stood there, with a vein throbbing in his forehead. Words seemed to form but nothing came out. A contorted expletive rose and then died.

"Half an hour, you goddamn hoople!" he finally decided.

I hobbled to my desk, logged on the video display terminal, and launched into the story of Berlin, using brochures and other handout stuff. At least here, alone at my machine, I could function. No crazed Claudettes picking at me, no missions over The Wall, no love-mad *B.Z.* reporters shooting at me. Any decent ink-stained wretch, of course, can write a pushover thing like a travel article in half an hour, whether he's been to Berlin or not. The whole trip, let's face it, was just a trivial interlude.

I wish I could tell you that Claudette Barry sold *The Green Room* and repaid me and the *Daily Press* promptly. Unhappily, when she went to the State Department to rescind that forced signing away of her documentation, the State Department came back and told her the Soviets were having none of it.

"What did they say?" I asked her as we sat in Costello's.

"Fitz, they're bonkers!" she declared righteously. "They say they confiscated those papers from us because they have the real *Green Room,* and that mine must be a fake."

"What?"

"Yes! They still say it wasn't stolen, and now they have documentation to prove it, and I must be an adventuress or something."

Well, I thought, they were partly right.

"So you can't pay me back yet?" I asked miserably.

"No, but the State Department is filing a vigorous claim," she went on. "And as soon as that's settled, I can sell it, and everything will be terrific."

I sipped my mug of beer and wished I was deaf as a graveyard headstone.

"So, listen," she said, turning around on her bar stool and knocking against my leg. I flinched. "Oh, I'm sorry. How is it?"

"Coming along," I muttered.

"All we have to do now," she said, "is get some stories going about this thing!"

"Stories?"

"Sure! I want you to go after them hammer and tongs in the *Daily Press,* and the whole thing will be settled in a week! Now, I've got lots of stuff for you to take to Ironhead, and . . ."

We walked back down Second Avenue to the *Daily Press* and in through the lobby, past the big, slowly spinning world globe, up on the elevator to the seventh floor and the reception desk, where Denny the copyboy from Ireland sits and keeps out lunatics.

"Denny," I said, "this is Claudette Barry."

"Ah, yes, how do, ma'am?" he said liltingly.

I told Claudette I'd talk to her later, but was unable to keep her from giving me stacks of papers that would prove to the Louvre, the State Department, the Supreme Soviet, and the United Nations that *The Green Room* was her rightful property.

When she finally got into the down elevator and vanished, I limped back over to Denny.

"Denny, did you get a good look at her?"

"Ah, yes! Quite a lovely young lass, Fitz."

"Yes," I conceded. "But get this, and get it straight. She's an international Soviet hitwoman!"

"She's a . . ." Denny's gentle Irish eyes narrowed.

"And don't you ever, ever, ever let her into this goddamn office again!"

I hobbled into the city room. My leg was beginning to feel better already.

If you have enjoyed this book and would like to receive details of other Walker Mystery-Suspense novels, please write for your free subscription to:

Crime After Crime Newsletter
Walker and Company
720 Fifth Avenue
New York NY 10010